THE PARIS NETWORK

BOOKS BY SHIRLEY BURTON

HISTORICAL FICTION
Homage: Chronicles of a Habitant

THRILLERS
Red Jackal
THOMAS YORK SERIES:
Under the Ashes - Book One
The Frizon - Book Two
Rogue Courier - Book Three
Secret Cache - Book Four
The Paris Network - Book Five

MYSTERY
Sentinel in the Moors
INSPECTOR FURNACE MYSTERIES:
Mystery at Grey Stokes
Swindle: Mystery at Sea

CHRISTMAS
Clockmaker's Christmas
Christmas Treasure Box

FANTASY
Boy from Saint-Malo

shirleyburtonbooks.com

BOOK FIVE OF THE THOMAS YORK SERIES

THE PARIS NETWORK

SHIRLEY BURTON

HIGH STREET PRESS

HIGH STREET PRESS
Calgary, AB
www.highstreetpress.com
First printing 2018

Printed in the United States of America and worldwide under license.
Available in eBook formats.
Design and edit Bruce Burton
Photo license Shutterstock.com.

Library and Archives Canada Cataloguing in Publication.

Burton, Shirley, 1950-, author
        The paris network / Shirley Burton

(Book Five of The Thomas York Series)
ISBN 978-1-927839-15-7 (pbk.). —ISBN 978-1-927839-16-4 (bound)
ISBN 978-1-927839-17-1 (ebook)

There is no such thing as an accident;
It is fate misnamed.
—Napoleon Bonaparte

THE PARIS NETWORK

One

Paris, July 14, 1789

Through the haze, the misty rays of sunshine struggled to peer through to wake up the city. As in recent months, Jean Claudet awoke tired and angry in his dilapidated tenement near the 14th arrondissement.

The overnight humidity over Paris was heavy, and Jean had slept in his work shirt streaked with blood, soot, and grime from laboring in the granite mines, then the nightly gathering with his peasant comrades to protest outside the Arsenal of Roquette. With centuries of oppression, they knew the boiling point for Paris had become climactic with passion and patriotism.

Jean's clothes clung to his body from sweat as he climbed from his quarters in a garret, shared with beggars, orphans, and sickly Frenchmen. The air was thick of stale lager and the stench of street sewers, yet he was grateful for the lodging offered by the owner of a livery in exchange for services.

Achieving his eighteen years without the providence of family, education or a nightly roof, Jean was ripe for revenge and retaliation, yet managed to stay out of the prisons, luckier than many other scavengers and pickpockets.

A seething hatred swelled among the peasant militants for the Bourbon monarchy and the bourgeoisie that had arisen and quashed all rights of the poor. Weeks before, King Louis XVI ordered reinforcements of gunpowder and muskets to the Bastille as the mob had threatened to break down the walls.

Jean knew that tonight would be different. The protesters were ready to go to the brink, whatever that would mean.

"Mother France, I will give of my blood for all Parisians to have liberté, égalité, and fraternité. I will stand with the brotherhood tonight and take back the Parlement from which we have been denied. Let the towers of Notre Dame rise up in the heart of our city."

As dusk fell, Jean walked in urgent strides, shoulder to shoulder with others, from the darkness of the granite mines, joining the chanting mobs at Bastille Square, bordered by the 4th, 11th, and 12th arrondissements. There they gathered in the thousands, forging an army of patriots.

Men, boys, and even women dressed as men eased toward the medieval fortress, carrying pitchforks, axes, shovels and a few with muskets. The revolution had begun months before in the hearts of peasants, but this night would be a landmark for French liberty.

On this sacred night, a mob of less than a dozen beseeched entry to Notre Dame and climbed feverishly to the belfry. From this vantage the lights of Paris burned in every window, an image to be remembered in a lifetime. The cry of battle pealed across Paris as they rang the great bells incessantly, while paupers and peasants surged like ants to the Square.

The Bastille fortress towered a hundred feet, protected by a treacherous moat. The military commander, Bernard René de Launay, conceded to discuss the peasant issues with two negotiators who were permitted inside the walls. However, several hours later, the mob was titillated to a full-blown riot and began cutting the chains that secured the drawbridge over the moat. It was too late when de Launay raised a white flag of surrender.

"To the death!" the mob ranted, spewing hatred and revenge against the monarchy and noblesse of Paris for its treatment of them, treated as slaves and dogs catering to the whim of stuffy, frilly, perfumed, and heavily adorned men and women of the upper class.

Finding the Bastille defenseless, the revolutionaries scaled the walls into the Bastille to lower its two drawbridges. In minutes, they were in control, loading the cannons and with no hesitation to confiscate the royal arms.

Battle culminated in the relinquishment by King Louis XVI of control of Paris in the night of massive bloodshed. As a symbol of royal authority, the anarchists destroyed the Bastille.

Desperate yet passionate Parisians defended patriotism above all else. Their heritage knew battle through the ages and it was in their blood to be defiant.

The economic costs to France from the American Revolution had sunk the treasury into financial depression and the noblesse of Paris had encumbered the poor with more taxes and less food, triggering the failure of the feudal system throughout the country.

Three months after the storming, the hungry and poor of Paris marched on Versailles and brought the King to Tuileries to enact a new constitution limiting monarchy rights and permitting the public to participate in votes. In 1793, Louis and his wife, Marie Antoinette, went to the guillotine for their crimes against the people.

The government's resistance was the prelude to a ten-year reign of terror and rebellion that led to Napoleon Bonaparte's coup d'état in 1799, establishing the French Republic. Napoleon was named Emperor of the First French Empire, to bring order to France, albeit while the Napoleonic Wars raged throughout Europe.

The populace became a veritable personality of defiance and resilience, ready to fiercely defend their freedom and rebound from oppression. This is the heart of the Parisian since the Middle Ages, valuing rights and liberty above all else, claiming and vowing, 'Vive la France'.

The poet Victor Hugo recounts the anguish and illustrious glory of Parisians in his acclaimed writings of *Les Misérables*. His own father served under Napoleon in the military during the time the Arc d'Triomphe was ordered to be constructed to serve as a reminder of the victorious Grand Armée.

Paris on November 15, 2015

The shouts and celebrations of partiers paraded through the town squares on Armistice Day, demonstrating their victorious spirit of historic survival and everlasting love for France.

The terrorist attack at Charlie Hebdo in January left its scars on the city, but Paris was ready to show the world they would not be denied their liberty. Marching bands with batons and vintage costumes of the ancient regime were flaunted and displayed, including marching Napoleon Bonapartes with the trademark slings while chanting 'Vive la France'.

Even on the hilltop of Montmartre, the highest point in Paris, markets sprang up in the commons at the close of the Dijon International and Gastronomic Fair of Paris. Vintners were already on their heels for Les Trois Glorieuses of Beaune, with its annual wine auction and fête. Food, music, and frivolity were strengths in the Parisian way of life, overshadowing but not forgetting the terror that hit the city ten months before.

The November evening produced a brisk wind, with misty strands of moonlight that drifted through the clouds. The autumn dusk had settled over Montmartre before 5 pm. and the crescendo of night revelers climbed the hills toward the Sacré-Coeur Basilica, merging up Rue des Saules.

The popular French quarter at the Place du Tertre had come alive in the cool night, now jammed with tourists and fledging art folk, with dreams of romance and ghosts of great artists of a hundred years that had lived on the streets.

The cabaret culture of Montmartre established the great art studio at Le Bateau-Lavoir where many struggling artists came to renew themselves including Picasso, Van Gogh, Brissaud, Matisse, Renoir, Degas, Dali, and Toulouse-Lautrec.

Its cobbled lanes were lined with charming provençale houses, with wrought iron balconies, flower boxes and colorful shutters, with many lofts atop quaint boutiques. Everywhere, dormer terrace doors were flung open tonight to invite the jubilation.

Thomas and Rachel had hired an office manager, Madge Bitteridge, for their detective agency, who in three years had already marshaled their lives into a better balance between romance and work. A woman of distinct command, Madge was a lovable, middle-aged widow, with grown children, who on more than one occasion had put her life on the line to save her two dear friends.

"It's just not my cup of tea, dear, why don't you and Thomas go," Madge said, pulling tickets from an envelope in her Queen Elizabeth style purse. "It's an American band, tonight, in the 11th arrondissement. My friend bought them, but can't attend as unexpected company arrived at her flat today."

"Oh, Madge. But they're yours to enjoy."

"Rachel, you just have a Friday night out—it will do you both good. I watch your lives often teetering on the brink of danger, and you need entertainment and laughter."

Madge's arms crossed suddenly and her voice became stern. "I think you've both become withdrawn from culture and fun."

Rachel nodded at the admonishment, and looking up at Madge, they both laughed.

"Bless you, Madge, you know I get homesick for the States." She held the ticket up to read. "I don't know this band . . . but yes, of course, we will be happy to go. You are a gem."

With a familiar hug, Madge waved her hand to dispatch Rachel out of the office for her own good.

"Tell Thomas we're going out tonight and he should be home before six, will you Madge?"

"Yes, yes. Now get going. Do some shopping. I have everything in hand here."

As the agency door closed, Rachel heard the phone ring but decided to leave the matter. With a spring in her step, she bounded down the stairs like Christmas morning.

Leaving the office at Champs-Élysées, Rachel Redmond wasted no time getting home, striding uphill from the Metro, and bursting into their second-floor loft over the flower shop on Rue des Saules. Collapsing onto her sofa, she placed her hands on her temples, with time to think over her day.

Her work had been tedious for weeks, tracking relations of an orphaned child isolated from her family, and she was up against a brick wall when it came to clues. She rifled into her handbag and grinned at the surprise evening with Thomas.

You're right, Madge! Thomas and I don't get out often like this. We've had limitations since moving here from Albany. Someday we'll be free from the New York identity program.

At six, Thomas York arrived at the loft in a sweat from the climb up from Abbesses Metro station at the bottom of St.

Pierre's hill. The tram had passed him on the grade, but he preferred to be alone with his day's end thoughts, a time for silent consultation.

"Rachel, Madge says we're going to a concert tonight at the Bataclan," Thomas called from the door. "Which club is that?" Rachel danced from the bedroom wearing new designer denims, a white silk blouse, tan Fendi heels and a new burgundy leather jacket. Her eyes twinkled with energy.

"You look fabulous Rachel. Looks like you did a little shopping on the way home." Thomas teased walking toward her for a tight embrace. After three years of marriage, they were still very much bride and groom, yearning always for the safe harbor of each other in their hazardous career. His arms wrapped around her, and she finally broke the silence.

"Do you like it?"

"Of course I do."

She reached up and planted a glossy lipstick imprint on his lips. "Now, scoot and get yourself ready."

"What is the group?" Thomas called from the shower.

"The Eagles of Death Metal from California. It's going to be such fun, Thomas. I love the vibes of Montmartre and French music, but we need to spread our wings once in a while. We haven't been out other than for dinner in the longest."

"I hope that isn't a complaint," he called out again, over the shower noise.

"I'm only guilty of wanting to keep you to myself," Rachel teased. "That's our date tonight!"

At her makeup mirror, Rachel paused for an instant to listen to Thomas whistling in the shower. It was *Que Sera*, his favorite, and she smiled her pleasure at their life together. She resumed primping her auburn hair into a French knot, pulling small curls down in front of her ears, then a light spray.

With a dab of French perfume behind each ear, she was ready for a night on the town.

Running late to get the Metro to the 11th arrondissement from Montmartre, Thomas unlocked their tiny Renault Twizy. "I'll park it at behind a friend's near the club zone. We can hop the tube from there, not far to the Bataclan."

Rachel said, "Oh, and my new shoes and I agree! Driving is best tonight!"

"Heaven forbid we call an Uber," Thomas joked.

With the car at his friend's carport off Rue Charonne, they headed past La Belle Équip Café that was already bustling with night patrons. A short line queued out onto the street, and they were forced to squeeze past a Volkswagen van, parked with its wheels taking half the curb.

The van was rusted around the wheel wells and the exterior was painted with offensive graffiti, boasting of Death and Liberty, with symbols of guns and blood.

"I'm surprised that is even allowed on the streets," Rachel said, scrunching her nose.

"Hopefully he'll get towed."

The passenger window was down a crack, and as he passed, Thomas turned his head to see two occupants inside, talking excitedly in a foreign language.

"Did you hear them?" he whispered to Rachel.

"I heard rapid voices, that's all," she said. "Was that Turkish, maybe? Or Syrian?"

Thomas shook his head. "I don't know."

The night air was humid with a mist of rain now hurrying them toward their destination. The sidewalks at Rue Voltaire were congested and bustling as a celebratory crowd squeezed and excitedly moved together toward the club, a three-story 19th-century theater. The warm-up music was loud, as they made their way to a bar for lagers to take to their seats.

Thomas teased, "Ah, I would have thought Madge would have seats for us directly in front of the band."

"No, we'd be sure to lose any hearing we have left. First floor tables will disappear and dancing and singing will take over before you know it. I'm glad our seats are in the balcony. The acoustics will be exceptional in this vintage building."

"Here, we are— the second row," Thomas said. "And on the aisle, with extra room for my lanky frame.

Settling into the red velveteen-cushioned seats, Rachel sighed, "Ah, this is good, even if my new shoes are killing me."

Throngs of patrons of all ages, types, and occasions pressed into the seats and up the staircase to the mezzanine overlooking the stage—music fans, husbands and wives, young lovers, mothers and daughters, friends and business socials, birthdays and anniversaries—anticipating a festive night.

At 9 o'clock, Jesse Hughes, the lead guitarist nicknamed 'the Devil', and Josh Homme, the original founder and drummer, walked on stage leading the other band members to an eruption of boisterous applause. Everyone was standing, cheering and urging the startup of their unique blend of bluegrass slide guitar and stripper drum beat.

The audience was already swaying in eagerness through the welcome monologue and erupted at the band's first chords of *I Only Want You.*

"I do remember this one," Rachel squirmed and began to swoon with the beat.

With each of new songs, the excitement became louder, with inhibitions gone as patrons danced in the aisles, singing in English and French.

By the fifth number, something distracted Thomas over the noise—a loud rumble from outside, and he looked instinctively at his watch. It was 9:40 p.m.

He elbowed Rachel. "Hear that?"

On his phone, he opened a news app, horrified at a flash that four miles away terrorists had attempted to blow up Stade de France during a soccer match between France and Germany.

"Rachel, read this. At least one suicide bomber triggered a bomb in the outer arena."

Their eyes scanned the report together. French President Hollande and German Foreign Minister Steinmeier were safely escorted out and whisked away. The soccer match appeared to continue without warning fans, for fear of panic and stampede among the thousands.

The band had finished *Cherry Cola* and *Silverlake* when a burst of staccato pierced the acoustics. At first, many clubbers thought the sound effects were part of the band's act but Thomas saw Hughes dive to the floor and exit backstage. Homme crawled out the same way.

This isn't part of the act. Something is very wrong.

From the balcony, Thomas' eyes followed three unmasked men in black clothing, blazing Kalashnikov German rifles. He recognized the weapons from military training and knew mass murder was imminent. As bullets erupted over the audience, the scene switched from revelry to bloodied chaos, and the terror of screams couldn't muffle the staccato of bullets.

Rachel's head was huddled low for protection, and Thomas pulled her hand. "Follow me now. Every second counts."

Numb with fear, she locked onto Thomas, crouching toward an exit light. Some balcony patrons had already been struck and were frozen in panic, hovering over companions.

With heads down, Thomas shouted to those around, "Go to the roof or down an outside ladder. Don't go down to the lobby."

Other calm men and women were helping patrons to crouch low as they skulked behind the seats, with many already bloodied. With the unknowns, it would be the blind leading the blind.

A pregnant woman stood in delirium by the level's exit, and Rachel gripped her arm to keep moving. In the hallway, Thomas jammed open the 'Authorized Personnel' door to the third-floor roof and ushered a line of patrons to follow up.

"There should be fire escape ladders, but help will come and you're safer up there, believe that."

Outside, an echo of sirens added panic. While those in the balcony dealt with survival, the plight of those had become horrid, with the main floor covered with blood and bodies. Some that tried to save lives of girlfriends or boyfriends drew the attention of shooters. Their cries were silenced in return, with those lives also fleeting in an instant.

The horror was too much to process, but instincts kicked in for Thomas from training in military tactics.

From the fire escape, concertgoers knotted shirts and clothing to make a chain for repelling down the outside of the brick building. Some waited on window sills or at balcony railings, while others took a leap of faith jumping to those below. Adrenaline was at its peak and the weak gathered strength to become mighty at the moment, clicking on reflexes.

Police and pedestrians now waited with nets and pads below to catch any miss-steps, and to scurry them to a safe zone behind the line of red and yellow striped emergency vehicles. Overhead, helicopters surveyed the roof to evacuate remaining huddled patrons, and drop medics and snipers.

Thomas squatted to grasp the top of the man-made ladder over the outside balcony. "Rachel, it's your turn. Lower yourself slowly . . . I'm not far behind."

She looked at the fledgling knots, then into his eyes, but there was no time to argue. "I love you, Thomas York." Rachel closed her eyes, silently fearing they could be her last words to the man that held her heart.

Thomas remained at the top of the rope that was anchored to an inside radiator, and one by one, folks chose to trust the makeshift evacuation. Barricades popped up on the perimeter, and organized columns of rescuers were preparing to move victims toward the ambulances.

Fierce gunfire on the main floor hadn't stopped and Thomas knew it could be moving in his direction soon. Over the edge, he saw Rachel being comforted by an ambulance worker, insisting she is taken on a stretcher. Her blouse was bloodied. At that moment, he knew he had to be with her as a flashback flooded him of the Webster bombing at the Euler office, with the image of Rachel on a stretcher, limp and bloodied, and near death.

Rachel pushed away from the medic. "No, I don't need to go to the hospital. This isn't my blood. Others need your help."

She squinted into the darkness at his ID. "But I'll always remember your kindness, Ethan."

The man nodded. "I've never seen anything like this."

"Bless you," she said, "and thank you so much."

"Everyone counts," Ethan said. "Remember 'Je suis Charlie'. The French people will overcome. Napoleon said 'Victory belongs to the most preserving. Liberté, égalité et fraternité'," the medic said, reaching for an emotion he was professionally bound to keep at bay.

Rachel shivered as her voice cracked, speaking over the background of piercing sirens. "Merci. I'll remember those words, emblazoned in French history."

As she staggered to her feet, Thomas ran to her side. "Mon Dieu, Rach, there's blood on your clothing. Are you wounded?"

"Don't worry, Thomas. It's not mine." She looked back to the medic again, but he was already back in the Bataclan.

Thomas cupped her face in his hands and wiped a smear of blood from her cheek. "You're my hero and my faithful soldier,

Thomas. I can't imagine what I would do if anything happened to you."

"Honey, you know I need to help here."

"Yes, of course. You wouldn't be the man I married if you didn't live your life following your instincts. You need to help save lives. I'll get out of the way and go over to the fountain to wait. Maybe help the Red Cross people."

On the street, time became locked in slow motion. An eerie calm swept those that escaped, still in a state of numbness between tears and grief. Inside, the terrorists escalated their threats. The Brigade of Research and Intervention were on scene and an elite tactical unit known as R.A.I.D.

After negotiations failed, the police assault commenced at 12:20 a.m., three hours after the first shot, with the counter assault taking only three minutes. Two of the three attackers had blown themselves up with suicide vests. The third tried to escape but stumbled over bodies, and police fired at his suicide belt killing him.

Returning to the outside wall of the Bataclan, Thomas joined others carrying wounded to the ambulances and leading able-bodied to a police unit that was taking names of those leaving the club.

He glanced at a text from Rachel. She was safe, passing on news flashes. Early reports suggested a hundred casualties including the club and five restaurant sites.

A realization struck Thomas.

Those men in the van—could I have done something to change this?

Rachel shivered in the night air and cuddled a young woman who was sobbing.

"Jean is gone! I saw the light leave him—he is no more."

"What's your name?"

"Josephine. Jean called me Josie."

"Josie, you sit right here. See the Red Cross coffee cart? I'll get us a cup. Alright?" Josie nodded, her eyes closed tight.

A Red Cross woman stepped from the cart toward Rachel. "Here, Ma'am. Take a blanket for you and your friend. We'll collect them later when you're ready."

Rachel glanced at her phone to read a short reply from Thomas. "He's okay. Thank God for that."

She couldn't believe the carnage, the blood running on the streets pooling at the storm drains and the mournful sobbing of survivors. Shooters had taken hostages inside and the police were planning drastic measures to save their lives.

Rachel flipped to a long list of shootings on the phone. It wasn't just the Bataclan. Patrons had been murdered at Le Carillon and Le Petite Cambodge near the Saint Martin canal, then shots at Café Bonne Bière on Rue de la Fontaine-au-Roi, killing five more. And moments before the Bataclan, a drive-by shooting in the 11th arrondissement on the terrace restaurant of La Belle Équipe killed nineteen. She read the news to herself, frozen in the horror.

The van! Mon Dieu!

Josie was warmed by the coffee and blanket, and mostly that Rachel stayed.

"I don't know what to do. I don't know how to find Jean's family."

"The lady at the Red Cross said there's a team to help everyone over the coming hurdles, with emotional support and financial assistance. You are safe now, Josie."

"My Jean saved my life. We were on the main floor. When the shots started, he threw his body over mine and told me he loved me. I knew he was going to die."

Rachel squeezed her hand to console without words for his heroic act of love.

Distraught onlookers walked aimlessly out from behind the concrete barriers, some showing phone photos of missing loved ones. A man in his twenties with shoulder-length dark hair in a tail appeared desperate and stopped in front of Rachel and Josie.

"Have you seen my father? His name is Jacques Trudel."

Rachel's instinct allowed him his grief and she reached for the picture.

"You must be proud of your father, he looks like a good man—I see the similarity. There were so many people, I can't say. Where was he in the club? I was on the first balcony with my husband. Many of those escaped."

He didn't answer, and Rachel looked up into his anguished brown eyes.

"Register over there with the Red Cross tent. They'll do their best to match up survivors with hospital records and will be able to contact you. Add your name to any notes on poles and bus stops. Above all, pray and remain hopeful for your Dad's sake. If you come to a dead end, call me."

Rachel regretted saying 'dead end' and handed Jacques her business card. As he walked away, she felt regret that she hadn't even asked him his name.

A new sense of responsibility hit Rachel as she scanned the crowds and faces, deciphering their statuses.

Over there, the man by the Pharmacy. He looks detached and unfeeling. Just staring.

She memorized his features—underweight, a heavy five o'clock beard, cap backward and distinctive heavy-rimmed glasses like Waldo.

He's nervous. His hand . . . on his right pocket. Maybe a weapon.

Rachel's heart pounded with the urgency to flag an officer, but as she watched, two policemen in bullet-proof vests approached him. He became edgy but didn't run, and they left.

In the blur, Thomas didn't remember how they got to the Renault Twizy parked in the 10th arrondissement, then home to Rue des Saules. The roads all around were cordoned off and police searched every car and bike that passed the checkpoints throughout the 10th and 11th arrondissements.

All public transportation systems were shut down to inhibit the escape of perpetrators, and finally at 2:30 a.m., they walked through the door and dropped exhausted on the living room couch. Thomas reached for the remote for a news update.

"No, Thomas. Don't. We'll find out in the morning. Just sit with me for a while."

Two

The following morning, the sun rose minutes before seven, like every other November morning. But today, somber silence echoed dread for all of Paris, as muffled church bells pealed across the city in respect for the souls lost.

It wasn't a matter-of-course morning when windows would be opened to invite the flavor of the streets into homes, but today doors and windows were closed in grief. The chill in the air was unnoticed by the few that ventured onto the sidewalks, overshadowed by the sobering reality of the night.

Rachel eased the balcony door open, not to alert Thomas from his sleep. Curling up on a small bistro chair, she cradled her arms about her knees and let her chin rest there too.

She lost all concept of time until she heard the shower shut off and Thomas emerge with a terry towel around his waist. He noticed Rachel's shadow on the balcony leading from the bedroom. The sun was shining on her auburn tresses, hiding the emotion he knew burned in her heart.

Thomas pulled on jeans and a cotton shirt and went to join his wife. As every morning, he kissed her gently on the neck, her cheeks then her lips. Today she was icy cold and unresponsive, and he knew she'd been crying. They were two very different people, but both intuitive of each other.

He would guide her through their grief, with the reassurance that he'd protect her. She had been the core of his life since the day he saw her on the bus in Ely, back in upstate New York. While he suffered amnesia, she guided him back to his identity, and then his future.

"Honey, we'll get through this together," Thomas said, "Come to the living room and warm up." She offered her hand as she stood, and he held her in a long embrace.

"Thomas, would you mind putting up a small fire in the hearth. I need to burn my clothes from last night."

Over crumpled newspaper, he teepeed kindling, then watched it dance into an orange fury over the wood.

Rachel's clothing was on the floor, and she looked at it quickly with disdain. "I can't touch them, Thomas. Would you do it?"

The only sound was the crackling of the fire as he retrieved the discarded silk blouse and jeans tossed them into the flame.

"The leather jacket?"

She nodded, and he removed it from the back of the chair and placed it in the outside trash with the bloodied Fendi shoes. Then the same with his.

As Paris woke to the news, telephone lines and cell phones lit up across town, across France, and around the world. Today's news said the attackers were from within Europe and the plot was organized inside France and Belgium. With the exception of Britain, European nationalities were free to cross borders without inspection or customs declarations, but today Belgium was scrutinizing the influx of possible terrorists.

The manhunt had grown overnight, tracking the terrorists' movements from Paris to Brussels, with door-to-door searches in both cities. Raids were resulting in hundreds of arrests in Brussels. A ringleader, Salah Abdesalam, was on a Brussels security camera, renting a black compact Renault Clio several days before. A manhunt was underway to track him down.

Both Thomas and Rachel's phones were buzzing. One message was from Madge.

"Oh, my gosh, Thomas. We forgot about Madge. She'll be going out of her mind with worry."

"I'll call her now."

Madge Bitteridge was stocky in stature with a heart of gold. Without even a sick day since she was hired two years before, she prided herself on her tight ship at the office. Her children were married and lived away, so she had adopted Thomas and Rachel as her nearest kin.

Following her morning rituals, she rose and put the kettle on and let a warm bath run. Her morning paper was in the slot in her door, and she gasped at the front page littered with the first horrific pictures of a massacre at Le Bataclan.

Her hand covered her eyes as she lowered to a chair.

"My heavens, what have I done? I couldn't bear it if anything happened to Thomas and Rachel."

Thomas reached her on the first ring.

"Madge, it's okay. We're both fine. Sorry that we didn't call and leave a message. Folks won't mind if the office doesn't open today, and the police are asking wherever possible to remain at home. Rachel needs to have today at home with me. You understand, don't you?"

"Yes, yes, my dear. If only I hadn't given you the tickets. It must have been awful."

"The news is still coming out. Paris is in emergency lockdown with transit out of commission and many stores closed. A massive manhunt is looking for others claiming responsibility. The police are holding back information that might interfere with the capture of those who escaped. Stay home and call your friends to let them know you're safe."

"No, no, I'll go to the office. I'm best to keep busy."

"Thanks, Madge, but Rachel is adamant. You must stay home . . . and she says she sends her love. Okay, thank you." He put down his phone and nodded to Rachel.

"She'll stay put."

"Thomas, I should call my parents and Amy. With social media and cable channels, the bad news is instant. They'll know all about it."

With two piping coffees, they sat close on their comfy, beige corduroy sofa. His arm was around her shoulder and she hugged a large cushion.

Rachel said, "Also, your Dad will worry . . . and Bert too."

Thomas squeezed her hand, recognizing her caring responses and sensitivity in dealing with tragedy. He knew it from the past. "If you're up to it, we could stroll up to the Basilica and light a candle and offer a prayer."

"Yes, that would be the right thing," Rachel said, intending to reflect stoicism, but the trembling in her hand gave her away.

As they stepped onto the street, Marie, the shop owner downstairs, was placing out the flower pails and watering the planters. Marie was sixtyish and had become more than a landlady, but was a trusted friend.

She was wearing her familiar floral smock and gloves to protect her hands from thorny roses. Toby, her bloodhound looked up at Rachel from his noisy slurps from the water pail, debating between his thirst and an ear rub.

"Bonjour, Marie. Such sad news for Paris today, but Napoleon said: 'Victory comes to those with perseverance.' We must remember that." Rachel felt a second of guilt for stealing the medic's phrase.

Pushing a wayward strand of hair from her face, Marie left a smudge on her cheek and embraced Rachel, then Thomas. Her face was stern today with sadness. "Thank goodness you two weren't there. C'est tragique."

Rachel contained the pain that was still so fresh for her. "We're going up to the Sacré-Coeur to light a candle, I'd like to take some memorial flowers. Put something together for us, please."

"Of course, dear." In a paper tissue envelope tied with a red bow, Marie placed some delicate white roses and carnations.

"My mother told me as a child that the carnation carries great symbolism: white is reverence, and red represents deep affection, pure love and good, while the pink carnation is said to be the tears of the Virgin Mary. These will be from the heart," Marie said, then paused. "Light a candle for me as well. I won't take payment for the flowers, you understand."

Marie made a skedaddle gesture to them, and Toby started to follow, thinking he might get a walk out of Rachel. But Marie called him back.

Hand in hand, Thomas and Rachel headed uphill on the winding streets to the point where Rue Paul Albert goes one way and Butte the other.

On the seven banks of steps up to the Basilica, they stopped to rest on the landings, bordered by garden suites and four-story lofts with heavy doors, robust gardens, and trellises.

At the top, the magnificent Basilica stood at the highest point in the city, with fifteen-story arches and a promenade circling across the front. At least a dozen gendarmes in khaki uniforms paced the sidewalk, with rifles slung over their shoulders. A few naïve tourists, unmindful of the previous evening, posed behind the policemen for selfies and were shuttled away into the church without commotion.

Several street artists had set up easels along the stone railing with a distant view of the Eiffel Tower and the panorama of Paris. Before the acrylic would dry, their canvases would be sold around the corner at Place du Tertre, in the center courtyard of the artisan community.

It had become a romantic place to Rachel, and she often imagined Montmartre in the eyes of Henri Toulouse-Lautrec, who spent most of his life here, capturing the passion and energy of the bohemian community.

Her favorite accordion busker was playing a soulful rendition of the Italian romantic 'O Sole Mio' in tribute.

She tossed a few euros into a box at his feet. "Pierre, it's beautiful, but could I persuade you to play a French waltz that makes your foot tap, and puts smiles on our faces today?"

His lively jig filled the somber mood and others gathered in the square to clap hands to the rhythm.

"Merci, merci!"

The arrival of a white and blue tram interrupted the fun, bringing four carts of tourists from the base of the hill. The caboose's engineer tooted at a straggler as he pulled up to the side of the Sacré-Coeur to disembark.

Thomas moaned, "Let's wait 'til the tourists have had a chance at the Basilica. It's hard to say a prayer for those that died, with constant selfies and cameras flashing."

"Later suits me," Rachel said, pulling him back toward the artists. Passing a caricaturist and easels of more artisans and craftsmen, she stopped to observe the work of an artist she recognized, an older man, with a long, peppered beard and beret. She knew he was faithfully in the same spot every day, often with his half-smoked stogie. As she moved closer to admire his project, she smelled smoked sausage and burnt toast. He lit up to see their familiar faces.

"Bonjour, Emily and Joseph!"

Joseph and Emily Harkness were the assumed names for Rachel Redmond and Thomas York when they arrived in Paris in the witness protection program. An unscrupulous lawyer and his conspirators were serving long sentences in a New York prison, while Sanderson, the kingpin of an insurance fraud was on death row for murder.

As the tentacles of his mob were far-reaching, Thomas and Rachel had not yet been given CIA's green light to return to their own names. In their hasty exit to France, Rachel left her parents and sister, Amy, in the suburbs of Albany, and Thomas left his father in Florida, aging and in poor health.

"Bonjour, Émile. What are you painting today?"

"It must be of sadness, oui?"

"You're right, Émile. We can't paint over the truth that exists—it will be part of us from today forward and this pain should never be forgotten. We'll come and see your finished work later; please save this one for me, it will be my statue of the spirit of the Parisians overcoming adversity."

"Merci, Emily. It will be special."

From his pallet of brilliant colors, Émile touched a round brush to add a tint of black. The sun would not shine in his paintings today, replaced by clouds and tears and emotions of a passionate heart.

Their voices and footsteps echoed on the cobblestones as they neared their Patisserie.

"Madame, shall we stop for café au lait and zee chocolate croissants?" Thomas said with his best French accent. "That's me doing Chevalier. Could you tell?"

"Oui, oui, Monsieur. Shall we defer to La Boulangerie Pomponette?"

Rachel laid the bouquet on the table and cuddled the foaming cup in her hands. Thomas always delighted in coffee and morning croissants, and today was no different.

"What can I get you, Rach?"

"Ooo, a buttery croissant with jam. With this aroma, I do feel hungry after all."

Her blue eyes looked deep into his, and she brushed her hand over his.

He's my pillar today.

Rachel found a bistro table under an outside canopy and Thomas straightened some wicker chairs. With crowds now emerging to the streets, it was apparent that Paris would revive itself quickly.

"Ah, Thomas, it is good to be alive, non?"

"Oui, oui." He pointed toward a sudden boisterous cheer for an entertaining street busker. "With artists, musicians and tourists alone, France will survive. And Montmartre seems isolated from grief."

As voices raised at the next table in an argument about yesterday's soccer match between France and Germany, Rachel nodded. "Yes. Isolated indeed."

A tourist queue was starting toward the Sacré-Coeur at the tram's stop at Rue de Chevalier, but was loosely disorganized, snapping pictures.

"We'd better scurry and beat this line," Rachel said. At the door of the Basilica, the armed guards asked to look into Rachel's bag and to examine the floral arrangement.

"Excusé, Madame. Les fleurs must be outside the doors."

Rachel knelt by the stone wall and placed her bouquet beside other tributes. After a visual inspection, her bag passed through a portable x-ray machine and a fortified door frame.

The magnificent church dated to the Druids of Gaul's regime, and in subsequent centuries suffered crumbling and fire until the 12th-century resurrection when the chapel was restored to its glory by Gothic inspiration. The basilica stood as a political and cultural monument signifying national penance in the Franco-Prussian War of 1871. Construction of the chapel in 1875 was in tribute and was completed at the end of World War II.

Passing the bronze doors to the 19th-century chapel, Rachel stopped in awe of the dedicated stained glass and ceiling mosaics.

"It feels so reverent, Thomas. We should come often, it's so close to home."

At the votive table, they deposited euros for two candles. Kneeling on prayer stools, they prayed for comfort and strength for the survivors and victims' families.

"Yes, the tears of Mary. I am glad of the carnations," she said. "The Heavens do weep today."

Outside, Rachel wandered to the railing for a moment of contemplation. Through the remains of the morning mist, she could see a hazy Eiffel tower. But sunbeams were pushing through to brighten the clouds that blanketed Paris.

"It appears calm and at peace from here, Thomas."

"Yes, but it's far from the truth. Hidden in this beautiful view, the city is immobilized at metro stations and public facilities where large groups would gather. Even look behind us here at the presence of the gendarme guards, posted and eager to find a terrorist—to seek retribution." Thomas was the realist. "And down there . . . so many families are preparing to bury their own. The grief must be surreal."

"But the view is the same as it was yesterday," she mused. "We're standing on a historic parapet that will remember this day as it has so many others."

They lingered wanting to be in the embrace of Parisians who suffered. "It's odd the way sadness seeks sadness for comfort, isn't it Thomas?"

Rachel rested on the grand staircase to watch arrivals at the top of the funicular, an angled railway from the Basilica to the base of the hill. The ninety-second ride paralleled two hundred steps running up Rue Foyalier and served the metros at Place Saint Pierre/Place Suzanne Valadon and Rue du Cardinal Dubois, where Rachel and Thomas walked most days.

Her eye caught a man standing near the funicular. She looked away quickly then back again. His eyes were scanning everywhere, watching intently.

My intuition isn't good about this.

The man had a heavy five o'clock shadow and wore a backward cap, and heavy-rimmed Waldo eyeglasses.

Must be my imagination.

Thomas noticed her silent thought and intent gaze.

"What is it, Rachel?"

"It's preposterous, totally preposterous! That man was outside the Bataclan last night. I distinctly remember . . . he looked suspicious to me and persistently patted his pocket. I wondered if he was carrying a gun."

"The man in the ball cap?"

The Waldo impersonator had become aware of Rachel and Thomas watching and began fidgeting and pacing.

"Looks like he's waiting for someone," Thomas summed.

Suddenly, one of the gendarmes approached the man and took him by the elbow. With his arms over his head, the policeman patted him down while a second gendarme pointed a rifle at him.

"I haven't done anything. When is it a crime to enjoy the view of Paris?"

"Come with us now for a few questions." As the gendarme attempted to lead him, the man dug in his heels.

"No, no! I must wait here. You don't understand, it is very important that I be right here."

The guard wasn't interested in his explanations and momentarily gave in to his pleas.

A curious crowd was collecting in hearing range to watch, but suddenly everyone craned their necks skyward toward an overhead noise, a buzzing of a remote-controlled eagle kite drone. As it advanced, Thomas spotted a camera and a small payload in the undercarriage.

Three

Ornery and agitated, Waldo struggled to hold his position, anchoring his feet and locking his limbs, and forcing the gendarme to drag any movement.

The buzz grew louder as it closed in over the Basilica promenade. The initial crowd murmurs turned to shrieking as skittish spectators scampered for cover behind the trees and railings. Taking no chances, the guards pushed back on the perimeter of pedestrians.

"Get down!"

In perfect sniper aim, a soldier fired upward in a staccato of bullets at the drone, inciting the crowd into more panic. As the fragments of debris plummeted to the ground, a tiny cylinder dropped toward Rachel, landing at her feet. Thomas put his foot over it.

Other particles of the aerodynamic delivery unit were immediately claimed by the gendarme as evidence fragments. One shouted out, "Clear the area and don't touch anything."

An immediate security checkpoint was set up to clear the pedestrians, instantly reinforced by the second wave of guards racing up the funicular.

Thomas shuffled the cylinder behind his shoe and bent to tie his shoelace, rising with the tube in a closed fist.

Out of their sight, an Arabic man returned a drone controller to his backpack. He was distinctive in appearance, in his mid-thirties with a dark complexion and beard, slight early balding and a mass of long, curly hair. Climbing down a giant oak beside the Basilica and near the tram pickup point, he slithered unseen into the background with the ease of a magician and made his escape.

But he'd been quick to assess the intrusive pair who intercepted the drone, and his eyes moved to watch the gendarme, now forcing his accomplice's hands into cuffs.

Suddenly the suspect attempted to bolt from the guard's grip but was tackled to the ground.

"That is mine—it belongs to me. I didn't do anything."

His dark seething eyes scanned the ground, searching for the wayward cylinder, and burrowed into Thomas's eyes.

Two other gendarmes arrived to lead the man away, while another gathered more pieces of metal and plastic for later examination. The drone's camera, still intact, was added to the evidence pouch.

Thomas nudged Rachel as he slipped the cylinder into his pocket. She raised her brows and nodded, aware of the value of this fresh evidence. Discreetly, they scoured the ground for drone fragments, hoping for something of consequence that could be traced to a registration.

"Honey, if we scurry, we'll beat the tourists to the Botok Café for lunch," Thomas said.

Passing onlookers, they sauntered down to the outdoor café at Rue Paul Albert, at the conjunction of the staircase and the public park. The colorful patio umbrellas were raised, and patrons were arriving at the bistro tables, buzzing with gossip from the promenade scuffle.

From years of military training, Thomas was attuned to changes in the environment, and instinctively scanned the terrain and nearby tree roots, for any object, shadow or sound. His radar picked up on something out of the ordinary.

The patio was congested with sullen locals, drowning their grief from the night in a glass of wine or café. Chantal, a regular server recognized the pair and rushed to Rachel.

"Your favorite table is available and I'll clear it. It's crazy here today, but I'll be back in a few minutes. There's a saying that misery loves company." Chantal straightened their metal bistro chairs and hastened to the kitchen.

Before Rachel could ask about the cylinder, Thomas interjected. "First things first, Rach. I'm famished again. Their Beef Tartare is the best."

Rachel grimaced. "I'm good with the Nicoise Salad and an Americano."

"Ditch the coffee. How's a half liter of Chardonnay?"

"Better still," she sighed and laughed. "Now show me the cylinder."

Thomas grinned as he watched her curiosity peak, then spoke in an almost silent whisper. He looked across to the park and observed the patrons.

"Where a criminal lurks, partners can be nearby—it's possible we're being followed. We'd be naïve to assume we could intercept such an object without someone observing."

From the vantage of an ancient robinia pseudocacia tree across from the patio in the thickly treed park, a man blended into the low hanging branches, watching them. The man was dark-skinned with bushy black hair protruding from a black woolen toque. He took a small camera from his pocket and moved into a cover of the shrubs until he had a focus on the pair at the bistro.

The hair on Thomas's neck ruffled as he returned his gaze to the row of trees at the edge of the foliage.

Something isn't right. The oak tree . . . there's a shadow behind.

Leaning onto the table, he whispered, "The gendarme picked up a camera from the pieces. It's likely our faces are in the footage, and I'd be curious where the film ends up."

"What was it you picked up?" Rachel asked.

"A metal cylinder." The tube from his pocket was no bigger than a fountain pen, and he shielded it in a menu. "There's a cap or a lid here at the end."

Flipping it open, he tapped the tube on the table and a tight, rolled blueprint fell out.

"A blueprint!" Rachel whispered. "Why would someone deliver a blueprint at Sacré-Coeur by drone to a man standing on the promenade?"

Thomas turned to listen to a dog bark in the park and the rustle of a branch a few feet into the brush.

"We're being watched by the bushes. Someone who didn't want to be seen with the pickup man . . . perhaps he wasn't even known to the other man."

"Waldo was hardly inconspicuous," Rachel said. "If he hadn't been edgy, I might not have noticed him. We're just a couple having lunch, he can't hear us."

In spite of Rachel's protest, Thomas re-rolled the blueprint and returned it to the cylinder.

"When you saw him in Rue Voltaire did he speak with anyone else?"

"No, he made a point of keeping to himself."

"My gut tells me these two incidents are connected. If this is terrorism, it's over our head, Rachel."

"What do we do?"

"First, we'll take a look at the blueprint and see if we can identify the location. We'll do that back at the loft."

The waitress arrived with her tray of entrees.

"Steak tartare pour le monsieur et une salade savoureuse pour Madame. It's a sad day but nice to see a familiar face. One day the terrorists might come to Montmartre. No one is safe."

As Chantal recovered from the words, she turned away to a table, calling for a check.

"It's not safe to open it here, Rachel."

Her frown and grimace showed her impatience. "Looks like I'll have to wait."

"Yum, this beef is delicious. Next time you should have this instead of a plate of weeds and foliage," Thomas teased.

Rachel's face froze. "There's a definite movement in the park," she whispered. "Someone has just taken off running."

"Stay here, Rach. I'll check."

Under the colossal oak were considerable depressions in the grass and trampled cigarette butts. Thomas collected them in oak leaves as evidence, should they need it later.

"Rachel, the grass is worn with footprints. But no-one is there." He didn't mention the butts, avoiding needless alarm.

At the Rue des Saules loft, Thomas spread out the blueprint and anchored the curled corners with books, and they both bent close to study the print.

"Here, it says Denfert-Rochereau; and there's the Cemetery of Montparnasse," Thomas said.

"In the 14th arrondissement," Rachel nodded and looked up abruptly. "Montparnasse—it's the location of the Paris catacombs museum."

"Yes, I recall. It has a romantic history in the public square, Place D'Enfer, an evil place, with a wall built in the memory of farmers."

"Farmers?"

"An ancient regime built a guarded crossing from Paris for farmers trying to escape paying excise taxes in the 1700's."

Rachel laughed at his nerdiness and peered closer. "It would be eerie to venture into the catacombs." She winked. "I haven't been fond of dungeons since our adventure in Rouen."

"These are engineered mechanical drawings," Thomas said.

"Are those tunnels?"

Thomas found a magnifying glass. "Specifications show tunnels under Place Denfert-Rochereau, spreading all the way to Montmartre without any sign of the modern urbanization of the last century. I don't see an architect's signature or firm on the surveys. There's a small box here that almost looks like a hologram."

"Why would someone today be interested in these old tombs?" Rachel asked.

"We have to decide if we want to know the answer to that, Rach."

Rachel's pleading blue eyes opened wide. "We've never yet turned away from a challenge."

They gritted their teeth at each other playfully. "We do thrive on the edge of danger, don't we? Wisely or unwisely."

"That's what makes us such good detectives—we can't leave stones unturned."

Rachel paused in troubled thought. "Thomas, I don't really want to say this . . . but since we can't just go to the police with what we know, perhaps someone could help us."

"I know what you mean—and who you mean. The city is consumed in the search for escaped terrorists. They still haven't identified all the victims and our borders are being locked down. Even if we went to the authorities, this could get buried in a Cold Case file for years. All the Directorates and bureaucracies have been steered to the manhunt, and we have no contacts in those bureaus."

"We're on our own for the time being. Do you know where he is . . . Daniel, I mean?"

"He disappears for months at a time, but I have sources to locate him."

"I hope he's alright. We haven't heard since my aunt's wedding in California. He could be incognito here—perhaps take an underground mission."

"A friend at Interpol can put out the word for us."

Four

Montparnasse district, on the left bank of the Seine, was the center of culture and creativity, reminiscent of 1920's bohemian, bars and studios. Walls of the cafés still seemed to echo the sounds and sights of the likes of Picasso, Matisse, Dali, Degas, and Chagall.

The Boulevard still houses historic establishments of La Rotonde and La Closerie, where Hemingway wrote *The Sun Also Rises*. At Le Dome, Gertrude Stein had hosted Saturday night soirées, with private inquisitions on empathy, suffering and above all passion.

In the roaring twenties, poverty was a respected luxury, with popular restaurants and cafés of Montparnasse eager to accept the art of impoverished painters to hang on their walls in lieu of tabs, many remaining today to the envy of Europeans.

In the afternoon's lingering daylight, Rachel and Thomas set out on the metro from St. Pierre on an exploratory trip to inhale the arts on Montparnasse and pace the surroundings of Place Denfert-Rochereau.

The next morning, they rode the same metro route to meet their contact. The Denfert-Rochereau garden was shedding its fall leaves, and horse chestnuts littered the lawns that were encircled with maple and black locust trees.

Magnificent, handsome stone buildings stood on the outskirts, and remnants of two guard towers graced the entrance to the wall.

Rachel waited at the museum threshold, standing at a giant marble pillar, while Thomas stayed in the shadow of a maple, sheltered to survey the crowds of tourists.

Rachel wiggled an earphone with a direct connection to Thomas. "Can you hear me?"

"Loud and clear, Babe."

"Do you see him?"

"Not yet, but he'll be here. He's never let us down."

"Relax, Rachel, and behave like an interested tourist," Thomas joked. "Your beauty is like honey attracting the bees."

Striding across the lawn, with masculine conviction, a tall and dashing lean man headed toward the museum. He was like a chameleon, seen when he chooses, but could disappear when the wind of bureaucracy came too close.

Years before in New York, when Thomas York first met his later counterpart, Daniel Boisvert, circumstances led to a life and death situation for both of them. Thomas would never forget when Daniel reached into the Hudson to save him from drowning.

When the threesome of Daniel, Joseph, and Emily reunited in Paris, they established a bond of trust and friendship, although at times suspect. The brotherly bond was even stronger now.

The first clue of recognition to Rachel was Daniel's jacket, pulled up in the November wind, and his black turtleneck. He was cleanly shaven with a fresh haircut.

"It's him," she proclaimed.

"Yes, and I bet he still has a whiff of cherry tobacco," Thomas teased Rachel, then silently left her at the museum and moved across the park behind Daniel, surprising him with a slap on the back.

"Hey, old friend, glad to see you!"

Daniel swung around with fury. "Don't ever do that, Thomas. I almost gave you a judo flip. In my line of work, I am extraordinarily sensitive to touch and movement."

In seconds, his face lightened up.

"I forgot the rules of etiquette between rogues," Thomas laughed.

"Where's your better half?"

"I'm glad to see you too. Rachel's at the museum waiting for us. We've missed you, pal, and finally found an excuse for a reunion. What have you been doing?"

"Here and there with the organization. You know I can't tell you specifics, but as always I keep a balance of danger in my life."

Daniel's eyes twinkled with mischief. "I'm still waiting for the day you'll join me in saving the world."

"Hmm . . . it's a tough choice between you and Rachel," Thomas mocked.

As the pair walked toward Rachel, her heart fluttered.

My goodness, what a handsome pair of men. Dear Daniel has saved my life a time or two, but Thomas—he saves me every day.

Thomas scrutinized her expression as they neared. He was well aware of the special and unique connection between his wife and his best friend.

If anything happened to me, I know Daniel would swoop in to rescue my wife.

"Daniel, what name do you go by these days?"

"I don't expect to cross paths with anyone who'd know me from my past or present, so we can stick with Daniel here."

His eyes flashed with a seething soul of a vagabond. Rachel reached up and embraced him for longer than Thomas liked.

"Let me take a look at my girl." Daniel stepped back and surveyed Rachel. "Beautiful as always."

Thomas interrupted, inserting himself between the two. "Now that we're reacquainted, let's find a pub for an ale and a long discussion."

Daniel sat across from Thomas and Rachel at a booth as he inspected the blueprints. His brow was tight with concern, realizing the extent of the underground web before him.

"How did you come by this? It's highly classified and kept under lock and key in the President's office. This is a significant security breach for the French government. These should be in a sealed environment at the Palace of Justice."

"We found it exactly as I explained on the phone—dropped by a drone at the Basilica."

"Are you two prepared for where this might lead? It's not going to be a treasure hunt. Once you deviate from the marked catacombs, it's an unmarked precarious territory. I've heard stories of hauntings and ghosts, of people going in out of curiosity and overtaken with unsolved mysterious. Over the years, many have disappeared, with bodies not found for decades or even centuries."

Thomas replied, "We understand. But it could be a clue to a terrorist plot connected to the Paris shootings or a future plan. Would we be good citizens if we passed up the chance to intervene and possibly save lives?"

"Do you both think that's the case?"

"I had a risky encounter," Rachel said. "It was a man outside the Bataclan, who then reappeared on the Basilica promenade the next morning. "He was disturbed and paranoid. Isn't that enough to be concerned?"

Daniel looked at her pleading and sparkling eyes.

"Thomas, do you put up with this every day?" he joked.

"Yes, and I love it."

Downing the rest of his ale, Daniel got down to business.

"I did some research yesterday and hacked into the museum schematics of the catacombs and tunnels. It's recorded that more than four hundred miles of a labyrinth of tunnels and chambers lie under the Paris streets, besides these catacombs."

"Should I be taking notes?" Rachel asked without intending sarcasm.

"No. You just need to keep me close by."

"Alright. Just lay out the plan," Thomas said.

Daniel zoomed in on the blueprints with his smartphone.

"See here . . . these marks don't appear on the museum plan." He paused at the fine print in the corner. "And these initials belong to highly classified personnel. Curious how they got into the hands of a drone operator."

"Over here is a metro line, Daniel," Rachel said. "Do you think we can get through to those tunnels from the catacombs?"

"First things first, kids," Thomas said. "Let's agree on the premise for this hunt. It's all based on preliminary information of a suspicious man at the Bataclan and the Basilica that might be connected to the terrorist massacre. We assume he's a terrorist. What would he want with a blueprint of underground tunnels?"

"It could lead to a stash of weapons," Rachel said, "or a hideout or an underground railroad of sorts."

Daniel thought for a moment. "I agree, it would seem this has something to do with the terrorists. The police focus is on a sect operating out of Brussels. Was the man French, Rachel?"

"I didn't speak with him. I assumed so but could be wrong. Paris is so cosmopolitan now, with its increasing immigrant population."

"Let's take a catacomb tour in the morning and take measurements using the blueprints." Daniel stood suddenly, ready to go his way.

"You're welcome to stay with us at the loft," Rachel offered.

"Thanks, but I have a place of my own already."

"Then would you join us on the hill later for dinner?" she said.

"Thanks, I'll take a rain check." Daniel was gone.

In the loft, Thomas delved into internet facts about the catacombs history as an ancient cemetery in the 18th century near the old Appian Way. As cemeteries became overwhelmed with a need for private plots, the catacombs became a practical storage for skulls and bones and isolated the spread of rampant diseases by closing channels and strengthening the old mines.

The Paris government re-evaluated the cemeteries, and between 1787 and 1814, skulls and bones were removed from dedicated cemetery land and placed in depleted quarries to fortify the roadway system later known as the catacombs.

At various times in history, the catacombs were used as a sanctuary of secrets, concealing a great portion of prohibition for bootleggers that built stills and brew houses in the tunnels.

Later, when technical sources and electricity found their way into the tunnels, police search regularly for vagrants living in the depths, finding illegal cinemas, bars, and restaurants.

In 1999, the Arènes de Chaillot were discovered under the Palais de Chaillot, when a group defying authority thrived in small theaters, tapping into the city's electric system. It had become trendy to conquer the tunnels and steal electricity and conveniences.

'The Painted Lizard', the fascist Paris underground leader, was Lézard Peint, who sanctioned a world or expression without rules and consequences. Its sanctuary of secrets was the same world of Jean Valjean of Les Misérables, and the police sent units under the Trocadero in the 16th arrondissement to shut down the subterranean theaters. For years after, the tunnels were closed until renovations in 2005, with the museum and catacombs becoming a tourist attraction.

Thomas searched the gallery of photos of its network under the limestone sections of Paris. Chalk tunnels and barren caverns were relatively untouched except for the adventurous spelunker and homeless vagrants.

"Rachel, check these pictures. It is eerie, but I'm definitely curious about the history and use of these tunnels. They were used by the French Resistance in World War II as a bunker to hide from Germans."

Rachel leaned over his shoulder at the pictures, momentarily distracting him with her Matchabelli Wind Song cologne. He took a deep breath of it and she teased him with her eyes before he continued.

"I'll print the map that Daniel hacked from the museum and we'll make an overlay for the blueprint."

"Oh, my goodness, Thomas. Are those skulls and bones jammed into mosaics on the wall?"

"I said it was eerie. And yes, each is a deceased person. Many attempted to conquer the depth of the tunnels that are joined by rabbit holes and occasional ladders dropping or rising to other levels. At many points, you can't stand up straight and you could walk for hours, hunched in watery trenches. Are you sure you're up to doing this, Rachel?"

"We have a blueprint and two strong intelligent men that I trust to lead the way," she teased. Thomas didn't react.

"We'll need a couple days to collect supplies for the journey," he said. "At an army supply, I'll get mine helmets, gumboots, and lanterns. Look here on the overlay . . . we'll be traveling a long distance before they connect."

Rachel stood behind Thomas and massaged his neck. "How do we get in?"

"The museum is open Tuesday to Sunday from ten to eight, with the last tour at 7:30. They check bags at the entrance and exit to search for anyone pilfering bones. We'll have to avoid checkpoints as our equipment is suspect, but we won't exit with a tour group. We'll deviate into these tunnels."

Locking onto spots marked 'X' at conjunctions of the map, Rachel marked in red ink what appeared to be ladders or access points to railway tunnels, basements of hospitals or churches, or into the drainage system through grates and manholes.

She didn't want to admit her fear. "I'm wondering what Daniel is really doing tonight, Thomas?"

"As always, he's peculiarly evasive and reclusive. He's the kind of person you wonder about. Did he even have parents and roots once?"

"Let's order dinner in, I don't feel like going out tonight."

Rachel couldn't admit how scared she really was in this adventure. Mentally taxed, she drew a bubble bath and took an aromatic candle with her to retreat.

"Chinese or baguettes?" Thomas called out.

"Chinese, but have it delivered, I don't want you going out without me. Call Marvin at St. Pierre's. I like their egg roll."

Thomas knew she was worrying and needed him to reassure her. He understood when she needed time like this to herself to reason with her thoughts, and when it was best dealt with in a bath.

"Of course, I won't go. Take your time. I ordered and they said thirty to forty minutes."

"Thanks, Honey. I love you."

"You too, Babe."

Rachel put on freshly ironed, baby pink silk pajamas and waited for Thomas at the dining table. She found it enchanting that he had laid out the good china for her, with two tall candlesticks. She watched the flames flicker and realized how lucky she was.

At the sound of the downstairs doorbell, Rachel shuddered. Thomas kissed her on the cheek and bounded down the stairs. As he unloaded the containers from a paper bag, she placed her arms on his shoulders. "Am I dressed suitably for the occasion?"

"Just the way I like my dinner companion."

"Then dish our plates; can we watch the news as we eat?"

Thomas gritted his teeth into a smile. "You know there's no good news today, don't you?"

"Yes, but life goes on and I don't want to live in denial."

Video horror still suffocated all the channels. Watching a clip of survivors running outside near the fountain, she jumped up. "Hold that scene! Replay that last portion?"

They moved closer to the screen, studying every movement. "Freeze that, Thomas. See behind me by the wall. That's the man—that's Waldo. Perhaps if we had a picture, Daniel could check it through his sources."

"Saved. I took a photo and I'll send the video tonight."

Rachel went to sleep exhausted from her emotions. Haunting images of the club massacre rushed into her subconscious as she fretfully tossed in and out of a nightmare.

With a crush of thousand ideas in his mind, Thomas knew he wouldn't be able to sleep yet, but he laid down beside Rachel and stroked her hair. Gently rubbing her back, her breathing slowed and her muscles relaxed into a slumber.

In the glow of his phone, Thomas continued to search news updates on raids and roundups. The day of blood had been carefully orchestrated, with a chain of soldiers moving about Paris.

A man named Abaaoud, who had recruited a network of accomplices, was killed in the police raid, but his two brothers Brahim and Salah Abdeslam were on the loose. Their known acquaintances were being arrested in France and Belgium, with some released, and others under house arrest. Police had already raided more than two hundred locations, seizing multiple weapons.

Fabien Clain, an ISIL representative calling himself Brother Omar, bragged of a successful attack on Europe in return for its treatment of Muslims, in accordance with their vows for jihad vengeance with blood. Even while serving a prison sentence, he established a recruitment network before making his way into Syria.

Clain had been in the news in April, before the Bataclan, taking responsibility for a planned attack on a southern Paris church that was foiled by the ineptness of an accomplice. Each time the terrorists succeeded, Clain praised ISIL for the blessed attacks on the French Crusaders for striking insurgents in caliphate with their aircraft strikes.

Searching every possible link, Thomas took note of a drug raid in an abandoned warehouse in Brussels.

This will be worth checking out.

As the free world continued in shock, a service was announced for the following day at the Place de la République, as a focal point for mourning, floral tributes, and candles.

"Mon Dieu, what is the world coming to? Should I postpone our meeting with Daniel at the park? The French President asked that residents stay indoors for safety."

He mulled it over for a long time before concluding. "No, that is the way of cowards. I'll not give them victory in forcing me to be afraid."

But the visions of the blueprints kept Thomas awake. His automatic reflexes examined and re-examined the various scenarios, and at 2:30 a.m. he sat bolt upright.

It can't be!

Five

At six on Monday morning in Montparnasse, on the left bank of the Seine, the church bells of Saint-Germain-des-Prés pealed from the Romanesque tower across the 6th arrondissement echoing into the 14th.

Daniel was already awake, having left the windows open overnight. From his window on the third floor of the Lenox Montparnasse, he could see the magnificent Petit Luxembourg Palace and the surrounding acres of elm trees and gardens.

He watched as the streets below began to stir. First, a street washer motored past, collecting the residue left in the gutters from the street bars overnight.

Toward the east, early morning crowds surged toward the Vavin Metro, heading to work, and today, some Parisians that rarely attended church services were appeasing guilt by queuing up for first mass.

"I might as well get up, since you are," Daniel groaned toward the window in a long stretch.

Half an hour later, he stepped through the quaint lobby to a breakfast room, impeccably designed with peach colored, square armchairs. The aroma of bacon drew him in, and taking a table for two by the window, he settled in to review the news on his iPhone and an issue of Le Monde that was folded at his table.

"Just the one text; everything else is as expected."

Daniel Boisvert was a handsome man of almost thirty years. Dark brown eyes and short-shorn hair with a swag of loose curls captivated attention, whenever he could use it to his advantage. He had continually shown Thomas and Rachel an uncanny skill to disappear into the background, and his physique excelled in any brawl they'd seen.

Bachelor life suited Daniel's style of traveling and mystique since his days of training and recruitment into Interpol, previously going underground to bring out villains by gaining their trust. This time, he came to Paris from Moscow on short notice at the appeal from his friends.

Rachel and Thomas . . . or are you Emily and Joseph Harkness today? It was good to see you well. I value the adventures we've shared. Are we the Three Musketeers of the 21ˢᵗ century?

At 7:30 a.m., he strode down Rue Delambre in search of the café Auberge de Venise, the onetime historic Dingo American Bar, in the Montparnasse Quarter.

The Dingo was where Ernest Hemingway and F. Scott Fitzgerald first met amongst peers and literary critiques, and here James Joyce wrote *Finnegan's Wake,* becoming a grazing ground for authors. Other great writers languished here in flowing champagne and inebriation, inspiring *The Immovable Feast* and *The Great Gatsby.*

Many believed that great art came from poverty, when the senses are sharper and emotions deeper, touching an inner depth of beauty. The Dingo was popular twenty-four hours a day in the 1920's and 30's, and revived again in an 80's reprint of *This Must Be the Place: Memoirs of Montparnasse.*

In recent years, remodeled as L'Auberge de Venise, it became a fine gastronomic establishment. Daniel wanted to go inside to enjoy the journey of admiring posters and memorabilia, but his appointment was on the patio.

At a bistro table, he opened today's edition of Le Monde and checked his watch.

"You're late," he announced.

"Who's late?" A tall, nondescript man slid into a chair at the adjacent table. Neither looked at the other. "What brings you back to France, my friend?"

"You know darn well, Leopold."

Daniel didn't acknowledge his cohort but continued the ruse of reading the paper as he sipped an Americano.

"It's not looking good. The Terrorism Research Analysis unit has tracked ISIS cell communications, messaging to each other through a PlayStation. We're like cats chasing our tails. They are associated with the Paris 20 Cell, operating with three units of three men each. The fiends have disappeared into the woodwork like termites."

"I have a reliable lead from an old haunt," Daniel said.

"Go ahead, I'm listening."

"No recordings, agreed?"

"You've got it."

"There's a woman who saw the man you call Fernando Valois. She calls him Waldo for lack of knowledge of his history, as a man of his description has surfaced in the seedier world, in previous criminal activity in France."

"Fits the general appearance I would say."

Daniel slipped a photo into the newspaper folds. "Here's a snapshot that my friends found on a newsreel last night. From his nervous movements outside the Bataclan, he drew police attention and was taken away, but obviously, he was released.

Find out why the police let him fall through their hands that night?"

"I see."

"The next day my uncanny friends were at the Basilica in Montmartre and witnessed the same man in a kafuffle with the gendarme. Something about his drone being shot out of the air."

Daniel took a slow sip. "From the drone debris, my friends prudently collected a spy cylinder. Appearances suggested it was to be delivered to Waldo, and as he became agitated, he was taken away for questioning. He fiercely protested that the contents belonged to him.

"The gendarme collected the pieces, including a spy camera. Could you intercept that and scrutinize the footage to confirm that Valois was at the Bataclan. My friends will be in that video as well and I wouldn't want the wrong people to have it."

"Oui, of course. Now I suppose you're going to tell me what was in the container."

"It's a classified blueprint of the entire catacomb system. Clearly, a breach has taken place in security at a high level for these documents to be pilfered out of government offices, past their high clearance and monitors. My friends are smart and intuitive and knew it was conspicuous. Perhaps the discovery of the blueprint isn't a reason for alarm, but the calculation of circumstance is to be investigated."

"Have you seen the blueprint?"

"I have, at a glance. The draft shows the detailed labyrinth of tunnels and every access and exit point that any terrorist movement would die to get their hands on. The initials on the corner of the document suggest the Charles de Gaulle era."

"So what are you going to do?" the agent urged.

"I'll meet them shortly at the Denfert-Rochereau Museum to check it out. I thought it would be prudent to have a backup should things go sour. If it were just me, I wouldn't bother, but these people mean a great deal to me."

"You did the right thing, Agent. Have you activated again with Interpol?"

"I'm underground with the organization, but I'm prepared to deviate for this mission. You realize that with access to this network of tunnels, terrorists can cover over four hundred miles of Paris. Imagine a domino of explosions in a circuit under the city. Paris would be decimated in seconds." Daniel regretted his words, awestruck as it became a horrific image in his mind. "An entire city!"

"Incredulous! Let's hope it's just something like a weapons cache or smuggling route. When do we have contact again?"

Daniel rose and glanced at the surroundings, satisfied he wasn't being observed. He chucked the newspaper in a trash can and left the Dingo patio.

Moments later, on Leopold's subtle wave of the hand, a streetwalker delved into the can and walked away with Le Monde under his arm. A cleanup man of a different kind.

Leopold was distraught as he pondered Daniel's final words. He ordered another coffee and stretched his long, thin legs under the bistro table.

I've always trusted Daniel, and this is no different. But maybe this will only be petty theft or arms and ammunition. I'll hold back and see where it goes.

Over the shrill whistle of the cold November wind through the window cracks, Rachel heard the baying of a bloodhound.

"Toby, Toby, Toby. Marie must have gone out and he's lonely." She climbed out from the warm covers, and pulling on a pair of loose cotton pants, she sauntered barefoot to the kitchen. Thomas was in front of the TV with his eyes bleary and clothes disheveled.

"What is it, Thomas? Did you even sleep a wink?"

"Sit down, Honey."

Thomas took both her hands together and held them. "You won't like this, but I think you should go into the office tomorrow and help Madge. I can do this one alone with Daniel."

"Not on your life, Thomas."

"Madge sent a text that a man came into the office with your card. He said he met you outside the Bataclan; his name is Jacques Trudel, Jr."

"I can see right through you, Thomas York. Yes, I did give the young man my card, but that isn't what this is about."

"You've always told me to trust my gut. I have a premonition. This could be dangerous and I'm not willing to risk any danger coming to you again."

"You have to get over the Webster case. I survived and recovered fine and dandy. Madge can start Carter on the Trudel case. His father was missing, but it wasn't just the night of the Bataclan, it's been for a while. Poor kid is left to raise his siblings without parents. He's hoping that if they could find a body matching his father, life insurance could help. My hope is that he is just a vagrant Dad . . . and not involved."

"You didn't mention anything about that."

"It didn't seem relevant until now."

Rachel looked into his pleading eyes.

He really is scared for me.

"Let's have our first assessment with Daniel at Denfert and we can make decisions then. You and I work best as a team," Rachel said.

"What can I say to sway you otherwise?"

"Nothing." Rachel leaned in with a wet kiss.

"We're meeting at the Café Daguerre on Avenue du Général Leclerc at ten. I don't anticipate we'll be going far underground today, but we'll see what resources Daniel has been able to solicit," Thomas said.

"I'm ready. I found batteries and flashlights last night, and we can stop on the way for miners' helmets, carbide lamps and ventilation masks at Vieux Campeur. We should drive, as the Metro lines are still under guard. They've been shut down in Saint-Denis, searching with dogs and armored vehicles in the area."

Rachel disappeared to the bedroom. "Twenty minutes max to be ready," she called out, then giggled, "Fashion won't matter in the tunnels."

Without a word to Rachel, Thomas sent Daniel a text of his latest analysis without a word to Rachel, then followed her to get dressed.

In less than ten minutes, Rachel was waiting at the door in hiking apparel with a backpack of supplies.

"Was that packed under the bed? Is your weekender always ready?"

"As a matter of fact . . ."

Thomas wiggled the Renault Twizy out from behind the delivery doors of the flower shop so Rachel's door would open. Fifteen minutes later they crossed the Seine and passed Notre Dame then drove toward Montparnasse. Rachel was glued to the GPS.

"It's the café on the corner. We're passing it. See the orange umbrellas?"

Thomas swerved into a tiny spot. I'll park here for the day and we can walk to Denfert-Rochereau."

Daniel was already seated at a railside table for four. "Sit down. We need to talk," he said. He pointed at his café au lait and motioned for a barista to bring a tray."

"You going camping somewhere, Rachel? I've never seen so many pockets on a woman before."

Rachel scowled and kicked at him under the table.

Daniel and Thomas were on the same keel from viewing the blueprints last night, and their looks to each other showed their agreement not to breach the concern with Rachel. But they would be naïve to think she hadn't noticed.

"Rachel has another case this week, so I told her she was expendable," Thomas said. "She didn't take the suggestion well."

"Why you two are indeed Mutt and Jeff," Daniel said. "But Rachel, what's your new detective case?"

She wasn't about to be sweet-talked or sidelined.

"I met a kid at the Bataclan. He was overwrought that he may have lost his father as a victim of the shootings. I gave him my card, and he's now called the office for a follow-up. Carter can manage it, so I'm not concerned."

Daniel's fingers tapped on the table, soft at first but soon faster and louder. As he looked over his shoulders, Rachel decided that was enough; his behavior was covering something up.

"I know when you do that you're holding back, Daniel. We've been through a lot together, the three of us. Time to put all the cards on the table, gentlemen."

Thomas and Daniel passed another look, like two deer in the headlights.

Six

"Alright, cards on the table," Thomas said. "I studied the blueprints against the museum's mapping schematics, and there are vast differences. The blueprint shows so many access points and exits without going through the catacomb museum. It's a vulnerable situation, with the underground's eternal layers of caverns and tunnels."

"And I have the same conclusion as Thomas," Daniel said. "It could be catastrophic. The Paris and Brussels police are working to decode the terrorists' communications, but the messages have few footprints. The news says something big is going down today in Saint-Denis, with terrorists cornered."

"But I don't get it about the tunnels," Rachel said. Is it a plot to smuggle terrorists into Paris and on to Belgium?"

Thomas and Daniel looked at her with pained anguish.

"It's much worse that than, Honey."

Rachel paused, then it landed on her like a ton of bricks.

In the shock, she blurted out, "Oh my God. No, not that! The whole city? Exploding from underneath?"

Daniel looked behind, but no one appeared to notice her muted outburst.

"This is too big for us alone," Thomas said. "Waldo could be an ISIL sympathizer and not part of a conspiracy, but the alternative can't be ignored, considering what we've found."

Daniel said, "My friends at Interpol can trace if he's tied to a terrorist group. Did you pick up any drone pieces? A registration number might be on it."

"The gendarmes were there and got them first," Thomas said. "It was simple luck that the cylinder bounced my way."

Rachel whispered, "Is there a chance we're jumping to conclusions, connecting the tunnels to terrorism?"

"It will generate serious Interpol interest, should this prove to be bigger than we hope. First things first. Today's Monday and the museum isn't open 'til tomorrow, so we can't access the catacombs," Daniel said.

"The map shows other ways for us to get in," Thomas said.

Rachel gripped the backpack on her lap. "The helmets and flashlights are here, but once underground, we won't have any communication."

"For the first run, we'll stay together and get our bearings," Thomas suggested.

Daniel slowly shook his head. "I know you don't want to hear this, Rachel, but it may be efficient if we have a guard or relay in place on the surface."

"And you think because I'm a woman, it should be me?" Rachel's eyes flashed at him in anger, then to Thomas.

"No, not because you're a woman," Daniel said, "but because you're the least conspicuous and most intuitive."

Rachel stood, gripping her backpack.

"I'm ready, and I'm sticking with the two of you today. If you want, we can argue again tomorrow."

The trio set off, cramped in the Twizy for Montparnasse Cemetery on Boulevard Edgar Quinet. Through the entrance, they drove onto Rue Émile Richard. No other cars were on the lane, bordered by monuments, tombstones, cenotaphs, crypts, and statues.

"It's quite beautiful for a morgue, isn't it?" Rachel observed.

"We're not here for the scenery," Thomas grinned, but unamused.

"There's an X on the blueprint over Lot 12."

Thomas parked on Rue Raspail under a great, red maple. "This shouldn't be conspicuous if we're down there long."

Montparnasse Cemetery was abundant with lime trees, maples, ash, and conifers, and manicured flower beds still in an autumn glory. An old windmill overlooked the western end of the cemetery, and each lane between was numbered and named. Pacing over a grassy mound, they stopped at a 19th-century monument for French Revolutionary Soldiers beside an unmarked crypt.

On his knees, Daniel ran his fingers through the grass for the four cornerstones. "Rachel, check the ones at the top and I'll take the bottom. Press and push and hopefully something will happen."

On his second attempt, a lever triggered the lid to the crypt, and peering into the dark chasm, they saw nothing but the top few rungs of a metal ladder.

Rachel shone a light on it. "I see a lever on the stone inside that should release again when we come back. So we should get back out okay." She gritted her teeth at her bold assumption and looked at the others.

"We didn't check for security monitors or cameras," Thomas said. "We hardly look like grieving family members."

"It's clear to go," Daniel said. "Nothing showed up on my scanner."

Daniel was the first down the ladder. He looked across the gardens for a last mental list of visitors in the distance, then turned on his helmet's head lantern. Rachel eased herself through the opening next, catching a snag on her fisherman's sweater. "Oh well, it's a piece of wool as a marker when I come back."

Thomas was last and pressed the lever to close the crypt, putting them in darkness before they adjusted to the dim lighting from the helmets.

"There's a landing about thirty feet at the end of the ladder," Daniel echoed.

At the first T-tunnel, Rachel made a blue luminous mark on the wall. The limestone was cold and she was shivering from the damp air, but would never tell the others. After a long stretch in the darkness, they reached a reinforced door frame entering into the next section.

"I have cell power," she announced. "My GPS is alive and well so I can set in any location."

At a partially collapsed wall, Daniel stopped. "Careful. Here, immediately to the right . . . it's a small chamber."

Waving the light into the room, they made out a small, metal framed cot with springs still intact, and an old chair.

Rachel knelt down and pulled a small carbide lamp from her tools, screwed the components into place and lit the gas. Instantly, the room was fully lit and easy to see every crumble and crevice.

"Funny though, the chair doesn't have dust," Rachel said. "Look over there—a World War II munitions box. They're made of pine. I know because my grandfather had one to sit the old Sylvania television on. Soldiers carried them around the battlefields, taking ammunition to the front lines."

Thomas bent to explore the box. "This is newer than the bed, but I can't make out identifiable markings on the outside."

They all leaned close. The box was full of munitions rounds, and Thomas removed some from the top. "They're for AKM assault rifles."

Daniel stretched under the bed frame for a long wooden box and pried the lid open. "The same vintage as the box and these are four present-day AKM rifles. It's not looking good."

"At least there are no plastic explosives or suicide belts," Rachel said.

"We'll return everything to its exact location," Daniel said. "We're a few blocks walk parallel to the old train rails to Vavin Metro?"

"GPS says thirty to forty minutes," Rachel said.

The next alcove was a large cavern with stone steps leading down to a lower level under Montparnasse Boulevard. Outside the cavern door, a rabbit hole opened through a crumbling stone wall. The trio froze as the silence was pierced by water dripping below.

Thomas raised his hand, with his finger to his lips. "Turn off your lamps."

"What is it, Thomas?" Daniel said.

"Down there, to the right . . . a glimmer of light. Is it the Vavin Metro?"

"It's flickering like someone is walking with a lantern. Let's hope we haven't been spotted."

"I'll go ahead a few feet," Daniel whispered, deftly portaging the rubble of fallen rocks. "The light is moving away. Rachel, what's the closest access showing on the GPS?"

"It would be Vavin."

Crouched by the deteriorating wall, Thomas and Rachel waited for more from Daniel, but were met with silence.

"It's eerie," Rachel said, "and where's Daniel?" She flung her arm around in the darkness for Thomas.

"He's over there," Thomas whispered.

"I thought we were going to stay together."

"Take my hand, I see him."

With no light, they stumbled over Daniel, lying prone at an open parapet.

"Down!" Daniel mouthed in silence, then spoke softly. "The light is coming closer again. With my night binoculars, I can see at least one other person. They're working with a crude hoist of boards and rope, levering a pulley with a crate. Maybe raising it to the upper tunnel."

Rachel's heart pounded, as she contemplated an imminent discovery. After ten agonizing minutes, the din of voices ceased below.

"We're still in a trajectory to the catacombs. We've cleared the cemetery," Rachel said.

"I didn't expect an encounter so soon. I hope it isn't one of many more," Thomas said. "Rachel, what do you see ahead?"

"The GPS doesn't have specifics for the tunnels, just surface landmarks. But here's a sewer line access marked X. That's significant."

"We can't stay here or we'll surely be found out, whoever they are," Daniel warned. "Let's get back to the last vacant chamber. We can follow the wall with our hands without lights or words."

Thomas took the lead, with Rachel close on his heels. At the gap in the wall, the three huddled in the darkness, listening to the echo of voices grunting under the weight of the crate being hoisted by hand.

"They're at the top of the stairs, and out now. We'll wait until the coast is clear," Daniel said. On the return to the crypt entrance, he placed a transmitter under the metal of the cot to monitor future activity. Once above ground, they gave a sigh of relief.

"That's enough for today. I'm going to dig up an old contact and get some advice. Can we meet later?" Daniel asked.

"Since our conversations should be better shielded, why don't you come to the loft tonight for dinner? Remember, I have a diploma from the Cordon Bleu cooking school."

"How can I refuse? Just don't serve one of those tiny quails on top of a few tablespoons of pilaf."

Rachel laughed. "I always make something hearty for my men."

In the dark alley by the flower shop, a man's shadow waited, staring up at the iron rails of the balcony of the loft. His hand caressed a revolver in his pocket, repeatedly placing his forefinger on the trigger.

"So this is it . . . the loft above the florist. Perhaps I should have been more discreet at the café. I watched and listened from the grand oak tree, unseen. Clever of me.

"I have the eyes of an eagle and an elephant's memory. Were you not curious about the man on the roof of the Basilica? I am not without my own tracking resources. You have no idea what you are up against. Haha, stupides petits détectives."

The buzzer rang at ten to seven. Rachel bounded down the staircase, flipping on the outside lamp as she opened the door.

Expecting to see Daniel, she was stunned to see a dark man with strands of black, curly hair emerging from under his toque. But it was the evil in his eyes that unnerved her.

Foolish of me not to have used the peephole.

The Arabic man stood glaring at her before speaking in an almost inaudible gruff voice.

"I'm looking for a detective lady that was at the Basilica recently. She perhaps lives here? The revolver was warm in his pocket and Rachel examined the protrusion now directed her way.

Taken back by the ruse, she felt her face becoming numb. "No, you have the wrong address," she enunciated with force. As she began to close the door, his foot jammed it.

Both their heads turned suddenly to the lane, as the putter of a twenty-year-old Renault closed in on Rue des Saules, its headlights exposing the dark visitor. Aware he'd been observed, he slunk back down the alley.

Rachel returned to the kitchen, keeping her head down, lest Thomas would see her shaking. She didn't want the exchange to alter the optimism of the evening.

Minutes later, the lower doorbell buzzed again and Thomas went downstairs, expecting Daniel. Beside him was a tall man in a business suit.

"Thomas, I want you to meet Leopold."

"Pleased to meet you," Leo said, showing an embarrassed, sheepish look. "I apologize that my manners are out of sorts, but Daniel insisted I would be welcome for dinner."

"By all means, come in."

Seven

Rachel looked exquisite in a soft, yellow cashmere sweater and casual écru tie silk pants. Daniel wasn't subtle in noticing every detail, and Thomas observed his silent assessment.

Wiping her hands on her stark, white apron, she offered her hand. "Welcome, Leopold. Any friend of Daniel's is ours too."

Leo timidly offered Rachel a box of Jean Charles Rochoux truffles, and she smiled with delight recognizing the famous chocolatier. My goodness, Leopold, my favorites. How could you have known?" She gave Daniel a quick glance as he shielded a smirk.

Their heads all turned toward the kitchen, drawn by the bouquet of aromatic flavors that filled the loft, and Rachel watched their eyes.

"Braised brisket with lyonnaise potatoes, buttered spring carrots, and broiled tomato, Daniel. There are seconds and a homemade focaccia."

"Does your Cordon Bleu instructor approve?" Daniel asked.

"Jacques Charles can make whatever he wants, but it's my guests that I want to please. It's my UN special, a blend of Germany, Italy, France, and America."

Thomas made sure Daniel and Leopold got comfortable in the living room, part of a great room including the dining area. He opened a Nouveau Beaujolais from the pine buffet, and Leopold rose to join him.

"Let me open the bottle, Joseph. I rarely drink when working, but this menu calls for a fine Nouveau."

Daniel raised his hand. "My apology for a sloppy introduction. Leopold is my Interpol contact I mentioned today. And Leo, these are my partners in crime, Emily and Joseph."

There was no reason for Daniel to explain to Leo that Emily and Joseph were aliases used by Rachel and Thomas since arriving in France from Albany under an American witness protection program.

Emily returned for the tail end of introductions, balancing vintage plates of foie gras, with fragrant truffle mushroom sauce drizzled over delicate toast points.

The men took chairs expeditiously in anticipation, and Emily removed her apron and took the seat beside Joseph. "Dinner first, then we'll get down to the blueprint. I had it enlarged plus two copies made. It never left my hands during the process."

As they dined, Leopold's eyes took in everything, inspecting the couple and making his own assessment. He sat back between courses and said little.

Joseph, in turn, observed Leo as a reserved man, prematurely grey with a haggard look, perhaps from a life on the edge between good and evil, assuming his tragic eyes had seen his share of the unthinkable.

Emily offered seconds until the last morsel was removed from the platter and a mere crust of bread remained.

"Mmm, Emily, that was the finest meal in a very long time," Leo said. "It's not often I get a home-cooked meal."

Emily blushed. "I'm honored and so glad, Leopold. An early lesson from the great chef, Paul Bocuse, was to buy the freshest meat and produce from the markets. 'Market to table', he says. It gives me pleasure to see a man's belly well-satisfied."

With the table cleared, Joseph spread out the enlarged version of the tunnel schematics.

"Leopold, did anything come from the gendarme interrogation of Waldo?"

Leo and Daniel looked at each other with apprehension, considering what they could share.

"The police have him under surveillance," Leopold said. "Evidence shows he became radicalized last year at Mosul, the northern Iraq ISIL training compound, and we have footage of him in Brussels with the Paris 20 members.

Valois is known to authorities but is more valuable left on the streets. He supports aging parents and a disabled daughter, and we monitor that residence. We watch where he goes and who he meets, and hope he'll lead us to those responsible for the drone over the Basilica. He's a weak pawn in the overall scheme and one day he will squeal to save himself."

"We lucked out with the cylinder but didn't get any debris with a registration tag," Joseph said.

"Too bad. The gendarmes searched again for pieces, but sweepers had already cleaned the area," Leopold said.

Daniel said, "French Aviation requires drones operators to have a visual contact at all times and not interfere in public spaces or take pictures of individuals on private property. It's logical to assume another person was in sight of the Basilica."

"He was near the railing by the funicular," Emily said. "Tourists were everywhere when the drone buzzed in over the trees from the north. I think it came over the roof of one of the domes."

"We can't do anything about that day now," Leopold relented. "By the way, Waldo does fine for a nickname, but to authorities, he is Fernando Valois. The sender of the drone would have seen you with the cylinder, Joseph, and considering the threat of this document, you'll need to watch your back. You're in serious danger. Both of you."

"I like using Waldo. It's clear who we are talking about," Emily said. She knew she sounded defensive, but stood her ground. "We are all experienced detectives, yet we all have our weak spots, right?"

With the conversation now more candid, Emily recounted her unexpected visitor early in the evening. "And no one followed us from the Basilica, yet we were found."

Leopold wrote as each one spoke, and finally, Joseph could no longer withhold the pocketed cigarette butts and added the evidence to the table for consideration.

"DNA," Leo said. "Excellent."

Emily said, "I have some information to help too. Last year working with a Department of Protection Security team, I took a seminar on aerospace threat detection at the University of Paris. Joseph was away on a case. A Rhode Island team demonstrated their Airport Cooperative Research. Guess where they did the test?"

Before they could answer, Emily's adrenalin urged her to stand and become more animated.

"Gentlemen . . . there is definitely a way to track the source."

Leopold raised his eyebrows. "Tell me more."

"If you hadn't guessed, the Rhode Island demonstration was here at the Sacré-Coeur, instead of the public training areas that are crowded on Sundays with the countless recreational drones in Paris. Here's what I learned about drones.

"In the States, they're a hazard to airspace, even threatening light aircraft, a risk that started with lasers. Under the auspices of Worldwide Terrorism Tracking, the Rhode Island University used a portable prototype to detect drones within a five-mile radius."

Leo looked up from writing when she stopped.

"So weaponized units can come under immediate scrutiny," she concluded.

Joseph said, "And there's detection capability . . ."

"Yes! But there's more. The detection unit with a solar panel was to stay at Montmartre for a period of time, for results to be recorded for International Aviation. When an offender enters the zone, the registration number is recorded when it's within 400 feet of the ground.

Daniel was on his chair's edge. "You mean there might still be a recording system at the Basilica?"

Emily's eyes were still wide. "Leopold, would you have authority to investigate this? It might give you the source."

Joseph watched Emily's tight smirk as she sat again, satisfied that she'd put herself on an even keel, and Daniel quietly observed her stubborn sense of humor.

Leopold allowed a deserved compliment while maintaining control. "That's very good, Emily. Nonetheless, keep a low profile in Montmartre."

"Perhaps Daniel didn't tell you of our first meeting in Montmartre, Leopold. Never underestimate me nor my wife."

"Yes, Leopold. And Joseph is my match in both wit and brawn," Daniel added. There was no time for one-upmanship, and Leo relaxed his posture at the emergence of this new duo that Daniel praised.

"Alright then, we have an understanding. We are now a unit of four. No secrets and no deviations. From time to time, I will review the case and dangers with my boss, but for now, we operate in a clandestine mode."

Leopold's words were convincing, but Daniel knew he would not back down entirely.

Joseph felt he had just passed an exam and tried to see it from Leo's point of view. "Leopold, we'll discuss the situation and let you know if you are in or not."

Daniel winked at Joseph as Leopold's jaw tightened.

"Leo, he's pulling your leg," Daniel laughed.

Leopold's eyes widened at the blueprint.

"I never knew this existed. When we find the drone owner, we'll track the source of the document." As he snapped photos of access and exit points, he examined an initialed seal. "It's from the Department of Defense and is classified. Another breach."

Still rebounding from the trio's rebuke, Leo looked at them for any objection. "We should break into two teams and come from opposite points that meet at a tunnel conjunction. I suggest we start with a tourist viewpoint of the catacombs to assess vulnerability."

"The museum opens at ten," Joseph said. "We can meet at the entrance."

"Under the circumstances, I'll go to headquarters first and have the drone technology verified with the Basilica, and check on the prototype that Emily laid out. The three of you should proceed if I am late. After the forty-five minute tour, we'll meet at the Dingo Café in Montparnasse."

Daniel added, "The Dingo is a hot zone—it's ripe with spies. The trash is picked up every half hour if you get my meaning."

Almost out the door, Leo turned back to Emily. "Excellent information, Emily. Do you remember any of the names represented by the Department of Protection and Security?"

"Not off the top of my head, but it'll be in my material."

The next morning's sun was barely up when they left the loft together, Joseph heading uphill to the Sacré-Coeur, and Emily down to Place St. Pierre, then on the Abbesses Metro toward the Champs-Élysées. The detective agency had been closed for two days, but she felt compelled to consult with Carter on the Trudel case.

But when the metro lurched to a stop on the south side of the Seine by the Notre Dame cathedral, an announcement blared that it would reroute for security reasons.

I could walk from here but something else is going on.

Putting on earbuds, Emily picked up the BBC discussing a raid on terrorists in the night in Saint-Denis, with suspects cornered in a barricaded apartment. An interviewed officer said police were ramping up using extreme measures.

At the train station, there was a mixture of crowd panic and confusion as the gendarmes descended to the tracks and directed passengers to the exits.

A dark-complexioned woman was at the end of the platform listening to an Arabic man in his mid-thirties. Emily recorded his look in her memory—a three-day heavy beard, early balding and a mass of long curly hair. In her imagination, she wondered if he could be the unseen man under the Robinia and from the roof of the Basilica or even the man who dared to darken her door at Montmartre.

The distraught woman was sobbing, and through the tears, it was difficult to ascertain her age, sheltered more in a heavy wool coat and a paisley kerchief tied over her head. At first, she blended into the crowd like a vagrant, but her piercing eyes were coyly on Emily as she stepped out to block her path.

"I can't find my husband," she mumbled. Inching forward, she was close enough to touch Emily, who stopped to offer comfort, as she was always compassionate to a soul in need and willing to listen to the woman's pleas.

The woman's coat and thick, black shoes dragged as she walked. Her eyes were stained with tears and at the first glimpse of Emily's interest, the crying started again.

"Ma'am, is there anything I can do to help?"

"No one will listen to me."

"About what? I'm a good listener." Emily already had her hand on the woman's elbow to nudge her forward. "Why don't we cross the street for a cup of coffee?"

She had always been quick with sympathy and the first to rescue a lost cat or puppy. Joseph was continually warning her not to be so trusting, but to be suspicious of everyone when working a case.

"Thank you. That would be lovely."

On closer examination now, Emily considered the woman to be about forty and of African descent. Her head kerchief was knotted in a Ukrainian style and the coat's pockets sagged as if with concealed weights.

"I worked the night shift last night. My husband and I have a flat in the north section of Paris. Do you know Saint-Denis, the corner of Rue de Corbillon? It's not the best area, but it is our home."

"Yes, of course. There was a police raid there last evening."

"So you've heard. My husband called me at work in the early hours of the morning and said the streets were crawling with police, and shots were firing all around without ceasing. Over a hundred commandos surrounded an apartment building in the next block. He was afraid he would be killed."

"It's a good thing then that you weren't home. It would have been a great worry to your husband."

"That's nice of you to say. Bek . . . Herman would have wished it." The woman extended her arm for a weak handshake. "I'm Isabella."

"Nice to meet you, Isabella," Emily replied without offering hers to a stranger. She had noticed Isabella fumble with her husband's name and let it pass, as it was logical with the woman's fear.

"Security forces surrounded several houses firing assault weapons and tossed grenades," the woman said. Residents were told to evacuate or stay in their bathrooms, and the street below was barricaded from traffic."

"Did your husband leave? Is he alright?"

"The last we talked, his phone battery was dying, but he was going to make a run for the police line. When I called back, there wasn't an answer."

"Perhaps his phone died."

"The police won't let me back into my house to check," Isabella said. "The apartment building looked like an earthquake zone, and the police carried out body bags. The street is covered with blood—they say that two suicide bombers activated their belts."

"The morning news said the security threat in Saint-Denis is still active, and that part of a building under attack has collapsed. Some police were injured, with terrorists killed and others arrested, but there was no mention of neighbors or pedestrians injured."

"That's a relief. You have been kind to listen to me. I don't know what to do."

"Go to the gendarme station on the next corner and tell them your situation; they'll have answers. Many charity groups offer shelter and support. Will you do that Isabella?"

"Yes, yes."

As the African woman headed toward the depot, Emily phoned Joseph about their first visit to the catacombs.

"Can we advance the meeting in Montparnasse? I have new concerns in light of events overnight in Saint-Denis."

"As a matter of fact, Daniel just texted with the same gist. I'll bring the car and meet you there," Joseph replied.

A buzz in the sky caught her attention.

By gosh, it's a drone. I hope I'm not his surveillance target . . . or any other kind of target.

As she walked slowly, the object remained a hundred feet overhead staying in her sight. Within seconds, pedestrians began to scream and run in all directions, escalating the panic and chaos. Emily's instincts slowed it down in her mind, freezing time to separate the pandemonium from still life.

That left three people: a man on a bench, possibly the drone operator; another on a second-floor balcony; and a woman in a long heavy coat and boots bent over a backpack.

Her heart began to pound as her steps hastened.

"Something is happening here! And not a gendarme in sight."

Eight

Emily ducked into a nearby restaurant half full of patrons and grabbed a frazzled waiter.

"Please, I need to exit through your back kitchen door. It's urgent," she panted, speaking rapidly while scanning back over her shoulder.

Astonished by her boldness, he stepped in front of her to prohibit her from advancing to the back.

"No one's allowed in our kitchen without permission of the chef," the waiter instructed.

"Well then, may I speak with him to get his permission?"

A tall man named Jean-Paul, in a greasy apron and surgical cap, overheard and came to the kitchen door. "Why do you want to go through my kitchen, Madame?"

Forcing spontaneous tears, she blurted, "My boyfriend. He follows me everywhere. I don't know why he doesn't trust me. I need a restraining order. Please—if I leave through your front door, I will be followed."

With arms crossed, he sized Emily up.

"I don't believe one word you've said, but if it's important enough to lie to me, you may go through my kitchen."

With gratitude, Emily raced through the aluminum door, pushing past a congregation of confused cooks, then out into the back alley.

Seconds later, the front door burst open, with an Arabic man with a ponytail in pursuit. Jean-Paul was not having any of it and irately brought the man down with a heavy copper pan over the head. Instantly he was on his feet again, barreling through the cooks.

Emily ducked behind a dumpster for protection, hoping for mercy. Footsteps of the man were loud and she knew he was close. Then they stopped. She listened to his heavy breathing, knowing a physical barrier was feet from her, and she dared not move.

"Come out, Americano, I know you're there," he ranted.

Peering out, she made eye contact with the man, furious and glaring at her. His arm rose high, ready to swing a pipe down onto her head, then his face became a grotesque distortion, as Jean-Paul leveled the weight of the copper pan again on the perpetrator's head.

"Sorry, Madame, that I said you were lying. He's no good for you. Now get out of here, you're going to need that restraining order when he wakes up. Anytime you need an escape, come through my kitchen and I will help."

Emily admired his chivalry but had no time to spare. Crossing over to a parallel street, she dipped into a millinery shop and purchased a wrap for her head and shoulders to alter her appearance, then scurried along the sidewalk with her head to the ground.

Arriving first at the Dingo Café, she insisted on an inside table. Leopold was next to arrive and saw she was flustered.

"I'm glad to see you, Leopold. I've been followed."

"Are you okay now? Is someone still following?"

"I'm fine and the man was brought down as I fled. I don't understand how it happened. I left my loft and walked down to Place St. Pierre to the Abbesses Metro. The train was deterred at the Notre Dame stop because of the Saint-Denis situation. I stopped to talk with a distressed woman . . ."

The two words reverberated in her mind, and she looked up at Leopold, horrified she'd been duped by a woman in disguise beseeching her sympathy, long enough for a tracker to be put in place.

Leopold took a silver pen from his pocket.

"Did the woman touch you? Pass this pen over your body. If it beeps, we'll know that she left a target pin on you."

She remembered Isabella had given her a hug and knew what the reaction would be.

Beep, Beep. She gritted her teeth.

"It's under my collar." She tossed it onto the table.

"Take the pen, Emily, as you might need to check it often."

"Thank you, Leopold. I understand what happened but I can't believe I fell for it. The woman, Isabella, must have been a decoy, making me a target for the drone operator. After we talked, I noticed buzzing, then a drone about a hundred feet overhead following me. I ducked through a back alley and finally dodged the tail. Would they know that I am here with you?"

"Not likely, the jammer covers three or four blocks."

He handed her a remote car key. "Take this too, and if you've been photographed or recorded, point the key at the medium and it will erase any incriminating data."

Leopold opened his phone for screens of photos. "Is the woman here? Any of these?"

On the first screen, Emily saw the woman, without the kerchief. "Yes. Her. I don't easily forget a face. If she followed me on the train from St. Pierre, they know where Joseph and I live."

"Good. The surveillance on our friend Waldo has given her up as a contact, before his escape. As an operator had been on site with the first drone, it's likely you were followed on foot or by another drone without drawing your attention. On a busy, tree-lined street, the drone can roam under a hundred feet without being detected. They could fit in a pocket or be as big as a helicopter."

Daniel arrived next, then Joseph. "Sit down," Leo said, "we have a lot to talk about."

The two were stunned at the morning pursuit. "Are you sure it's safe to discuss these matters here?" Joseph asked.

"As a hot zone, Interpol has jammed all outside interference and telephone signals here. There's no need to look around, but more than half the patrons are Interpol or other agents, here to transfer information or find safety."

"Have you learned anything overnight?" Daniel said.

"We successfully gathered data on the Basilica drone thanks to Emily and recovered tapes and digital codes to identify the registration number. Even if you'd recovered the identification plate, I suspect the number would have been sanded off. But this detection was accurate.

"The drone was purchased a few weeks ago in Brussels by a Syrian, Youssif Didier. He's a jihadist and militant, but not clever enough for high authority. We're convinced he follows the orders of Salim Benghalem, the ringleader, and executioner for ISIL."

"I found the business card for the security defense contact I met at Sacré-Coeur," Emily said.

"Do you have a Paris location for Didier?" Joseph asked.

"Abu-Khalid is another ISIL mastermind that Didier works for. He ordered a dozen more Phantom 4 drones. They were picked up by another man; the warehouse dispatcher didn't have a name but provided ID numbers. He was reluctant to give up his Chinese supplier, but we were persuasive." Leopold looked at Daniel. "You know your friends are in grave danger."

"I am skilled at becoming invisible. I guarantee that I'll pick up any tail and keep my friends safe. They are pivotal in tracking this insurgent group, whether it's an amateur copycat or skilled terrorists. They will remain key components of this investigation."

"Very well, Daniel."

They all hushed to hear more of Leo's findings. "Using Interpol resources, we intercepted signals at a private airfield, getting radar images of low-flying objects near a recreational field at Paris Le Bourget. It's an abandoned meadow in the north used for drones, and with cliffs for hang gliding. Valois was sighted here with a group of aviation enthusiasts."

"And Interpol continues to leave Valois free to do as he pleases?" Joseph's face was stern with irritation.

"It's like setting cheese out for mice. We want to round them all up, not just the first. We permitted his escape in the pretense of being lax until we know all the contacts. These are devious evil people, capable of doing who knows what."

"Capable of planting bombs throughout Paris for one big fireworks show!" Daniel said.

"We don't know if that is the plot. They could be using the tunnels for arsenal storage or bunkers to move unseen. Over the years, the tunnels were occupied by secret societies and political groups. It would be naïve to assume they are empty long halls, not yet to be explored."

Emily leaned toward Leopold. "You've seen a great deal in your life and no doubt lost people that mean the most to you, right?"

"That's true. And your point?"

This isn't a game of Risk with a winner. These are the lives of Parisians, and of me and my friends. We must all be more certain with our calculations. Perhaps you are not using the most intriguing resources at your disposal."

Leopold overlooked her comment and wrapped up his comments. "If any of you ever need help and can make it here to the Dingo, fold a decipherable note in the current issue of *Le Monde* and place it in the trash can outside the main door. It must be *Le Monde*. Your message will be treated as a priority in our safety net."

"Good to know," Joseph said. "It might be useful. Are you coming with us to the catacombs, Leo?"

"No, if you'll excuse me, I need to locate some *intriguing* resources." Leopold winked at Emily. "I'll get in touch."

Joseph and Emily were left alone observing the backdrop of agents and espionage in their midst. A mist filtered from the street lamps and glistened on the cobblestone street, and Emily listened to the laughter of after-theater crowds surging towards the row of restaurants.

Sipping on a last dreg of coffee, she peered across the street, then at each patron on the patio.

Curious people, we all are!

"This is fascinating, Joseph. About twenty feet from us . . . a waiter has been wiping the same table for an abnormal amount of time. Now, look across the street at the woman leaning against a gate, smoking a cigarillo. They don't move until someone sitting on this patio waves a hand in the air. Then it's like a movie set, then they spring into action. Newspapers disappear, limos suddenly arrive and everything slows down."

"Incredible. I hadn't noticed," Joseph said.

"Ah, it's like Poirot says—it's the little grey cells that tell you so much," she teased.

At 11:30 a.m. the trio arrived at the museum. The tourist line was short for tickets, and small groups of students, tourists, and families were released at timed intervals. Gasps echoed through the cavern as the crowd eased in slowly, keeping tight lest they disturb the dead.

Emily slowed to read the wall sign.

Bags will be searched at the exit
Please respect the dignity of the dead
Don't touch the skulls or bones

I'll look for a place to stash the carbide.

The tourist line descended down a staircase, with Emily, Joseph, and Daniel at the back. A guide explained that two hundred years before, the quarries were filled with bones from surrounding cemeteries in Montparnasse, generally moved at night. To ease the burden in providing land for graves, structural support was provided to the empty tunnels when the quarries ceased to be productive, and in the late 20th and early 21st centuries, sections were further reinforced.

The walls were lit with banks of high-wattage lamps, and each new section had a directional sign indicating what surface street lay above, and occasional framed signs described the cross-section. It gave a momentary sense of security to know where you were.

Emily zipped her jacket tight and shoved her hands into her pockets, shivering with the chilly underground dampness. The air was still musty, convincing her that she could taste the death in the tunnels.

"Are you alright, Honey?" Joseph said.

"I'm fine. But we're journeying into the Land of the Dead. It's rather macabre."

They came to a section with skulls and bones arranged in symmetrical rows of mosaic patterns that lined the walls and alcoves. A few channels had respectable monuments, crypts and worship alcoves honoring historical figures, politicians, and artists, while other areas were gated to prevent visitors from proceeding further.

The lead tourist group moved at a decent pace, stepping it up to get to the end and rise to street level. Some innocent stragglers had to be warned from trying to pry open the tunnels from the grated doors cemented into the floor.

"Come along," the guide barked to the mischievous ones. "Authorized Personnel and No Admittance means what they say."

After a workshop with tables and display cases, they came to a cavern with magnificent arches leading to a jutted cliff. Standing at the edge, Emily felt a dizzying sensation as she looked into a bottomless pit in a lower chasm. Over the arch was an etching in the stone.

C'est ici l'empire de la Mort

"It's eerie. One Halloween my parents took my sister Amy and me to a Haunted House in Albany. I was frightened before I set foot inside, yet in the end, there was nothing to it. Just a coordination of moving objects, lights and sounds—all in all disappointing. But this is different, with real bones."

Emily attempted to shrug off the unnerving sound of silence mixed with the death of souls, leaving bones as souvenirs of their existence. For an instant, she wondered if the smell would cling to her clothes forever.

"Joseph!"

"What is it?"

Emily pointed across the cavern. "Can't you see it? Another old stone staircase on the other side, to a darker opening. It's not on the tourist route, but I saw a blur of movement there."

Turning back to see where Joseph was, she flinched.

A threatening, unshaven man was behind him, glaring angrily with black penetrating eyes. Emily wanted to move on, but her feet were frozen by the man's sudden appearance.

"Monsieur et Madame, do you have the time?"

Emily whispered in Joseph's ear. "Where's Daniel?"

"Ten o'clock." The answer was meant for Emily, not the inquisitor.

Squinting in the dimness, Emily focused on the man, who was now deliberately hiding his face. His scarf was pulled up over his mouth, but she recognized the glasses. Daniel was silently edging along the wall about six feet behind the intruder.

"No, I don't have the time." Joseph was sure it was a distraction and couldn't see if there might be a second man. He pulled Emily around behind him, realizing the perpetrator could lunge at any time.

"I want my cylinder back. You had no right interfering."

"I don't know what you're talking about."

"You were at the Basilica prying into other people's business. I saw you pick it up."

Valois leaned forward and poked Joseph in the chest. "You have no idea what you have done and the price you will pay for your medaling."

Daniel yanked Waldo's extended arm behind his back and slammed him to the stone floor, then straddled him to restrict his movement.

"Who sent the drone?" Daniel bellowed in the offender's ear.

"We have followed your friends, the cowards that stand behind you! We will track our enemies to the death." the offender gestured toward Joseph and Emily.

"It's you that is the coward, sneaking into Paris through the underground," Daniel bantered.

"Death to the Americans! Death to France!" Valois sputtered.

"Pour quoi do you talk of Americans to me? Je suis Francais." Daniel kept the pressure of his knee against Valois's back until a crack said it was enough. Writhing in pain on the ground, he surrendered.

Daniel dialed Leo. "Cleanup in the aisle . . ." He looked up at the entrance to the next section. "Aisle Henri Roi Tanguay."

Turning to Joseph, he said, "You two go on. The authorities are coming and we don't want you to have to answer questions. It's simply a tripping accident. Fernando here doesn't seem cooperative and his memory is going to be extremely poor." Daniel grabbed his hair at the back and smashed him to the ground again.

Joseph and Emily scurried to catch the guide at the exit, where concerned staffers waited.

"We thought you were lost. When the meter counters at the entrance and exit don't match, we send a search party for any wanderers. It means closing our exhibit, causing expense and a waste of time."

"We're sorry to have been any trouble," Emily said. "We should be the last, I think."

"No . . . one more," the clerk insisted.

"There might be one more coming," Joseph agreed.

Emily whispered to him. "Shouldn't there have been two? If the missing person were Daniel, then Waldo must have accessed the catacombs by secret tunnels."

"I hope Daniel has it under control. Possibly our attacker wasn't alone."

"Leo will be here soon to take care of things."

"We have the whole afternoon ahead of us, Joseph. Can we drive out to see the airfield he identified?"

Nine

Fifteen kilometers northeast of Paris, Joseph slowed their Renault Twizy at Route Nationale 118, near the Saclay Plateau.

Emily saw the sign for the airstrip Paris-Le Bourget, then the symbol for the Game Studios where flight simulators were built and available for training.

Emily googled as they approached. "It says right here that there's a historic statute commemorating Lindberg's 1927 solo transatlantic landing by the front entrance.

"Wow, Joseph, do you know what this is? It's where FSX Steam Edition is developed for gamers. It's now in shutdown, preparing for an air show."

"You're a walking encyclopedia. I've heard of the gamers' sites. They'd be an ideal camouflage for terrorist use. I understand that messaging on games and social media is now a lane of communication for terrorists, and in some cases, decryption is extremely complicated to monitor."

Emily shuddered. "That's scary. Technology is wonderful for health, science, and knowledge, but it's a black hole that frightens the socks off me."

Beyond the FSX building was a massive administration structure, then a row of airport hangers that faced the landing strips. A shuttle aircraft was landing from Orly, and the runway had business jets waiting. Beyond a mirage of parked jets, Emily could see the helipad with a helicopter rotor spinning.

"Joseph, it isn't a coincidence that Le Bourget offers air traffic controller training on its simulators. What better place for Didier's drone flyers to practice and hack into air traffic patterns and manoeuvers. The field is open to the public on Sundays for recreational drones."

"We should stop on the way back from Van Dame's farm," Joseph said. "The airport's a base for the Paris Airshow Demonstration flights. It's like a museum, with private planes, helicopters, and even competitive barnstormers. For an aviation nut, it's like a pie with ice cream."

The full moon was casting long blue shadows on the farmers' fields that were silent after a long day of work by the combines and irrigation wheels. Each field was like the last, with golden brown strips tied with winter thatch, and mounds of hay waiting to be hauled away to silos. Every barn had a red roof, faded from many summers.

Nostalgia inspired Joseph's memory. "As a kid I asked my Dad why all the barn roofs were painted red. He said that whenever he went into town to buy fresh paint there was always a sale on red. One day when he was in the hardware store, a paint salesman came in and my Dad asked him why. It's because the stores always run out of red paint that we make more." Joseph chuckled mostly to himself.

"I didn't realize that your Dad had been a farmer."

"He never was, but he always liked to tell that story."

Emily gave him a polite teehee and he elbowed her gently.

"It's so peaceful here," she said. "Remember Rouen's and Monet's masterpieces of the haystacks? These fields remind me of those . . . and of the art forgeries case too." She gritted her teeth in fun.

Focused on each farm as they passed, Emily began to second-guess their direction.

"According to Daniel, we should turn onto a rough gravel road at a sign marked 'Van Dame Farms' just past the red barn. Another sign will have a small aircraft or hang-gliding symbol."

"Did he give a mileage marker?"

"Daniel hasn't actually been out here but looked up the directions in some farming registry. All I have is 15 km northeast of the Paris perimeter on Highway 118."

"We'll find it then."

After the next red barn and through the shrouds of dust, she saw a barn with a grey roof and a red-capped silo.

"Slow down, Joseph, this should be it. The fence post says no access past the electronic gate without permission and there's a pass swipe box."

Joseph got out to jot the phone number, and Emily joined him at the gate.

"Private airfields are usually controlled by local farmers, without regulation. Farmers sell rights to use ultra-lights, gliders, and drones for annual fees. It adds income to their struggling resources. Too often farms are being bought out, with industrial buildings popping up in their places."

"Does that mean that we're expected to pay to drive down the road?" Joseph joshed.

She poked him. "The GPS grid shows a gravel quarry or construction zone on the other side of the Van Dame Farm. On the road behind the farm, the field connects to the back lot of the Games Studios, but they're separated by a barbed wire fence, with security lights on both the airport fields and the farm."

"The porch lights are on, Emily, and the living room is fully lit. Someone is there. I'll call the number and ask permission to view the airfield. If I need an excuse do you have a suggestion?"

Emily shrugged her shoulders. "Ask him point-blank if he's a terrorist."

"I'd like to see his expression, but I'll try something else."

A woman answered at Van Dame Farms on the fourth ring. Joseph thought she sounded edgy or cranky.

"Can I help you?"

Joseph said he'd bought a new drone and needed a place to try it to train for the fall drone competition at Champs-Élysées.

"Wait a minute, I'll get Alain."

She'd barely gone when a husky voice came on.

"What do you want? This is a private facility for members of the club only. Are you a member?"

"How do I become a member? A friend of mine in Paris recommended this place."

Alain paused, confused about a recommendation. "If Didier told you to come, then it's him you gotta deal with . . ." Joseph repeated the phone number aloud as Emily wrote it.

"Thanks, Monsieur Van Dame."

"What makes you think I'm Van Dame? Did she tell you that?"

Joseph disconnected and turned to Emily.

We've pressed someone's buttons!"

The Twizy's window was down, and Joseph heard a whirring sound above. From the top of a utility pole, a camera was pointed at them.

"It's recording us, Emily."

In an instant, she pulled Leo's remote car key from her bag, aimed at the camera, and pressed the auto button to trigger the data erase.

"Leo gave this to me," Emily smirked. "Spy equipment. I just erased the pictures."

Joseph's eyes widened at her new toy and he let her savor the moment.

"I'll drive ahead on Highway 118 toward the next farm. Take pictures and we'll enlarge them later for detail."

The adjoining property was vacant, with a demolition sign posted by a construction company, claiming to be the future site of a University campus. A collection of backhoes and bulldozers was parked in the yard around mounds of gravel and removed soil. No one was in sight, and a good distance across the field they could see the training field.

"We'll park here and walk in."

Near the backline of the fence, a concrete building on the Van Dame side had a sheet metal roof with an attached triple garage with overhead doors. Emily photographed a cluster of aerials and wires that seemed out of place.

"The concrete building will surely prohibit frequency interception or outside interference. It's a clever setup."

"And no animals in the farmer's field," Emily said. "Yet this area is all crop and dairy. That stands out."

Hearing a car, they lowered themselves into the overgrown weeds, then watched as the high beam headlights of a grey Peugeot stormed in their direction, then raced down the gravel lane. It skidded to a stop beside several other cars at the cement house, kicking up a cloud of dust. A dark-complexioned man, dressed in black, exited the vehicle and slammed the door.

Emily trained her binoculars on the vehicles. On the far side of the barren field was a wooden control tower with a viewing stand. A row of posts rose from the ground twenty feet apart, and at the top of each was a small platform, perched like a podium. Only two of the stations were in use, where drones, camouflaged as eagles, prepared for launch.

Emily whispered. "These drones are like the Phantom 4 used at Montmartre."

"Can you identify the men?"

"No, they're all in black with bandanas. You have a look."

"Did Leo give you a receiver to pick up their conversation?" Joseph queried, knowing that *he* should have been better prepared for this espionage outing.

Emily made fun in return. "Where's your trusty QPro, Joseph? You always come equipped with listening devices. Do you even have the loft bugged when you go out?"

"Now there's a good idea!"

She focused again with the binoculars. "In the back section, there's a helipad, but no chopper." A thought hit her and she googled instinctively.

"Police have cordoned off a helipad in Brussels where criminals had been arriving. The terrain is too rugged for aircraft. Is it possible to take a helicopter from here all the way to Brussels?"

"Look that up too," Joseph said.

"Could be a puma, a small chopper that can fly up to two hundred miles as fast as two hundred knots. Brussels would be too far. But here it is . . . an Apache Attack chopper covers from 1200 to 1900 km. without refueling. That could do it."

"That's military issue. I know of it," Joseph said. "Have we overlooked that there are militants for hire from jihadi sectors? A few years back, they supported Hamas fighting in the Gaza Strip, smuggling weapons through tunnels, and converting them to bunkers. The Mexican cartel uses similar practices."

"Would the Djinn terrorists have choppers and weapons access?"

"It's alarming when the Syrians have their hands on our military equipment. Text Daniel," Joseph said.

"I'm on it." She winked. "The military wouldn't always inform the press when airfields have break-ins, or when

American or Russian equipment is stolen. But it must happen often. Last year, a British Airways plane spotted an airstrip on Reunion Island, stocked with missing or abandoned equipment—right in the Indian Ocean where no one would think to look."

"I'll ask Leo. He'll have access to data."

Daniel was waiting outside the Montparnasse police station when Leopold arrived.

"Leo, it's time for Interpol to take custody of Valois. If he's out of the picture, another will step forward to take his place and we'll work our way down the chain of command. He's a dedicated criminal but doesn't think for himself. He just follows orders."

Leo balked at the idea. "He's now only being held as a public nuisance, with a French passport and simple assault. We don't have evidence to hold him longer. He'll be out by tomorrow morning—it's not a crime to be a Syrian and a citizen of Paris. The flow of immigrants went unchecked in recent years thanks to the Schengen Agreement. Europeans could travel between countries under the radar. Interpol won't expose themselves without a concise connection to the international crime.

"We'll be careful with him. He could become an informant if the price is right. His father is ailing, making him vulnerable to a payoff and safety guarantee. It's kind of like swatting at a hornet's nest—if you don't win, they all come looking for you."

"Are you planning on a personal interrogation?" Daniel asked.

"I'll give it another go, but he's obstinate and refuses to name anyone. He has a well-paid lawyer; we aren't privy to their conversations. Downloading data from his phone is proving to be interesting. The GPS download shows access points that Fernando used to get into the catacombs today."

"Have you identified who sent the blueprints?" Joseph asked.

"Government House security is reviewing tapes of the last few months, for a breach of their classified materials. Next, the screening of all their employees with access to secured data will be required. The spy business will never be obsolete as long as there's motivation . . . and a commendation of valor."

Daniel interjected, "And a fortune in payoffs."

"What concerns me is how Valois knew that Joseph and Emily would be in the catacombs."

Daniel frowned. "Emily was followed from St. Pierre by the accomplice of Didier, and your sweep at the Dingo found a target pin on her. A logical explanation is that they know we're getting closer to a nest of terrorists using the tunnels for running arms and mercenaries."

"The pin would only bring a tail into the area. It's more likely the latter, Daniel. Could you ask Emily to do a sweep at the loft for any listening devices? I don't see how else they would have known about our plans today."

"We should all sweep repeatedly," Daniel said.

"Absolutely. The firewall for the jammer is impenetrable. However, for extra security, I've arranged clean burner phones for the three of you that can't be hacked. Here's yours."

"Joseph and Emily are heading back to town, and tomorrow we'll access the tunnels from Vavin Metro where we left off. Did you read my report?" Daniel asked.

"Good work. This team situation seems to be working out alright."

"We'll coordinate at Daguerre and have lunch. Will you be joining us, Leo?"

"Yes, I enjoy the young woman's spunk. She challenges me."

Daniel smirked.

"I know the effect."

Ten

The foursome rallied in the morning. An entrance to an old Vavin train line through a sewer grate led them to an overgrown hillside garden near the ruins of a historic hotel converted to flats.

Climbing through thorny thickets and shrubs, Joseph tore away enough to pry the grate open, and the team slipped through into a damp hole.

Drip, drip, drip.

"That sound is annoying," Emily laughed. "So annoying that they use it in torture chambers to break a person."

"Let a cheery tune overtake you," Daniel teased. "Like 'Build Me Up, Buttercup'. I promise you won't hear any outside noises."

At the T joint, the group stopped. We'll break into two teams," Leopold said. "We'll cover more ground that way. Remember there are four hundred miles of tunnel. Emily, I'd be honored if you would be my partner this afternoon."

Joseph and Daniel looked at each other, shocked and with raised eyebrows.

"Tomorrow she's on my team," Joseph snapped, expressing his displeasure. But Leopold didn't notice.

"Alright then," Leo said, "Emily and I will go left."

"Daniel, do you have GPS since I'll be losing my guide?" Joseph grunted.

"Yes, my signal is strong."

He poked Joseph with a look of amusement.

"I'll be *your* guide."

Seconds after splitting, they heard a rumbling, far off at first, then overhead. As the crushing roar of a train entered Vavin Metro, the carbide lanterns flickered, and bits of debris fell from the crumbling ceiling.

"The arches aren't reinforced like under the cemetery," Emily said. She brushed off her helmet and continued on Leopold's heels. "This section of the tunnel is older than yesterday's but the graffiti on the walls is new. Others have been here recently."

"Yes, and just because they didn't enter from the grate doesn't mean they didn't come from another channel," Leo said.

Plodding through the narrow passageways, they came to an opening.

"That stretch was long with alcoves or chambers," Emily whispered. "And I hear running water."

"Look. There are footprints in this culvert." Leo bent and shone his flashlight on the imprint. "Two men."

"How recent are the tracks?"

"Within twenty-four hours."

Emily stiffened. "Should I turn off my lamp?"

"Good idea. Here, hang on to this tether." Leo handed her a long leather strap from his pocket. "As long as we have it, we won't be more than ten feet apart. Take a few minutes to let your eyes acclimatize to the darkness."

"Don't move," she mouthed. "I hear a commotion ahead."

They froze for what Emily thought was an eternity.

My back is aching. Pull the tether and we'll go, Leo.

"Coast is clear," Leo finally whispered and tugged.

Trudging down the tunnel in the darkness was painstaking. Emily continued to mark her X's on the wall until they were within the sound of a pair of men at a cross joint. Along the way, they stepped past the sign of vagrant occupation with charcoal and an old cooking pot, rusting tins and rat-infested blankets.

Emily moved up beside Leo to listen. The first man spoke in Arabic.

"Be careful. This is live ammo. We don't want to blow up the tunnel with us in it." He laughed sarcastically. "At least not yet!"

The other voice was younger. "When is the big day going to take place, Didier?"

"We have four weeks to load the explosives and build our fleet of drones. Secrecy is on our side, so you won't be given any more information than you need for your assignment. Our orders come from ISIL headquarters, and none of us here knows the complete plan. You wouldn't be here if you haven't been trained in Syria and pledged to be a suicide bomber if asked of you. Correct?"

"Yes, I vowed my allegiance to the Djinn insurgents. I volunteered to serve as a suicide bomber on the day of equalization, the day that ISIS rules over Europe. I am joyful of the mass devastation that will fall upon Paris. Allah will prevail."

"Tonight, a convoy will arrive from Brussels by train, bringing an arsenal. You are to be at the Notre Dame station to help unload it when the church bells ring at midnight. The crates have guns and grenades to be packed into coffins and marched in the ceremony tomorrow of Bataclan victims. There are at least twenty funerals tomorrow. Spectacular revenge and so unexpected! The irony is pleasing, is it not?"

The pair laughed at the evil visualization.

"How many of us serve the Djinn cause?"

"It is not for you to ask."

"Yes, a true soldier follow orders. Orders of the great Salim Benghalem." The younger man's voice shook hearing the name of a man of such terrifying power over his troops.

At a clicking sound, the two men stood and listened to the silence.

Didier reassured him. "We are alone with sewer rats. Leave these boxes under that pile of bones and we'll go back for the next run."

When they'd gone, Leo moved in on the boxes, placing a mini tracking mechanism in the hinge of the lid.

Emily was itching to tell Leopold about the conversation with Alain Van Dame, but not knowing the men's distance, she didn't make a noise.

Joseph and Daniel followed the GPS to the north side of Boulevard Saint Germain at Rue Lecourbe and exited onto the street through a tight obscured opening in the back of a monument, hidden by a broken barricade. Close by, Emily and Leo climbed out through an alley manhole on Boulevard St. Michel, near the Sorbonne.

The spires of Notre Dame Cathedral were to their north, and Emily surveyed the grand bridge that spanned the Seine, the main artery through the city. "Ah, good to be back on land," she sighed, inhaling the Paris air while stretching her arms behind her back.

In a momentary trance, she turned to find Joseph walking toward her. She was overwhelmed to see him.

Ah, beautiful golden brown curls and the most romantic eyes, he makes my heart patter. How I long to have some private personal time with the man of my heart.

As their eyes met, she rose on her toes to kiss him.

On the edge of the bridge, the four discussed findings from the airfield and tunnels.

"The blueprints have been scrutinized by my forensic people," Leo said. "This is not only one blueprint, but an overlay of several going back to the Souterrain of Ville de Paris in 1855. It appears to have been taken from the original held in secured archives at the Palace of Justice.

"Each adds a crust of truth, but as we peel back the layers it is less daunting. There's no advantage to terrorist groups deviating from the main routes, so we can eliminate most of the offshoots."

Joseph listened to Leo's words with suspicion; something was unsaid. He was about to challenge him when Daniel interjected, "That is good news but it is a mammoth project."

Emily moved closer to Leo. "My friend, we have not known you long, but I can read your eyes. You saw something else there in the maps, what was it?"

Leo swallowed hard and looked at each of them. "There's a lone marking. Certainly, it cannot be, and it could be my imagination as that of a child seeking a treasure."

His friends waited in silence.

"I heard it once said that the King's map held the blood of Napoleon. See here . . ." Leo opened the map and pointed to a smudge, a thumbprint in a small box. I suspect that a forensic examination would open a pandora's box of antiquities; a national treasure, no less!

"This map shows a cache, however, it has disappeared from the other layers. When we're finished, we'll defer this to the Treasury Department. Perhaps this is as much a treasure map as a terrorist blueprint."

"Great scot! The terrorists must know of this too, and not only want the map but the treasure," Joseph exclaimed.

"Perhaps," Leo said. "But there is no point in us joining a treasure hunt when national security swings in the balance."

"Dangle a carrot and snatch it away," Emily laughed.

"Perhaps tomorrow, I will have better news. Unfortunately, we have an impending crisis threatening victims' funerals tomorrow. Emily and I overheard a planned attack during the ceremonies," Leo declared.

"If it's true, they'd load grenades into coffins and remotely set them off with mourners in attendance, the project begins at midnight," Emily said. "Where is the memorial site?"

"I'll ensure enough security for tomorrow. The terrorists will not have their way, I will see to that," Leo said aloud with his thoughts, but his far-off demeanor concerned Emily.

"Are you alright, Leo?"

"Yes, yes, fine . . . Emily, would you consider going undercover, as a plant, at the Directorate of Intelligence and Investigations? The reports for Interpol need a more detailed interpretation of the chain of command, and our information suggests a Djinn mole within our system. I have a contact that will arrange it if you agree." He looked pleadingly at Emily, and in turn, she looked at Joseph. He didn't say anything, but she knew and smiled, hoping the reassurance would ease Leo\s mind.

"Of course, Leo. If it helps to expedite our activity, I'm in. We're all part of the same team."

Joseph and Daniel both knew it would be pointless to express their objection to Emily without a fiery backlash about treating her as a woman.

Distracted, Leo stepped to the curb without looking back and hailed a cab to headquarters.

When Leopold had first entered the International Criminal Police Organization at the Lyon headquarters he was an undercover agent. His advancement up Interpol's ranks had racked up countless successes, but not without loss and alienation from friends and family.

His first case was assigned ten years prior, on a complex terrorist plot threatening London's financial district. During the investigation, he made a critical mistake and was tracked to his residence, unbeknownst to him.

Returning home one night, he found his house had been bombed, and his wife and son murdered inside. Blaming himself for the loss of his family, he poured himself into tracking terrorist operations to the point of avoiding close relationships and confidences.

He would not be at peace until this vendetta was revenged. Riding in the taxi to his office, the event of ten years before was fresh in his memory, and his knuckles were clenched and white with anger. His mind switched to Emily and Joseph.

Interpol agents know our risks, but with this curious pair of detectives, we must use caution to protect them. The background search for them only goes back four years. Who are they?

Joseph and Emily drove to their detective agency off the Champs-Élysées, before heading back to Montmartre. Taking the elevator from the parking garage, Emily reached for his hand and surprised him with a cheek kiss. As the door opened on their floor, she giggled at the sound of Madge chattering to herself inside the office.

"Hello, Madge!"

Madge was at the front desk, matronly and professional in a navy business suit. Her silver hair was twisted into a French roll with an ivory pearl comb, and her spectacles had moved to the end of her nose, and fell to the floor when she jumped up to give Emily a hug.

"I'm so glad to see you both. I can't tell you how sorry I am about the tickets."

"Don't give it another thought, Madge," Joseph reassured. "Oddly, we've had significant developments since that night and we've been dragged into a new Interpol sting."

"Sounds exciting, I love a good case. I won't press for details, but you will tell me about it when the bad guys are carted off to jail, won't you?" Her eyes gleamed with the taste of adventure.

"I promise, Madge. How's Carter doing with the Trudel boy?"

"They've struck up a unique friendship, and Carter is dealing with the life insurance company to appeal a waiver. Seems the father became indebted to the wrong people and became coerced into a life of ill-repute; so to spare his family, he deliberately avoided contact with his sons. The night of the massacre, he saw the opportunity to retire from his obligations, and texted his son to say he was in the club."

Emily said, "That would be a good foil. But I understand that all the bodies have been identified by family members or passports. Jacques Trudel wasn't among them. When were Jacques Senior and Junior last in physical contact?"

"A year or more, he says."

From her desk drawer, Emily retrieved a business card for Madge. "Call Mr. Tessier, and say we need advice on declaring a person officially missing. Is the son over twenty-one?"

"Yes, recently."

"Perhaps he could apply for guardianship of his siblings and ask the court to seize his father's assets, then sue for child support," Joseph suggested. "The family might qualify for a government pension. Madge, if the family is suffering, take some money from our benevolent fund, and be discreet so he won't be embarrassed."

Madge beamed. "Good angle; I'll get to work on that."

Emily collected her bag again and slipped her arm into Joseph's. "Give our best to Carter and Jacques Jr. You'll not see much of us over the next weeks, Madge, but we'll check in. You can catch up on your knitting."

"Knitting, my foot." Her face was flustered, and she stood and waved her hands. "Go on now and get out of here."

"What is it, Madge? You're holding something back," Emily said.

"Yesterday a man was loitering in the hall when I came to work. He was dark-complexioned with eyes that could light a fire. I saw into his soul when he took off his weird heavy-rimmed glasses. He had a knitted toque . . . I notice those things. He watched me unlock the door. The frosted pane in the door restricts details both ways, but I saw his shadow pass back and forth for a while before coming in."

Emily was alarmed. "He came into the office?"

"He wanted to know where you were, saying that it was important."

"How was he dressed?" Joseph asked.

"Unshaven, not at all business-like. He wasn't particularly tall, but the frames were distinctive. He insisted that I give him your home address, but of course I didn't."

"Thanks, Madge you did the right thing. Text us if he comes again."

At five o'clock, they crossed the bridge, heading north in rush hour traffic. "Glad the car's so small. I could even mount the sidewalk in a jam if I needed to," Joseph boasted.

"This is Paris, not Rome."

His eyes were on the rearview mirror. "We're definitely being tailed by a grey Peugeot. Sweep for a tracking bug? I know you have a bag of tricks that Leo gave you."

"Yes . . . there's something under the back bumper."

"Can you disable it?"

"I'll give it a try."

Joseph sped through a lane change at the intersection and turned at a construction route. "They've dropped back. Your jammer is working."

At Montmartre, he drove up the hill the back way, and into the alley from the street behind the flower shop. Easing into his reserved parking spot, he pulled a protective canvas tarp over the Twizy.

"We'll go up the back roof ladder. I have a bad feeling."

"Sure, Babe. I'll go first, and you catch me," she said.

"Yes, but don't turn the lights on yet. I'll be along in a few minutes. I'm going to hang out here as a lookout, and see if anyone comes along snooping."

"If you're not up in ten minutes, I'm calling Daniel," Emily threatened.

Maybe we should move to a hotel near Daniel or Interpol. If Emily picked up a tail at St. Pierre, they know we are in Montmartre. Then again, Waldo appeared at the agency. It's not a huge area to disappear in. I'll get Em to pack a bag.

Joseph texted Daniel and got an instant reply.

"I agree, Joseph. I'll book a room here. It's close to the hot zone. Come to the Lenox Montparnasse by taxi and leave your car where it is. I'll inform Leopold."

When Joseph tapped on the balcony door, Emily was standing, ready with two overnight bags.

"Will this be enough for a few days?"

He took her wife in his arms and hugged her. "I love you so much. You realize this means you'll miss the Christmas market in Montmartre. I know how you look forward to that."

"There will be many more, but we're in danger now!" She kissed him again.

"Come on then, m'lady."

Eleven

An hour later, Emily and Joseph were at the Lenox Montparnasse in the center of Paris. The boutique hotel on Rue Delambre was elegant even from the street, with ornate balconies, tall dormers, and gargoyles of lions and goddesses.

The cab driver parked their bags on the curb and departed to find another fare in the nearby theater district. The late evening street mimes and musicians were on the walkways serenading pedestrians and tourists enjoying the night air.

Check-in was immediate, and they were directed to a junior suite on the top floor. The tiny hotel elevator was reserved to transport luggage, or at best one or two patrons at a time; otherwise a narrow winding staircase would suffice. Opting for the elevator, they were relieved to reach the fourth floor.

The room's ambiance delighted Emily, and she crashed onto a plush bed, waiting for a second wind. The décor was old French Provençale with antique inlaid furniture enhanced with gold gilt, and heavy fine tapestries and flocked draperies.

Sounds of music and gaiety wafted through the balcony window from the street below. A fruit basket and a bottle of Bordeaux lured them to a Demilune end table by the window.

"There's a card," Joseph said.

"It's from Leo. At first, I found him too authoritative and controlling, but that's his job. He seems to be a nice man with a good sense of humor. I see how he and Daniel would be friends as they're both mysterious and hide their past. Other than that, I don't know anything about him."

"Don't get too attached to Leo. Tomorrow I claim you as my partner in the catacombs." Joseph squinted as he said it, wanting it known that he was jealous of today's pairing.

"Your wish is granted. I'm famished. Here's a brochure from the Italian restaurant next door where we met with Leo earlier. If I order for us, do you mind picking it up and we'll dine in our room? I'd like to remain behind a locked door considering the tails tonight."

"Call and place your order, Honey. I saw a wine boutique outside the front door. I'll go there first."

"There's Bordeaux here already, with glasses."

"We'll get to that later. Tonight I'd like the Nouveau Beaujolais. The season is short and I missed the wine auctions in Montmartre. You remember I have obligations to the Order of Beaujolais since I was inducted into the cellars of Lyon?"

"How could I forget, Darling? You remind me every November."

Emily greeted his return in her soft pink silk robe. The table was set for a romantic dinner, with a lone candle and wine glasses that sparkled from the city lights.

Paris was bustling outside the Lenox at 6:30 a.m. when Joseph got up to close the window. Emily was still sleeping, and he brewed a pot of coffee on the desk.

Last night wasn't the first tail I've seen. I woke up again today sweating with heart palpitations and the reenactment of the Bataclan. The sounds and smells will be with me forever, and the stranger's glaring eyes at the Basilica haunt me in my dreams. Staring into the soul of a terrorist.

His agitated thoughts were interrupted by Daniel's text.

"You up?"

"I am, but Emily's sleeping, exhausted from yesterday."

"Meet me in the breakfast room downstairs off the lobby."

Daniel was sipping coffee at his regular window table as Joseph slid into a peach armchair facing him.

"You don't look like you slept, Joseph."

"Did you?"

"It was a good decision for you to leave Montmartre," Daniel said. "We'll be more productive here. So far, we've only marked two caches in five kilometers, and the mathematics don't look good. So we'll pick up our pace."

"I'm glad you're here, Daniel. I know you run as a lone wolf, but when you're absent for long periods, we wonder how you're doing. It was a lifetime ago in Albany when you saved my life. I'm forever indebted."

Without a reaction, Daniel returned to his newspaper.

"We serve ourselves from the buffet, is that right?" Joseph said, pushing back his chair.

"There's a tureen of scrambled eggs, and if you want them a special way, the girl will get them for you."

"Scrambled is good."

Daniel watched Joseph across the room. realizing the sense of attachment and bonding that he had for Joseph and Emily.

Joseph filled his plate with meats, cheese, fruit and some croissants, and Daniel followed. They delved into their plates in silence, both in deep thought, then got to business, Daniel first.

"Leo says an undercover security interception unit is in place to monitor airfield transmissions. The name Youssif Didier came up there, as well as in sensors from our bugs in the tunnels. Interpol has a profile on Didier; he's high in command in ISIL in Belgium and France, but not high in the Syrian masterminds. He's passionate about Djinn Insurgents, a festering startup group working on new recruits and investments.

"Didier's description sounds like the man at the Basilica—Middle Eastern, dark hair tied back. He wears a folded bandana over his forehead, but he is clearly balding as Emily described. Leo overheard Didier's name yesterday in the tunnels too."

"What does Djinn stand for?" Joseph said.

"It's simply pure evil," Daniel said. "It's at the opposite spectrum of principles of Christians and their God. The man that Alain Van Dame referred to as Didier at the training club is the same man. The equipment and facilities don't come cheap. I wonder where they get their money."

Daniel stopped and looked around the room, then sipped coffee as if he were through.

"There's more, isn't there?" Joseph said. "I can see you're either distracted or worried."

"Yes, there's more. This group is more complex than following orders, planting bombs or drone attacks. Leopold did an Interpol search on you and Emily, according to protocol. Someone is trying to make life difficult for you. SWIFT is a Belgian company that tracks suspect transactions into terrorist accounts throughout Europe."

"A search on us?"

"You have already been blacklisted—a sizable sum was deposited and withdrawn by these criminal channels, with the loans in your names."

"No way, Daniel."

"Check for yourself. The problem is that you have been targeted. Valois and Didier want revenge on you for taking the blueprints, and this is a way to ease his responsibility and earn redemption in the eyes of his Syrian leaders. If you are exposed, it gives them a financing vehicle and they expect authorities will hold you, making their way clearer. Interpol picked up some chatter mentioning your name."

"So if Valois gets taken again, he'll turn the tables on me and say I paid him to do what they're planning. Is that the plan?" Joseph said.

"It won't stick, but I'm letting you know how things stand."

"Go on, Daniel. What else?"

"It's likely that the deposit came from Syria, as Interpol tracked a loan on an Asian bank in Molenbeek Brussels. The State of Islam uses loans to fund immigration, recruitment, and training. The British, Canadian and American governments refuse to pay ransoms for hostages, so the insurgents can't count on ransoms for cash flow. In your case, they used these funds to purchase explosives and more attack drones. Right after the deposit, a transaction paid for a drone shipment."

"This is ludicrous. My witness protection identity Joseph Harkness didn't even exist four years ago, so how can it get a large loan like that? We have a secured credit card for travel and expenses using our aliases Joseph and Emily and we don't rack up traceable debt. We pay taxes but have no traceable credit anywhere."

He no longer had an appetite. "You realize, Daniel, this scenario leaves Emily and me vulnerable to international exposure. The hounds will come looking from the past. Can the deposit be tracked and reversed?"

"Leo is looking into that. He knows it's to frame you and keep you out of the way. They want the blueprint and they need leverage to bargain with you. With this level of activity, we know they didn't have a copy. Backtracking security footage of the Presidential office compound, there was a breach two days before you encountered the drone.

"A man in a dark toque overpowered a guard late in the day when the building had emptied. With the guard's uniform and stolen credentials, he moved freely to steal the documents. We don't know how they knew of the existence or location of them but they were in and out in minutes. It's embarrassing to the government, and there was no press leak. It couldn't have happened without inside co-operation."

Joseph shook his head in disbelief.

"So a mole is somewhere in the government, sympathetic to the insurgent cause? And I am the government's patsy! That's the reason Waldo is not behind bars."

"The government had a difficult choice—ignore it and spare their formidable image of tight security, or shame themselves in the press. An easy answer."

Joseph was absorbed in thought.

The classified blueprints are the least of my problems. If these people have inside access to do this sort of thing, our exposure in the witness protection program leaves us vulnerable. Emily's in danger!

Emily woke to an empty pillow and Joseph's note and dressed quickly to join them in the breakfast room.

"Good morning, may I join you? From your faces, I've missed something important."

"Daniel was telling me about the terrorists rounded up in Belgium and Germany. It's plausible to believe that the Brussels cell didn't draw suspicion and cued the authorities."

Emily's silence was punctuated by her analyzing stare at each of them. "Is that story yours as well, Daniel?"

"Don't let the breakfast get cold, Em," he fumbled. "We're going into the catacombs promptly at ten."

"Hogwash, the two of you. I've always been straightforward with both of you. Perhaps I should pair up with Leo today, and not tell you about our findings at the rendezvous."

Joseph nodded to Daniel. "She's right. Tell her what you've told me. We're a team and trust is paramount."

Daniel reluctantly gave Emily a shortened version of the new risk. "And furthermore, from now on you are Joseph and Emily. Right?"

Emily was more agitated than he'd seen. "We know the risks to our lives and witness protection IDs better than anyone. Thanks for trying to protect me by withholding news, but don't."

She stalled in thought at the buffet bar and returned with only a croissant and jam, and a slice of fruit.

"At this moment, three's a crowd," Daniel said. "I'll meet you both in the lobby at 9:30 to go to Denfert-Rochereau."

Alone at the table, Emily said, "We're in trouble, Joseph."

"Leopold is dealing with it. I'm sure it will get sorted out."

Leo was eager to see them arrive at the museum. "We tracked a shipment of three dozen Phantom drones on the way to Le Bourget, and an old American-made Apache Attack helicopter is being fueled in Brussels with the cargo on board."

"I'm game to be there for its arrival, Leo," Joseph offered. "Now that I'm implicated, I promise you I will redeem myself, and get a bit of vengeance as an enticement. We've been to the drone airfield and I can find it in the dark."

Leo looked at Daniel. "What's this about?"

"I briefed Joseph and Emily on the illegal loans done in their names."

"Yes, yes. But don't preoccupy yourself with the little stuff. However, your little red car is rather conspicuous. I propose we use the sedan and take up coordinated posts."

"What? Emily piped. "Don't think that the team won't back each other up. Joseph and I will go back into the tunnels at the Sorbonne and work our way north as far as possible. No need to wait 'til the museum opens; I've saved my GPS movements to match up with the blueprints."

"Yes, backup is key," Daniel exclaimed.

"Agreed," said Leo. "At six tonight, we'll dine at the Dingo to review everything. I'll reserve a booth inside, then we'll go to the airfield under the cover of dusk."

"What security plan will prevent grenades in caskets today?" Daniel asked.

"A perimeter with security scanners will detect any gas, and everyone gets checked. The area continues to be swept. We intercepted two cars coming into Paris packed with explosives, and insurgents are in custody but are tight-lipped so far."

Emily sensed Leo's quiet evaluation. "What's troubling you, Leo? Tell me."

"We'll talk later, Emily. I'm getting your security credentials for the Intelligence Investigations unit. We're certain a mole there is stealing top-secret data."

Outside the museum, the four waited near an occupied bench. Nearby, a frightened child was at the feet of a tall man fiddling with a kite on the edge of the park.

He was chattering in Arabic and wore a black bandana, and to anyone watching, it would be obvious he was unfamiliar with the kite situation and the child. The man was careful not to make eye contact with Emily and reveal himself as the visitor at the loft on Rue des Saules.

Instinctively, she looked up at the kite. The sky was blue with sufficient breeze, but a sound grew louder.

Hmmm, hmmm.

Joseph shielded the sun from his eyes and looked too.

"It looks like an eagle, Leo! Did I mention the drones at the airfield wore eagle camouflage?"

Leopold withdrew a narrow flashlight and pointed it at the drone. In seconds, Leo's laser downed the drone, scattering pieces on the ground while frightened pedestrians dispersed in the aftermath. The kite man fled with the boy into the tree line.

The copper tag and camera were instantly retrieved. "Emily, quickly, do a sweep of Joseph and Daniel," Leo asked.

"Nothing. They must have tracked us another way."

In seconds, a unit of policemen was on scene to investigate complaints of a bomb on the street. Two of the approaching gendarmes carried drawn rifles, and few pedestrians stayed to watch, as most vacated the vicinity in disbelief.

"The three of you go ahead," Leo instructed. "I'll talk to the officer in charge and find you in the tunnel. If I get delayed we'll meet at Dingo as planned."

"I'll come with you, Leo."

Twelve

Descending into the metro, they were bunched up into the gendarmes' security checkpoint lineup. Emily knew her equipment could catch attention, with helmets, headlamps, and carbide. The inspector called for a second opinion, and the two officers looked at the pair in confusion.

"What is this equipment, Madame?"

Emily spoke in English, hoping for a tourist façade. "Oh, we're going to the catacombs. The salesman at Vieux Campeur recommended them, so I'm prepared."

The officers blurted in laughter that would normally be rude and waved them through the turnstiles. "Tourists!"

Exiting the metro at Cluny La Sorbonne Station near Boulevard St. Michel and St. Germain, Emily led them to the manhole where she last exited with Leo.

Joseph held the lid open for Emily to ease herself down the utility ladder, then took a last glance in the alley and followed.

The route was uninhabited through the back lanes, and bearing the lid's weight, he let it fall into its groove with a clank. Unsure of their surroundings, they stayed in one spot until their eyes adapted.

Joseph whispered, "BBC said today that UN Security forces recovered drones made in Iran with longer range and capability of dropping a small bomb."

"Doesn't surprise me," Emily said. "My seminar about prototypes and ID codes discussed light craft developments happening under the radar without piquing international interest. A fleet of recreational drones can go unnoticed even if their intent is sinister and capable of espionage with deadly payloads."

"'I'd have liked the seminar. Where was I?"

"In London, on an embezzlement case."

"Do you have a business card or contact with someone in the development of the hybrid example?"

"It'll be on the desk at the loft. But I can find it online."

Joseph flashed his light down the western section. "Let's take this way."

This older part of the tunnel was in poor repair, and they worked their way in a parallel route to the river, feeling trickles of water from above. At the conjunction, they split off to Notre Dame, finding another weapons cache. Joseph marked it with a scanning code to be visible with a monochrome reader.

After three hours in the damp underground, they surfaced for air and sunlight near the Musée d'Orsay and the Assemblée Nationale. Climbing out from behind a rusted grate covered in foliage, Joseph snagged his arm on a shard of rusted metal, leaving a deep gash. He gritted his teeth, knowing he'd been responsible to bring the forgotten First Aid kit, and he pulled his sleeve down to shield his arm from Emily.

"This doesn't look like a usable access point for insurgents," he mused, turning away to wince.

They stopped in the shadow of the grand Assemblée Nationale, with its distinctive pillars encompassing the 18th-century Hôtel de Lassay and Palais Bourbon. From a staircase leading to the Pont de la Concorde over the Seine, they paused to watch the innocent world of tourism pass by in a cavalcade of sightseeing riverboats. Every tourist was absorbed with smartphones, cameras, and selfie sticks.

At a sidewalk table at La Brasserie Bourbon, Joseph and Emily could relax, at last, fortifying themselves with French split pea soup with chunks of ham, baguettes, and café au lait.

"The Eiffel Tower looks so beautiful from here, Joseph. Remember when we dined there? So romantic!" Is it our lot in life, Joseph, to look over our shoulders wherever we go, for men in the shadows?"

Joseph was about to reply but hesitated.

"What is it, Joseph?"

"It's not important."

"We have no secrets . . . at least that's what I thought."

"Nothing concrete, just a feeling that Leo is troubled by us. I see him watching us with a look of distress on his face."

"It's odd you mention that; I've noticed it too. Will he know that we're really the Yorks? Are we are in danger of being exposed to that threat, even by accident?"

"All we can do is be careful and not slip up. Daniel would never lead us into that danger without investigating it. He's our guardian angel."

At nine p.m. the foursome departed downtown Paris for the Van Dame airfield northeast of the city. The sky was pitch black, with only a sliver of moonlight.

"Follow the 118 for 15 kilometers from the city limits, Leo. If you'd like, I could drive as it's so dark," Joseph offered.

Leo shook his head with mild irritation. "Just tell me when to turn; I follow instructions well."

The landmarks of a red barn roof meant nothing in the darkness, but the Van Dame farm was illuminated with a bank of lights in the backfield for night training.

"They couldn't be more obvious if they had sent up a flare," Daniel said.

Cutting the headlights, the black sedan eased onto the open field beside the gravel laneway, then cut the engine. Leaving the car near the entrance, they moved toward the control tower on foot, crouching into the tall grass, with Leo and Daniel leading.

Out of sight inside the cement house, an Arabian man in a bandana, black tee and greasy trousers was glued to the wall of security monitors. The windows were sealed with metal shutters and the roof was covered by a camouflage of shrubbery and old army tarps.

Each monitor relayed footage from the strategic cameras placed at the farm, on the highway, and even at points in Paris. The man crossed back and forth watching every screen. Suddenly, Camera 7 went black, with sporadic bursts of static.

"Bring up the film, Raymond! Camera 7," Didier barked.

"Sorry, Sir. There's nothing there."

"Send someone out on foot and check it out. I don't believe in accidents or mistakes."

At that moment, Alain Van Dame burst through the door.

"Alain, what are you doing here?"

Didier was on his feet, with anger flashing in his eyes.

"This is more than I bargained for," Van Dame said. "There's a field of insurgents all over my farm, and I didn't know about the attack chopper. You won't get away with this unnoticed; folks around here aren't blind and deaf. You can pay me off, but you can't bribe a whole community."

Didier's dark eyes penetrated into Alain's. Although Alain was taller and bigger, at this moment he feared for his life. Didier poked him, digging a finger into his chest, and he stepped back to regain his balance.

"Why did you come here?" Didier shouted. "I pay you well for use of the airfield. What I do with it is not your concern. All I ask is that you monitor poachers and intruders, and keep your mouth shut."

"The camera at the lane entrance is on the blink again," Alain said. "From my veranda, I thought a black sedan pulled into the drive. When I replayed the tape, there was nothing. The same thing happened a few days ago."

"What else?"

"Well . . . a nuisance fellow called me from the gate, wanting to practice with his drone. I said this was a private club. He insisted on paying for access, so I gave him your number."

"You did what?

"It was a fandangled miniature car. Red, and I'm sure there was a girl with him."

Didier stormed to the door and flung it wide.

"Get out!"

Didier nodded to one of his men, and in an instant, the farmer was dragged out the door to an uncertain fate.

The Interpol team heard it all through Joseph's laser microphone aimed at the cement house.

"I can't break through the firewall to pick up the control tower," Daniel said. Leo pulled another contraption from his pocket to point across the field.

"Try the tower now."

"Clear as a bell. An Apache 4 has a data request for landing clearance."

"Three kilometers from the helipad," the pilot radioed.

At the roar of the whirlybird, Youssif Didier stepped outside to watch an oversized chopper descend with a forceful wind blowing everything in its wake.

A dozen militants were lying in the grass that encircled the landing pad, crawling on their bellies with rifles in their arms. The lone controller waved landing instructions with red laser beams from the tower, and below, a man with green conal illuminated lights signaled the landing spot.

The tandem helicopter was a beastly, black hulk, flattening every blade of grass within fifty feet of the carriage as it hovered. Four main blades and four more on the rotor slowed to a hum then fell silently onto the helipad like a mother bird nesting. Eight men dressed in black and wearing padded ear coverings buffered the sound in the darkness.

On a signal, a dozen militants rushed forward to assist, then the detectives did the same close behind, coming to within a hundred feet of the Apache when the motor idled to a putter.

Didier's face was still livid from Alain's fumbling. He stood tall in the darkness with his hands on his hips waiting for the cargo door to open.

The co-pilot descended from the cockpit with the manifest, offering the chart to Didier. "Sir. Four Ababil Iranian drones, four Mohajer reconnaissance drones, eight military American drones able to carry light bombs, a case of 24 AK47 assault rifles, and a case of 12 AK104 carbines. The missiles will come by cargo plane and the grenades will arrive by land. Air decompression is too volatile for the nitrogen in the grenades."

"Excellent, my men will unload them." Youssif grabbed the paperwork to make an illegible scrawl.

"Emily, stay with Daniel, I'm going in closer to see if I can deposit a tracking pin," Joseph whispered.

Leo motioned, "Daniel and Emily, fan out to the right."

The unloading to the warehouse was expeditious, preparing the helicopter to depart in twenty minutes. "Get out of here so we can turn off the lights!" Didier barked.

Joseph and Leopold closed in on one of the militants that was lagging behind his group by more than thirty feet. Joseph signaled to Leo, then moved in with a chokehold on the insurgent, and in seconds, his muscles weakened and he lapsed into unconsciousness.

Joseph donned the man's clothing and bandana and merged with the others to plant three transmitters. Back in the long grass, he discarded the clothing in a foot ditch.

As he crept to rejoin Leo, he heard the click of a gun close to his ear and looked across the darkness at a man patrolling the outer perimeter. Another voice was about ten meters away, with footsteps thrashing closer through the grass.

"Robert! What are you doing over there?" the other man called. "This isn't the time to take a whiz."

The first man poked the gun into Joseph's face. "Who are you?" He kicked Joseph to the ground with a heavy army boot that smelled of diesel fuel. There was nothing to do but wait a few seconds, as Daniel surprised the gunman from the side, wrestling him to the ground. A few feet away, Leopold brought down the second man.

Leo tossed Emily the keys to bring the car closer.

"These men will tell Didier about us," Joseph said. "Our cover is blown."

"We have no choice but keep them quiet and drag them to the car trunk. Better that Didier thinks they were skunks that ran."

The helicopter rotors had started up, disguising the hum of the car engine. Emily popped the trunk and waited for the trio to stow the captives.

Emily reclaimed the driver's seat. "Where to, Leo?"

"Back to Paris while I figure out what to do."

"Only one saw me," Joseph said. "The other didn't see a thing."

"It won't be long before Didier knows that he's short two men," Daniel said.

Emily skidded out onto the road. "Long enough for us to be out of tracking range."

In the rearview mirror, a headlight was surging from the warehouse. "Guys, there's a motorcycle on our tail."

"Step on it." Daniel leaned out with his gun and fired twice.

"He's still coming."

Daniel fired again. A burst of flames lit up the sky, as the gas tank ruptured. In the distance, the motorcycle skidded into the ditch in a ball of fire.

"That's sure to get Didier's attention!" Leopold groaned, then sent a text.

"Here's the plan," he said. "Park in front of the Dingo Café. Interpol will clean the trunk. We'll split up and regroup in the morning. Joseph, give me the frequency codes for the tracking pins."

"We need a 24/7 stakeout team for Didier's movements and for the construction yard for future flights," Daniel said.

"And for ammunition and grenades," Joseph said. "We can't forget land shipments coming."

"It's been arranged," Leo said, ignoring their hints. "Interpol is already monitoring and tracking the chatter and transport."

Minutes after the sedan fled, Didier noted his troops had diminished and summoned his henchmen.

"Where are Robert and Marcel? I haven't seen them since the unloading."

"That's correct, Sir," one said. "There are six insurgents here, and it should be eight."

Didier bristled as he stared at the faces.

"You ninny! I've got eyes and can count. Spread out and tell the patrol unit. Search the grass for any sign of anything. Outlines in the grass, boot marks, clothing! Take the trucks and comb the area."

Livid that his makeshift army had faltered, Didier returned to the security monitors as the crew scattered, fearing his wrath. He froze the footage at a dark spot and bellowed to the security chief. "Here, what's this? Enlarge and sharpen it."

The black areas in the grass were in the shapes of humans, but not clear enough to show the images of the four spies.

Didier paced the room, shouting erratic orders. "Bring Alain back here!"

In minutes, Alain was yanked into the room with fresh bruises and plunked on a wooden chair, victim to the fist of Didier's muscle man. More blows to the jaw were meant to loosen him.

"I want details about the ones with the red car! Now, spit out everything!" Didier screamed. His eyes darted in a rage. "Don't leave anything out or you'll regret it, Alain. All you are is a sentry, that's not too much to expect."

Alain sat up, sputtering. "He spoke in French but it was a foreign accent, maybe American. The woman was just a silhouette, I can't describe her at all. When I looked out the window, he was back in his car, one of those new sporty things—cherry red. His hair was brown and curly, under a knitted cap like punks wear these days."

Didier walked toward the light, scanning through his cell phone. Producing a picture of Joseph Harkness, he asked, "Is this the man you saw?"

Alain knew he couldn't be positive from a distance, but an affirmative would take the heat off.

"Oui, oui, c'est l'homme."

With a bang, the door burst open. The guard aimed his gun, but it was only a beleaguered militant returning with the news.

"Sir, one of the patrollers set off on the motorcycle after a sedan. Looks like they shot out his engine. They bushwacked us."

Interpol picked up the full transmission from the pins and alerted Leopold.

Thirteen

Joseph's room phone rang on the fourth floor of the Lenox Montparnasse.

"It's Daniel. Meet me downstairs?"

"Sounds serious. Should I bring Emily?"

"We're all in this together now."

He turned to her to speak, but her intuition already said something was amiss. "Should I guess what Daniel wanted, or just pack my bag," she asked.

Daniel was alone when Joseph and Emily arrived, and his rare frown gave away his worry. He leaned forward on his elbows with his hands clasped.

"It's a good thing you left a bug at the cement house. Interpol picked up a transmission, and Alain Van Dame identified you from a picture Didier had of you picking up the cylinder at the church. Your cover is blown. It's not safe for you here anymore as Joseph and Emily Harkness."

"We can't go back home under our real names, it's not safe there either," Emily said.

"In the morning, Leo will take the two of you to a safe house. Didier has put out a contract on both of you."

"What about you, Daniel?" Joseph asked.

"I have my disguises; you won't need to worry about that."

That night, Didier advanced a trial run over Paris, launching a squad of six reaper drones from Le Bourget in a well-rehearsed fly-over.

Swooping with audacious confidence below the radar, they went undetected, until alarms went up, fearing a terrorist onslaught. The city of Paris immediately activated surveillance units, monitoring and tracking movements in the low airspace.

Twilight had drifted over the city. It was a romantic time when lovers stroll the streets arm in arm under the lights of the Eiffel Tower. From the North a tiny row of white lights moved nearer, bringing with them a buzz.

Parisians craned their necks toward the sky as they froze to watch the approach of these impossible drones. Other pedestrians scattered to find cover wherever possible.

The buzzing grew louder and the whirring closer until they raced overhead leaving those on the land reeling in the wind. It was not only over the Eiffel Tower but Bastille Square, the U.S. Embassy, the Place de la Concorde Bridge and the Invalides Military Museum. Sirens and emergency vehicles swarmed across the city Paris.

A final salute was made over the Presidential Palace with egregious mockery. Meanwhile, Paris Aviation was ill-prepared to get defense planes in the air to track and down the crafts before the drones disappeared into the moonlight.

"C'est merveilleux," Didier boasted, relishing the excellence of his prelude to terror. "Les imbecilles. They will be notified by the French Malou Tech's Army that this is merely a practice for La-Queue-en-Brie, a small town no one in Paris has ever heard of."

Leo Desjardins received a simple warning that the event was a training exercise.

"Don't be so naïve, Clemmons! Can't you see those are reapers and Go Pro Hero3's! Perhaps if you look closely under that stone you will find a rat," Leo said aloud at the Interpol headquarters. "Track down that dispatcher and you will find an unsettling truth."

Several nearby agents watched the look on Leo's face. He had been long known as a man of patience and steadfast under pressure. This outburst in expression sent a camp of computer researchers and detectives into delving for any computer trace of the Dispatcher.

"Oui, Monsieur Desjardins. The code name from the dispatcher is traceable to a Syrian named Tahir Sayed, and you are correct to assume he has ISIL training."

Leo outlined, "The Department of Protection and Security set up a working den to monitor all the transmitters we have placed, and every data source will be mapped. ISIL is ramping up to attack strategic points in France to retaliate for Britain's cooperation in stepped up airstrikes. Their intelligence backing is more than we anticipated."

Clemmons said, "Security points have yet to trace these mystery drones to their launch source."

Standing abruptly, Leo beckoned several agents working on his floor, at headquarters, to join him.

"Here, is this what you signed up for? To watch Paris crumble under our feet while we watch? Is this it?"

From the back of the room, a voice boomed. "Non, Monsieur, we are Parisians and we fight for our liberty and our children!"

"Any more? Heaven have mercy on us if it is only the man at the back of the room and I that believe in defending France."

Within a few minutes, mumbles became a rousing chant. "Non, les terrorists may not take Paris from us."

Copycat missions had already surfaced, going back to the eve of the Charlie Hebdo attack, and again before the Bataclan and Soccer Stadium. Government security was convinced that the drones had photographed sensitive facilities including power plants, government buildings and a bay in Brittany that housed nuclear submarines.

As a stand-by alert, extra military personnel were brought in, and France notified Britain, the U.S., Australia and other active allies against ISIL.

Leo texted Daniel, Joseph, and Emily of the threat. "Let's hope it's not a snide warning that ISIL is ramping up its target date. I have an emergency meeting before I meet you at the Lenox tomorrow morning. It's time for the military and police to secure the tunnels. Emily, we're ready to install you as an analyst at the Terrorism Research unit."

As he disconnected, an Interpol clerk tapped on Leo's door with a flash drive. "This is the information you wanted. I used your security clearance code as you asked."

"Thanks, but remember this never happened."

The disc brought up a raft of photos that included their real names, Thomas York and Rachel Redmond while in Albany, New York.

"I see, I see . . . you are both very clever and I never gave you enough credit."

At eight, Leo arrived at the hotel with two men, looking official in suits. At his request, they waited outside, as he joined Joseph, Emily, and Daniel in the restaurant.

"I understand Daniel informed you of the latest at the Van Dame farm. The insurgents are flexing their muscles with accelerated drone attacks. The terror alert for Paris has elevated to a critical level. Last night, we arrested men at the Montparnasse Cemetery trying to access the catacombs through a crypt—you know the one, of the French Revolutionary soldiers."

"I saw the arrests in the Daily Express," Joseph said. "All this is because I picked up a suspicious piece of metal dropped from a drone."

"Joseph, you did a good thing. Interpol is grateful, and we're on track to intercept a well-orchestrated plot. I can't fathom the impending destruction if you hadn't acted."

"What happens now?"

"We'll move you to a safe house, but we need your detective sense to hunt for the insurgents and unravel their plot. You'll both be given disguises and a temporary location, and I'll continue to retrieve you for investigations in the tunnel and for data interception from the farmhouse. Your American instincts have been most reliable in the past."

Leopold laughed to lighten the situation, then looked up at their eyes for a reaction.

"Leo, exactly what did you mean by that—reliable in the past?" Joseph asked.

"By profession, I turn over every stone. A confidential file found its way to my desk . . . it was enlightening about all three of you."

The three exchanged glances of panic at the disclosure. Daniel said, "Leo, you and I know that confidential files don't appear by accident. Did someone send it to you, or did you decide to solicit covert data?"

In a rare, gentle voice, Leo let his compassion show.

"When the financial situation came up with SWIFT, I was curious discovering that the background covered only four years. But now I have a clear picture of the situation and I assure you it will remain secure."

"We need to know where the leak occurred," Emily prodded. "You know our lives are at risk."

"I scanned the facial features into a classified bank and got a hit on the two of you with a disgraced agent named Deslormes. The file was quite complimentary, I should say."

"Who else knows?" Daniel asked.

"No one. Your secret is safe for now. I needed you to know the stakes have increased. ISIL has their own intelligence and there's always the possibility they'll make the connection. It would serve their purpose to share your whereabouts with the old crime conspirators."

"So what do we do now?" Emily asked.

"We continue with the safe house. Be extra vigilant, as I've grown fond of you."

"Thanks, Leo," Joseph said, "The *four* of us will be a tough unit to take down."

Daniel said, "I have more news. Your bank account was used to pay for a weapons shipment from Brussels and another from Iran. Interpol has requested a freeze on your accounts. You are on a blacklist somewhere."

"Ridiculous!"

Leo nodded. "Normally, criminal charges would have been laid against you for conspiracy to provide support to a foreign terrorist organization. I've interfered with such action, and provided a cover under the guardianship of Interpol."

"What are these new disguises you have in mind, Leo?" Joseph asked.

"The safe house has overalls and caps, branded Charonne Drains & Ditches. Emily, you'll need to conceal your hair and blend in as a worker. A cube van with that name will be outside your door at nine every morning, taking you as two workers to your tunnel access points. When you exit at noon, the van will return you to the safe house.

"A toolbox is adequate to carry your equipment, and either Daniel or I will meet you. Considering the vastness of the tunnels, Interpol has set up six teams at various points to scour for explosives and arsenal stashes. I'll give you a heat sensor showing a green image if a person is directly in your path.

"One more thing. Emily will not be with you full time, Joseph. I will take her to the research lab at Protection and Security to activate the mole situation. She will be perfectly safe, I assure you."

Emily was glad of the upcoming temporary promotion, but she could read the distress on Joseph's face.

"You have this well thought out, Leo," Joseph said.

"We can't have the mission interrupted. Chatter has increased about a plot on the Paris transportation system," Leo said.

"Are the men outside in suits taking us to the safe house?" Emily asked. "Can we still use the burner phones for contact?"

"Yes to both."

Minutes later, Joseph and Emily were back in the lobby to rendezvous with the suits. Joseph winced as he picked up her weekender, and she saw blood seeping through his sleeve.

"A scratch from the tunnel," he confessed. At the front desk, she picked up a first aid kit with wipes, bandages, and aspirin.

"Always tell me about your scratches, please."

She kissed his cheek, then covered his wound.

Didier drove alone from the farmhouse to his shabby, inner city apartment, where he had a room with another couple, Bekir and Isabella. He was agitated as he waited for a Turkish man, Farooq, to arrive and review strategy.

At a knock at the door, Isabella made herself scarce behind a bedroom door, listening to every movement and word spoken but remaining unseen.

The knock repeated, and under the shadow of the door, Didier saw more than one pair of feet and retrieved a handgun from the couch cushions.

"Who is it?"

The door didn't have an investigative peephole, and he waited with no reply. Yet the feet remained.

Since the Saint-Denis raid, he was edgy and distrustful, even of his neighbors, never offering as much as a nod when passing at the Carrefour or the smoke shop.

"Bekir, answer the door," Didier whispered from behind the door of one of the bedrooms, waiting cowardly.

Finally, a voice boomed out. "Farooq here, let us in."

Bekir looked at Didier for a signal and received a nod.

Slightly opening the door, Bekir recognized Farooq, but the second man was unfamiliar. "Who is with you?"

"He's okay. Tell Didier he is sent from Djinn in northern Turkey."

Didier came out to size up the newcomer. "Salim did not send word. Why have you been sent and who are you?"

"Munir is my name. I've been returned to Paris by Benghalem to consult with you. I was in the plotting of the fateful Friday, November 13th. Fortunately, I escaped and made my way back to Syria. I was right under their noses when I joined a family of immigrants that hosted me with food, clothing, and shelter."

The man sneered, embellishing his conquest.

"How did you travel to my apartment unseen? Do our leaders lack confidence in me, Munir?"

"Not at all, Monsieur Didier. They decided you may need access to a skilled arsenal. I'm trained in C-4 and grenades. We borrowed the car of a Turkish man in exchange for his life,"

Munir claimed with a scornful laugh, ensuring his sneer was seen. "The VW on the street is loaded with explosives for you to redistribute."

Didier was not yet convinced.

"I am intrigued, Munir, but it is not wise to invite strangers into your home or offer trust without a show of honesty."

"I'll vouch for him, Youssif," Bekir said.

"And you, Bekir, could be easily tempted, or do I have your commitment to wear a suicide vest on the day of reckoning."

"As Allah is my god, I agree."

"Okay, Munir. Your first mission will be to find a man that trespassed at the Van Dame farm a few days ago. It shouldn't be difficult to find a miniature red car. You'll start in Montmartre, looking for an American couple living above a flower shop on Rue des Saules. He is to be brought to me for questioning—I want the blueprints returned. You and Bekir must retrieve them."

Didier secretly coveted the truth of Napoleon's map and the taste of wealth, but never shared the confidence even with his closest friends.

Munir bowed in submission. "Oui, Didier, it will be done."

Isabella was now listening from the kitchen.

"Bekir, come here," Didier ranted. "A shipment of 150 kilograms of C-4 will arrive by a truck tonight for delivery through the Vavin Metro tunnel entrance. Along with Farooq's cargo, there's plenty to succeed in our plans. I will be late, but you should be there to receive the manifest and organize the men. The entrance to the train tracks will be guarded, and a heavy metal door will take you into the catacombs."

Farooq was stunned. "A hundred and fifty kilograms will surely decimate Paris and obliterate the metro lines. It will be like a game of dominos, one, two, three, booming in succession for thirty minutes or more in a network under the city. They will beg for death."

His laughter was evil, and Isabel shuddered at the sound.

"Boom! Boom!" Munir echoed the theatrics he envisioned.

Didier opened an intricate map of the tunnels. "The crates are stored here. It's damp and cool, a good environment for explosives until the day of implosion. Ensure movement is delicate to avoid a mishap.

"Furthermore, never come to my home again!" Didier's eyes were fiery with rage. "Neighbors might report to the police because we speak Arabic. Use cash, no credit cards or rental contracts—be invisible. If you need a vehicle or additional funds, we will supply some salvage."

Didier stood before the men and passed around the photo of the man at the Basilica. "This is him."

Munir, Bekir, and Farooq left together, and Didier turned to Isabella.

"You are to watch for the woman you followed on the day of the Saint-Denis raid. Check the metro line from St. Pierre near the Abbesses Metro, and ride the train continually until you find her. Her office is in the Champs-Élysées district, so that's where you'll start." Isabella gave a subservient nod.

The Metro ran sixteen lines across Paris with lines 4, 8, and 9 feeding into the Strasberg Saint-Denis station, a short walk from the insurgents' apartment.

Isabella dressed in a heavy wool coat, with a kerchief tied tightly about her face and started on the 4th line.

Joseph and Emily were delivered to a three-story limestone house on Boulevard Garibaldi in the 7th arrondissement. The windows were flanked with freshly painted blue shutters and a matching front door with a pushbutton doorbell. A narrow alley divided it from a five-level stone building, housing a dry cleaner and a neighborhood fruit market.

Two security agents lived on the main floor—simply called 'Black' and 'Brown' for discretion. Although invisible, they provided the first line of protection for the tenants.

"Black and Brown . . . easy to remember!" Joseph teased.

The Harkness second-floor apartment was starkly furnished with a private bath and shower, kitchen facilities and basic supplies.

"You have what you need. The third floor had two smaller apartments, but only one is occupied by a witness for an upcoming trial," the younger man stated.

The older of the two said, "There's no need to become acquainted with any others in the building unless you are in need of dire assistance."

With the window and door secured with locks, the couple was given the key with a warning not to leave without permission from Leo.

"Are we prisoners or special guests?" Joseph asked. Both men stood at the door void of personality, overlooking Joseph's remark. Emily checked the three rooms. The kitchen was aptly supplied with coffee, eggs, bacon, bread, and butter, with an assorted fruit bowl on the table.

"Am I free to shop at the market next door?"

"List what you need and someone will deliver it. When you want assistance, place the 'Room for Let' sign in the parlor window. If anyone comes to your door, say 'the dog needs to go out'. If the person is from Interpol they will reply, 'There's a dog park on La Motte Picquet'. Otherwise, don't open the door, but press this bell on the inside and the security guard will come immediately."

The two men were about to leave when the second turned back. "The van will be along within the hour. There should be uniforms on the bed. Good luck."

"I feel like I've been dropped off at Brownie camp for two weeks—it's an empty feeling."

She turned around in time to catch Joseph, who was staggering toward a chair.

Fourteen

"Thomas York, sit yourself down at the kitchen table and roll up that shirt sleeve." Emily didn't leave it open for discussion, calling her husband by his birth name. She disappeared to the medicine cabinet and returned with soothing ointment, gauze, and adhesive bandages.

"Yes, Nurse Emily. I'm ready."

"So, exactly when did this happen?"

"A rusty edge coming out of the tunnel. It's not more than a scratch."

Cleansing the wound, Emily was concerned about the red festered skin, then touched his flushed face.

"You're feverish, Joseph. Take this aspirin and get into a warm bath. I'll bring you scrambled eggs and toast in bed."

Feeling weak and headachy, he didn't refuse. Emily stood at the parlor window, using her index finger to pull back the lace curtain. The Eiffel Tower was in view to the north, and beside the walkway, the foliage was turning light shades of amber.

"Eggs and toast, Joseph, and a steaming cup of chamomile." She positioned his tray to sit upright and sat at the side of the bed. "Have you heard of septicemia or tetanus?"

In that tender moment, she rubbed Joseph's arm, enjoying the limited intimacy, then laid her chin on his burning forehead and planted a long soft kiss.

"I'm sure I had a tetanus shot in the last few years. Don't worry, Em. I'll be right as rain in the morning." He attacked the eggs ravenously, looking up at his wife between each bite.

"A tiny scratch is well worth it to get my own private nurse."

Phoning Leo, Emily requested an hour delay in the morning van pickup. "We'll be ready to catch up, I promise. Joseph needs to sleep off the fever."

Emily was awake early to change his dressing and determine if he had recovered sufficiently. At the scheduled time, she studied any movement outside and saw the white Charonne Drains & Ditches cube van arrive down the block. With helmets and toolboxes, they bounded down the stairs in their khaki overalls and orange caps.

A childhood tune was in Joseph's head. He whistled her a line, and she echoed back, "Hi ho, hi ho, it's off to work we go."

Emily did a kick of her heels to the jig before coming to attention outside the van.

"Hop in fellows."

It was comforting to see Daniel waiting inside. He passed her a café au lait and opened a paper bag with the aroma of pastries from the corner bakery. He too was dressed in matching overalls and reached to lift Emily's toolbox.

"Okay for this time, Daniel, but if you treat me like a lady, it will give away my disguise," she teased and tucked a fallen strand of hair back up into her cap.

The van was fitted with the latest surveillance computers, monitors, headphones, and GPS tracking boards.

Each tunnel access breached by their team was marked in green, and the three huddled at the screen. "This is the Vavin sector," Daniel said. "Note the green shapes of people moving into side chambers with crates."

"If this is real time, there are a lot of people in the lower tunnel," Joseph said.

"Leo has extra units in place, and the Vavin section has been covered thoroughly, leaving scanning dyes and target pins," Daniel said.

The technician was wearing a headset and pointed to a location on the monitor. "Watch this. Activity among the crates in the second chamber. It has buzzed near three of them, and a conversation is going on from one of the AK-47 boxes tracked from the airfield. Those transmitters are paying off."

"What are they saying?"

"Unfortunately the conversation is in Arabic, with only a bit of French. I'm afraid I can't interpret, but it's recorded and headquarters will translate."

"It'll be deciphered right away," Daniel said.

Emily took the jump seat behind the driver and sipped her coffee as they drove to the drop-off point near the Assemblies Nationale.

"Mmm . . . nothing starts the day like a good cup of coffee, especially in France."

As her phone beeped, she settled her coffee in a holder to read the text from Leo. His words were choppy and anxious and she read it out loud. "I've gone back to Vavin, activity there. Joseph and Emily, go back in at yesterday's exit. Daniel, backtrack and join me. Joseph and Emily, begin the underwater tunnel across the river to Grand Palais and Place de la Concorde. Bring equipment, as reports of gas smells."

She said, "He's got us scattering like mice!"

"Do you get claustrophobic, either of you?" Daniel asked as he readied a portable oxygen tank and masks from a bin.

Discarding the overalls, Daniel changed to jeans, a brown leather jacket, and French beret. "I'll walk from here to the Metro and text you within an hour. I assume you are both packing?"

Joseph pulled up his pant leg revealing a holster with a Beretta. Emily looked sheepish and put her hands in the air.

She shrugged her shoulders. "As we'll be using metro, I left it in my luggage. Can you spare something?" Her mischevious eyes looked pleadingly at Daniel.

Digging into a canvas bag, Daniel pulled out a .22 revolver and a small box of ammo.

"This is going on your report card," he teased.

Joseph and Emily continued alone on their assignment to the base of a marked pillar and pressed on a knobby stone embedded in the wall. It led into a cubicle of sorts.

"Muddy footprints, Joseph. This has been used within the last few days."

"Photograph the imprints and keep going. Are you alright to lead?"

"Of course, Joseph. What a question to ask of a detective."

He knew it and popped an aspirin to clear a headache.

"The air we're inhaling smells like death," Emily said, "and the water is dripping faster here on our helmets."

At the bottom of a long staircase, they leveled at a landing, then a spiral ladder took them further into the depths. Crumpled in the first wall indention they came to was a pile of ancient bones, either buried there privately or the decay of a vagrant.

"Someone made a home here. It's terrible that people resort to living underground to avoid the responsibilities of society," Emily said with empathy.

Joseph passed her a mask. "I see why Daniel gave us these. He must've been down here before. Do you feel the pressure of the water?"

"My ears are starting to ache, but I'm trying to ignore it. From the GPS, the tunnel is straight ahead with a dip at midpoint. No one would store munitions or explosives in here."

Water now covered the surface, and the pair continued deeper below the channel, trudging on through mud.

Their voices now echoed. "We're under the Seine. Scary that it would be an ideal target for a bomb placement. Look up at the ceiling. A tiny flashing light. I don't believe it!"

"My batteries have weakened from the moisture. I'll light the carbide. That will brighten the area," Emily said, fidgeting in the toolbox.

"I've got it. Now if the dang match will light."

"No Emily! Don't light it. There's a chance of gas in tunnels. I have spare batteries in my pocket."

Seconds later, the tunnel was filled with the white light, and Joseph pointed again to the ceiling. "Up there, Em. The beeping green light . . . it's a plastic explosive, set at the joist."

"There appears to be a timer, but we don't know what the trigger is. I didn't see any wires. Let's tiptoe out of here."

Water was trickling in rivulets down the walls, and the deafening thud of overhead traffic added to their concern.

"It'll be alright. C-4 needs a detonator and I don't see one," Joseph reassured.

"Is that it?," she whispered, pointing to a box a short distance from the C-4. "Can we assume it's a sleeper?"

"We don't know how much time we have or if it's even live. We'll notify Interpol. Under the depths of the great Seine; this is barbaric!"

Joseph took Emily's hand as they eased through the tunnel, retracing their steps. Back on the rocks at the pillar door, he phoned Leo.

"What color was the light flashing and did it change while you were there?" Leo asked.

"At first glance, I thought it was yellow, but when we lit the area it was green. Yes, a detonator, but we didn't stick around to find out anything further."

"Joseph, we don't have a choice," Leo said. "The Seine River! I'm sending in a hazmat unit. Stay until they arrive."

In seconds, a convoy of emergency vehicles arrived on the bridge for an evacuation. Barricades deterred local buses and riverboats, and on the streets above, traffic was redirected, starting a rumor of a bomb in the area.

A window passenger in a kerchief on the Red Line #4 bus took particular notice of the people at the base of the bridge. She snapped pictures including emergency and tactical team members, including a pair in orange overalls from the drainage company.

I've got to let Didier know.

Isabella was flustered and began yelling erratically at the driver. "Let me off! I must get off here!"

"Sorry, Madame, the police require that we go straight through. I'm not going to get a ticket on your account."

"Arrêtez! Stop the bus!" she persisted in panic, irritating the driver. Seeing a police patrol ahead, he pulled over and asked the officer to remove the woman.

Isabella was placed in handcuffs, resisting and struggling as she was forced into a police SUV. Its door was slightly ajar, and when the patrolman turned back to the chaos below the bridge, she slipped out and vanished into the crowd.

Twenty minutes later, she burst into the empty apartment she shared with Bekir and Didier, still wearing handcuffs.

"Bekir! Didier! They are at the bridge!"

On the bridge railing above the Pont de la Concorde, bystanders loitered to watch the commotion, until the security teams moved all pedestrians out of the area.

Several news choppers zoomed overhead for pictures and live news reports. Sirens wailed from across Paris, with local and international cable news teams and live reporting units on the scene.

Bekir and Munir had been dispatched to the chaos by the bridge and rallied with the crowd hopeful for a glimpse of a catastrophe. Parking their rented Volkswagen, they trained their binoculars on the access receptacle.

"There's a man there. Could it be the fellow from the Basilica?" Bekir said to his accomplice. From the base of the bridge, their conversation was intercepted in a security vehicle and relayed to Interpol Command.

Using a remote-controlled robot, Hazmat diffused the explosive that wasn't yet set to an active detonator.

"Someone meant to come back," Daniel said to a tactical officer, then phoned Leopold.

"Leo, are you watching what's happening here?"

"Of course. Bring Emily and Joseph to headquarters right away."

Daniel's gaze was elsewhere, observing a news cameraman. From Interpol files, he recognized the man known as Bekir approaching the journalist.

Using a fake name and backup cell number, Bekir pushed his way through and demanded. "Here's my card. Give me a still of the people on the bridge? Text it now."

Still in the orange overalls, Emily and Joseph sat in Leo's office for the first time.

"So this is how the higher-ups live," Joseph teased, looking around a tiny glass-walled cubicle stacked with files and evidence boxes.

"It's a tin can, and I know you've seen plenty of them," Leo said, unamused. "But for now I have an urgent need of both of you. Joseph, you'll go with Daniel back to the Van Dame airfield. With operations in the cement house, we've been unable to pick up conversations, and we need that current intelligence to be counteractive.

"Each day has brought an increase in chatter and movement of equipment, especially drones and C-4 explosives. With this escalation, Interpol has agreed to turn over the footwork in the tunnels to local authorities. It'll be hard to keep it quiet without alerting the terrorists or the public."

Emily's eyes were wide. "And what about me?"

"Remember the woman you encountered in Saint-Denis? She was seen observing the bomb team at the bridge. There was a police report of a woman taken off a bus. We believe it to be Bekir's wife.

We know she made a call to the Saint-Denis area and told another party that she recognized the pair in the orange overalls. She was arrested at the bridge, but slipped away."

"Is our cover blown?" Emily asked.

"Unfortunately it changes things. The cover in the tunnels is blown, but I'm ready for you to start undercover with our defensive tactics. Here are your credentials. You'll be Barbara Church—she's new to the department but comes with experience." He winked.

"I'll do my best. I do know about drones and surveillance tactics. The Department uses drones themselves for counter activity. I expect I can find espionage locations around Paris if that's what you are looking for, Leo?"

"That's a good start, but use your judgment. Anything of relevance, you understand. We'd like to identify the mole who's been relaying surveillance reports to the insurgents."

Leo delivered Emily to a nondescript building in the 14th arrondissement that was reinforced like Fort Knox. Inside the bulletproof doors, she was ushered into a full screening cage before reaching the front reception.

"Barbara Church. I'm here to see Blake Uberon," she said, presenting her new badge.

"Wait here, Madame. Someone will come for you."

Blake Uberon was a scientific man with the discipline to grasp every detail. He was well over six feet and suited to a job with order and instruction. With his dedication, he had few close acquaintances and little time for social engagements.

"Madame Church, thanks for pitching in here. We won't waste time, so I'll take you directly to your research station. This way down the hall, please."

Overhead cameras monitored every step and in a master room, someone was watching Emily's every step.

"This is where you will work. Sensitive data has been loaded onto your computer that cannot be relayed to anyone. Anyone means no one, not even a co-worker."

"Certainly, Monsieur Uberon, I understand."

After providing a series of access codes, Blake turned on his heels and Emily never saw him again.

Emily found that she was given full control of an espionage drone that could send and retrieve data. The ground control station would synchronize physical and logical periphery of the drones and aerial imaging for her review, at the initial regions of Le Bourget and the Luxembourg Gardens.

I have the ability to send a reconnaissance drone as far as the Van Dame farm. According to the logs, there isn't a drone placed in that area. If we can control an unseen drone, we could intercept their control tower and tamper with their own data.

Taking an independent tour of her floor, she discovered that her badge gave her carte blanche to all the active research rooms.

"What a terrorist wouldn't give for this badge!"

Tacking sensor values over Paris was a high-security issue for France. Under pressure, the analysis examined g aerial photography and videography from points across the city and in the countryside.

A hum of activity pervaded the halls, yet the employees were mostly unseen behind three-quarter partitions. On Emily's first day, twos and threes with heads together in consultation looked up to scrutinize the newcomer. When she returned a glance, the intrusive eyes turned away.

They all look like moles to me!

In no time, her experience with detection and spies sent up a red flag on her radar about a suspicious employee.

Barbara Church's desk was in a quiet corner and no one greeted her or initiated introductions. From across a partition, she felt the nervous eyes of one man studying her movements. He was not more than thirty, thin with a boney frame, coal black eyes, a dark complexion, and a wispy fringe beard. His ancestry was either Turkish or Syrian.

Emily squinted to read the cubicle nameplate.

'Stephen Cahill.'

Doesn't look like a Stephen to me.

On the way to the mapping room, she knew his eyes were following her

Clearly, he wants to see what I have. Maybe he's just overly curious about everyone—actually, it's a quality in this line of work.

The mapping room was beyond her imagination. Among the billboard charts was the same 1855 map of Ville de Paris, but the different markings and pins indicated an unfamiliar scheme.

With her arms crossed, she stood to absorb the markings near Montmartre, then felt the intimidation of someone beside her. It was Stephen Cahill, with his presence marked by strong body odor and a nervous cough in the throat.

"It's an incredible city, oui?" Emily said, before turning to face him directly.

"Uh-huh. What are you looking for?" His face was deadpan, but there was earnest in his voice.

"I don't know what you mean. It was simply small talk. My name is Barbara Church. I'm a temporary fill-in." She was relieved when he turned and left without offering his hand in greeting.

Employees came and went on variable schedules, with each computer locked down with access codes. When Emily prepared to leave, Cahill approached her. "Leave your computer on so I can use it."

His tone gave her a chill.

"Stephen, I received strict instructions about protocol. I cannot allow you to use my computer."

Cahill's face flamed with anger, and as he pivoted away, Emily slipped a mini transmitter into his cuff. From his cubicle, she heard his mumbling continue in another language.

He'll never find it there. I'll bet dollars to donuts, it will never find its way into a dry cleaner or a washing machine.

True to his word, Leo sent a car to retrieve Emily and deliver her to the Dingo. The others were in an intense conversation, and with gusto, Leo stood to welcome her.

"We'd like to use you as bait to locate Didier's hideout in Paris."

"Bait! How can I be bait?" Emily stammered.

"An assassination hit is out on both you and Joseph."

"Ridiculous," Joseph said. "What would they gain by that?"

Leo ignored the question. "We need the original blueprint, Joseph. We're working from your copy, but I want to investigate something I saw in your loft—the layering of a series of maps needs to be separated. On the 1855 map,

Napoleon Bonaparte's initial appears authentic. There must be another layer from the French Revolution as Napoleon died in 1821. Perhaps a chip is buried in the blueprint."

"Like a hologram?" Emily asked.

"We'll find out." Leo hoped his explanation would sell the idea. The last thing he wanted in dealing with the terrorist was a treasure hunt.

"I'd have to go back to Montmartre," Joseph said.

"No, we'll send a unit. It's too dangerous for you to be seen in the area."

"Have it your way, Leo, it's in a Ziploc in the mantle. Have your man feel for a wooden square projected on each side. Press the one on the left and it will pop open to find the tube."

"Then a unit will go to Rue des Saules this morning. This is good," Leo said.

"If I'm at the airfield with Daniel, who'll protect my wife?" Joseph asked.

Under the desk, Emily kicked him hard enough that he winced. "I can take care of myself; besides Leo won't let anything happen to me."

"Whenever Emily is not guarded at the safe house or at the Defense Department, two agents will be in the shadows. I assure you, two of my best," Leo said.

"Am I free now to discuss my drone activity, Leo?"

"Oui. Please, Emily."

"I sent an espionage drone to Le Bourget. It's safely hidden and can intercept Didier's frequency. Readings indicate a series of coded blips sent through his secure channel. They might be the same type that the Bataclan terrorists used on the gamers messaging system."

"If the drone were to be found, can it be traced to you?" Daniel asked.

"No, it is completely secure with a code to self-destruct. Like Mission Impossible," she grinned, then straightened up. "I'll download footage tomorrow to decipher the code."

"That will speed things up," Leo deduced.

On Leo's call, two undercover officers were dispatched within minutes from Interpol headquarters to the Montmartre loft to retrieve the cylinder. The oldest was a five-year veteran, and his partner, Ivan, was on his first stake-out. In a rental vehicle, they drove north from the Seine, with the Basilica high on the hill ahead of them, overlooking the city.

They accessed the loft using the back ladder to avoid detection.

The dusky evening provided cover of darkness. It was late and the bloodhound Toby had gone for the night.

Inside the loft, they worked in the dark, retrieving the map. As they returned to the ladder, they hesitated as Ivan raised his finger.

"Shhh. Footsteps on the stairs."

The floorboards creaked and they waited in silence.

Fifteen

Mid-afternoon under dull, grey skies, Daniel and Joseph arrived at Le Bourget in a common, dusty pickup. Their mission was to establish the stake-out from the construction lot. With lunch pails, work helmets, plaid shirts and worn out jeans, they felt 'in the role'.

The work site had no staff in sight. The fields were peaceful until a chorus of swallows burst from a tree line, swooping like a black cloud into the air, then landing again. Joseph felt the chill of the winter wind as he opened the passenger door.

"We should check the manager's trailer in the back lot for a vantage point," Daniel said.

"And if someone is there, do we apply?" Joseph laughed.

"Of course. Don't I look the part?

With high-powered field glasses, Joseph scanned the scene. "Trucks are parked across the field and at the security house. What's the plan, Daniel? The transmitters and receivers are in my bag. Should we flip a coin to see which one of us goes in?"

"Give me the binoculars." Daniel focused on the house, then the control tower. "The drone is near enough to the field house to record. A ventilation fan is spinning on the roof, meaning there's an intake opening into the house. Do we have a line to drop a sound receptor?"

"In the back, in the toolbox."

Joseph stayed low behind the truck cab, returning with a depth weight, several D-links and a spool of fishing line.

"I'll take them. Cover me from here."

"No way, Daniel, I'm coming with you. We're easily five hundred feet across the field to the target."

"If I get in trouble, Joseph, hotwire one of those tractors and create a diversion. If we both get caught, run!"

"Remember you're my backup. I'm the Interpol agent—it's me that has to answer if you get captured," Daniel said.

Outranked, Joseph conceded. "Fine, but I'll keep the binoculars. Wear the headphones and I'll have your back."

Daniel dodged along the fence line, advancing behind poles, stumps, and thickets. A gully bordered the fence perimeter, enabling him to rest and catch his breath without standing out like a stork in a field.

A hundred feet from the house, he ducked low as a lone patroller exited the house for a smoke. Frozen near the ground, he held his breath. The suspect ground the ashes of a half-smoked cigarette in the grass.

"Daniel, don't move. He sees me," Joseph whispered. "Might be a reflection of the binoculars."

"When you're sure he's onto you, go and start up a tractor. That will either convince him he was mistaken or at least we'll use it as a decoy while I go for the roof."

The patroller disappeared into the house and returned with binoculars. He trained them across the field and examined the vehicle. Joseph had already moved toward the tractors, and on reaching the first one, he revved up the engine. The man raised a rifle and looked down the long-range lens, then shot, with bullets bouncing off the tractor hood.

He kept firing—ping, ping, ping.

"Joseph, two more coming your way from the house. Keep up the distraction. I'm in the last rush to the house."

"If it goes sour, make your getaway. I'm trained in escape techniques and will survive."

"Okay, but don't be a hero. I'll be right back to help you."

The lead patrollers were now halfway across the field running on foot. Revving the tractor engine, Joseph raised the haul bucket part way. Letting his adrenaline rise, he locked on the first man.

Ping, ping. "I don't like being shot at!"

He glanced at the headlight of a motorcycle barreling his way from the house. Looking again, he saw Daniel's silhouette mounting the roof of the cement house.

Daniel flattened himself next to the ventilation fan, whirling at medium speed. His timing would need to be impeccable for the drop of the microphone and micro camera on two lines, ensuring they'd be high enough to be invisible. Slowing his heartbeat in military fashion, his fingers worked nimbly, knowing the measurements must be exact.

He blocked out the outside roar of the tractor engine as it charged across the field. Listening for more precise sounds and motions, and confident with his calculations, Daniel made his drops.

Believing the building to be empty, he swung down off the roof and entered it. Popping in a flash drive for a computer download, he donned black khakis and a jacket and toque from a wall rack. Running out across the field he pretended to rally with the defenders.

The men were bantering in Arabic, but Daniel understood every word as they planned splitting up to surround Joseph.

Daniel broke off to the right with another patroller, and the other pair went left.

"Alright Joseph, start your attack," he radioed. His partner turned abruptly. Hearing the English command, he raised his gun, but Daniel felled him before he got a shot.

Joseph found a tire iron under the seat of the bulldozer and jammed the prong into the gas pedal. Accelerating to its top speed, the aged equipment surged forward, holding at 20 km continuing across the field. Joseph crouched and tumbled out the side into the tall grass.

"I'm clear, Daniel!"

The rumble of the engine brought Alain Van Dame from his farmhouse, and with caution, he drove his pickup toward the commotion.

Three men continued firing without stopping as the bulldozer advanced toward them. Now within twenty feet, they had no choice but flee from the path of the driverless bulldozer.

Across the construction yard, Daniel and Joseph sped toward the highway. The mission was completed, with the frequency and camera activated inside the cement house. "It's all yours, Leo," Daniel said. "You should be able to intercept an enraged reaction."

"Don't return to Paris. Take refuge there and stay with your stakeout. You and Joseph are our only boots on the ground. We've picked up new fragmented conversations about more air shipments, and training is about to take place. I'll check with Emily about the defense drone intervention."

"Understood. We'll hide the car and retreat to the trailer."

Emily's burner phone rang at her desk. The ringing drew Cahill's attention and Emily ignored his effort to eavesdrop.

"There's a cable van outside, Emily," Leo said. "Take time out right now from the Department. It's the new cover for the

Ditch & Drainage façade. My men will drop you in Saint-Denis near the Metro."

"Leo, I have a concern here I'm hoping you'll resolve."

"Shoot."

Her hand cupped over the phone. "An employee Stephen Cahill here. We need a security check."

"Sure. Now get going."

Exiting the safe house, Emily wore the same street clothes from Montmartre that she used during her encounter with Isabella. Nearing the van, the side door slid open.

"Good afternoon, Madame. My name is Alexandre. I'll be shadowing you today. This is my partner, Christophe."

Recognizing the two men from the previous day, she teased, "Where's my café au lait and the pastries?"

Alexandre lowered his brow to a frown and pouted his bottom lip. Emily was ashamed, unsure how to read it.

"Non, Alexandre. I was joking."

He burst into a laugh. "Oh yes, I know. But a gentleman should still remember these things."

"Is there anything I should know this morning?" she asked.

Christophe opened a computer file with new photos and data. "This was taken at a Carrefour grocer yesterday. See the man in the background? We believe Farooq Razi is Isabella's cousin, a Moroccan terrorist. Examine his face closely, as you may encounter him if you cross paths with her."

Farooq was in his mid-thirties, with a heavy beard, round face and wire-rim glasses. In the photo, his eyes were on Isabella.

I wonder if he lets her out of his sight, but she is Bekir's wife.

"Where was this taken?"

"Not far from the drone incident the other day," Alexandre replied.

Emily leaned closer to the photo. "He's not the only one staring at Isabella. This other man is watching too."

"Very observant, Madame Harkness. As a matter of fact, he is one of ours. You have an eye for detail."

The van pulled to a side street in Saint-Denis for Emily to prepare to exit. "Is this near a tunnel entrance or exit?"

"Yes. Your GPS will take you, with my help."

"Do I get an earphone to stay in contact with my backup?"

"This earphone always connects to me," Alexander said. "But see what else you like." He opened a drawer of microchips, scanners, jammers, mini cams, sunglasses with a spy cam, and a remote door car key.

Emily picked through them and tried on the sunglasses. "Will your monitor show everything I see?"

"Yes, Madame. On the inside of the left lens, you'll even see if someone behind is following you."

Emily descended into the subway surrounded by a crush of pedestrians rushing to catch the next train. At the turnstile, a gendarme guard searched her bag.

Scanning the crowd for Isabella's familiar kerchief, she stopped to listen to a musician playing the flute. Emily tried out the glasses to observe behind her. Tossing a euro into the flute case, she sauntered toward the track as the train whisked into the station, creating a vacuum breeze of diesel fumes.

She watched the first train leave and returned to a newsstand for the late edition of Le Monde. Before she had opened the folds, she heard angry gibberish in a Middle Eastern rant.

Arabic!

A pair of youths pushed and shoved into the crowd as a decoy, as two others moved among the throng in hopes of wallets and watches.

A Frenchman shouted for the gendarme to interfere while struggling to take back his billfold from a kid with a switchblade. "Give it up old man!"

During the fuss, Emily noticed a man on the platform watching her. Then a second man gestured toward her.

"Alexandre, quick. Assess the man at the end of the ramp. Is that Farooq?"

"Possibly, Emily. Take the next train to the first stop. Our man will be close behind and take action if you appear to be in danger."

Whistles were blowing about the wallet scuffles, and the gendarmes warned they were ready to fire their rifles.

"Everyone stay where you are. Hands over your heads and don't move until you are dismissed."

The police began at the far end of the platform and released about a dozen after questioning. Within five minutes, the two criminals were caught red-handed and removed. Meanwhile, Farooq slipped into the background.

"Alexandre! Change of plans. I'm following Farooq," she said softly.

"Madame, it is not safe. He has seen you."

"You can watch where I'm going. I'm not worried, just keeping up, as he's trying to blend in, out of sight.

In Montparnasse, a cluster of familiar Interpol agents gathered inside the Dingo Café.

Leo's tone was solemn. "Here are the pictures. This is one of my men sent to recover the blueprints in Montmartre. A cowardly, dastardly act!"

Gruesome pictures depicted a man with a hood over his head. Without the hood, it revealed a young man in his late twenties, with a reddish crew cut, his hands duct taped, and blood from his forehead.

"He was found today in a cavern in the tunnels under the Louvre. A piece of paper in his mouth claimed victory for ISIS, and it's unusual they'd make a claim this way."

"Weren't there two of our men?" an agent asked.

"Yes, we haven't heard from our second man since they arrived in Montmartre. We're checking all video in the area from the last twenty-four hours."

"And the occupants of the loft . . . where are they?"

"They are safe, but I can't discuss details," Leo replied.

"Now that they have the original blueprint, does that change how we continue to operate?"

"No, but our check-ins must be more frequent, and our observation skills sharper. They're breathing down our necks."

Leo didn't share his belief that someone leaked information about the agents' mission to Montmartre.

There is a leak inside. Who can we not trust?

He remembered Emily's query about Cahill.

Sixteen

Emily hurried up the stairs to ground level to see Farooq dodging vehicles in heavy traffic. The second man was still with him, and in the jammed sidewalks, she had to jog to keep him in sight.

Where is he going in such a hurry?

"Do you have him in your sights, Alexandre?"

"Oui, oui!"

"Cool sunglasses. It's like you're right here."

Ten minutes later, Farooq was still traveling at a hefty pace, as Emily slinked in and out of doorways, remaining incognito.

Slowing down, he turned to look behind then spoke to the other man. At the corner of Rue de la Gaite, they stopped at the grand 19th-century Petit Montparnasse Theater, famous for historic pantomimes and Moulin Rouge cast-offs.

Farouq shook a locked front door under a billboard calling for orchestra auditions for a gala. Then at the side of the building, he opened a heavy maintenance door.

At the corner, Emily's eyes searched the building's exterior for security cameras, spotting one at her position.

She whispered into her shoulder, "Alexandre, I see only one outside camera, and I'm not sure it's working." She pointed the disabling remote key at it.

Thanks, Leo.

Easing her fingers under the bottom of the garage maintenance door, she got a grip and raising it a foot, she managed to slide through on her back.

"It's dark in here, Alexandre. I can't see much."

"Take off the sunglasses and use your flashlight."

Those were the last words she heard before entering a no service zone. On her right, she listened to footsteps becoming fainter down a decrepit staircase and quickly followed. The basement was musty and stacked with ancient trunks and props not used in recent times.

Retreating wouldn't be an option and she squeezed through the door of a walk-in vault, cemented in the wall. A rusted shank of steel had been forced into the latch and the door was slightly ajar with loose chain links and a broken padlock.

"Alexandre, I'm following Farooq. This has to be the way he went," Emily said. All she heard back was muffled static.

Her iPhone offered sporadic tracking of her steps, but she refrained from using the flashlight. Ahead, the men walked quickly, splashing in ditches, crunching over gravel and wall debris.

Odd—no sign of weapons storage or even a turnoff. But clearly, Farooq knows his way. There's something white ahead.

She strained to focus in the darkness, and slowing her pace, she shone her light on a street sign on the wall of l'ancien hôpital Laennec, barricaded with beams and boards. In the distance, she heard ominous echoes and sounds.

It's either Farooq or I'm coming to an old train tunnel.

Listening for any movement or breathing, she pressed her body into a narrow wall indentation over an eroding mechanical box. At last footsteps approached, then silence.

He is playing my game too.

A sharp whistle from further inside beckoned the dodgy accomplice to catch up.

Must be Farooq summoning his partner.

After the sounds of running, she heard another door close and sighed with relief.

Her cell's glow guided her to a steel door on her left, and she felt a vibration and hum on its handle. Inside was a short hallway, then a sliding wooden door.

I bet this was used during Prohibition.

Beyond the slider, she saw remnants of an old train track and on the ceiling the barely visible words Saint-Denis Metro.

This is the old track. Good . . . there are two shadows ahead.

Walking the rail line, Emily held back when the men did and otherwise kept up. At a platform, the men hoisted themselves up and Farooq stared back through the darkness. At first, Emily thought their eyes met—it was only an instant, but it seemed to her like time had frozen before he gave up and joined his partner.

She whispered, "I hope this isn't all on my account. We've doubled back to where we started, maybe to ensure they weren't followed. Are you listening to me, Alexandre? Hello?"

The earphone crackled back. "The line has broken up, but we have a foggy visual."

"They've gone up a ladder, and I'm going too. No one has seen me, and they don't expect anyone following them down here, right?"

"Emily, hold back. We have your location and the van will be there in minutes."

"If I quit now, it's all for nothing. This is progress. We're back in Saint-Denis. This is where the hideout is. Can you pick up any chatter?"

"It's not safe to go it alone. Give us three minutes. Wait for Leopold. He won't be content with one man, he wants his entire unit. The time is not yet ripe," Alexandre pleaded. "If they find you're tracking them, they'll disappear and we'll have to start over again."

Emily gripped the ladder and stepped up one rung, watching the crack of light above her. The manhole lid clanked into place over her head and dust reigned down into her eyes.

Waiting until it was safe to emerge, she eased the lid to the side. A rush of sunlight stunned her momentarily as she gained her bearings. She strained for the sight of the men but they'd gone, and she permitted herself to be lured to the safety of an alley that was lined with garbage bins and scurrying rats.

Yes, Alexandre is correct. This is not my mission—it belongs to France.

With no sign of Farooq or his accomplice, she examined the old limestone apartment buildings, with rusted fire escapes and the stench of dumpsters and vagrant urine. Most windows had broken glass panes covered with boards or tattered sun blinds.

I'll wait here for the van.

Emily assessed every sound, hoping for the vibration of footsteps, but hearing mostly scavenging crows and rodents. Near her, the silence was broken by a terracotta plant pot, tumbling to the ground. Looking up at an open third-floor window, she didn't see anyone, but the curtain panel was waffling outside in the breeze. Emily's ears caught a faint but growing sound of something out of place and turned her head to listen.

Classical music in a terrorist flat? Absurd! I know I've heard that before. Thanks for dropping your calling card practically into my lap!"

The cable van coasted to a quiet stop at the end of the alley, and close behind a brown Fiat emptied two plainclothes agents.

"Get in Emily," Alexandre said. "Looks like you might have found Farooq's nest."

Northeast of Paris, Daniel and Joseph hunkered in at the construction site, as dusk fell. The winter winds had sent farmers into hibernation, and construction workers were resigned to wait out the thaw. The two agents had laid low the last two nights in camp cots in the manager's shack, waiting for activity at Didier's camp.

Van Dame's pickup truck was the only daily movement on the narrow lane and across the back field by the helipad, with the runs recorded on Didier's security cameras.

Daniel checked the status of the intervention drone that ticked near them in the grass. The mechanism was programmed to launch and take aerial shots every hour, with a mission to identify the men in black.

Joseph was feeling hollow and longed for Emily. He always depended on her, and together they never tamed a mutual desire for adventure, sometimes even to the point of teasing danger. He was now trusting Leo to protect his wife and pondered the outcome of this grandiose campaign.

"How do you think this will end, Daniel?"

"Perseverance, Joseph . . . perseverance."

The two took turns sneaking out to get coffee and pizza, then played cards, often until they were too numb to continue.

The monotony suddenly ended and they jolted upright, disrupted by a roar from the farm. Three black trucks arrived at the airfield, and a handful of men crowded inside the cement house.

"The show is on, Joseph. Any second, we'll know if our transmitters are alive."

Settling in a ditch, they leaned with night goggles on a mound of dirt, and through static, they listened and recorded every sound.

Daniel recognized the voice of the leader, Youssif Didier. "Brothers, our vengeance is at hand."

Formal Arabic greetings then echoed from the rebels around the table. Joseph rotated the camera to see at least six men.

Didier was on his feet with his fist in the air.

"We are invincible," he shouted. "Abaaoud led the way as we rally insurgents from Morocco, Turkey, Yemen, Russia, Britain, Belgium, Libya, Jordan, Iraq, and Syria. Do I need to go on? We unite to fight for jihadist terror to avenge Allah."

Consenting cheers and raised arms boosted Didier to go on.

"ISIS is invincible. International Security Forces expect we're limited to Charlie Hebdo, or stadium and nightclub attacks, tourists in Tunisia or the Ataturk Airport. These are merely rehearsals, a distraction. We have them scattering like brainless mice in search of the cheese."

He roared with laughter. "They run from one scene to another oblivious to the journey."

The men joined in the celebration, bolstering Didier's spirits further.

"The Europeans put the minds of their leaders together to attempt to stop us, to cut off our financial resources, supply routes, and interfere with our recruitment. An impossible challenge and they assist us with open borders. We travel with bombs and munitions packed in our cars and trucks, rarely stopped or searched. We plant moles in the most unsuspecting places."

One of the insurgents was on his feet flashing a saber in the air. "Death to America!"

"Daniel—that is the original perpetrator from the Basilica. *That* is Fernando Valois! Waldo."

"He slipped through surveillance cracks," Daniel said sarcastically. "Observe him carefully. Leo hopes to recruit him as an informant."

Didier angrily continued his rant. "The bulldozer from the other day . . . has our security been compromised?"

"No, Didier. They were merely vandals from nearby farms. Boys, wanting to drive a bulldozer," a dissident said, hoping to calm Didier's ire.

"Unacceptable! There's no security footage of the incident. How is that possible? It must never happen again!"

The six insurgents were on their feet, chanting and praising, and working themselves into a frenzy.

Didier continued, "We are behind every security screen, we are pilots and war veterans. We dominate the controls of western society and yet they don't see us. Blending into immigrant villages, they welcome us while we recruit.

"Americans and Russians are at intellectual war with one another, yet they both provide us weapons and buy our oil. Merkel, the German lady, tries to unite wayward efforts to eradicate us, but it will never be.

"But a great day will be dawning," Didier said. "New recruits are funneled into France every day and we fester underground like a nest of angry red ants. The legs of Paris will be taken as we are always two steps ahead of Interpol.

"They congratulated themselves when a meddling tourist detective intercepted our blueprints, but we've taken back what was ours and they're no smarter than before. The codes encrypted in the scales are unbreakable and they haven't been the least bit curious. Fernando, well done, you were victorious in recovering our documents while they groveled for their lives."

Joseph looked aghast at Daniel. "That can't be. I hid them securely in the loft."

"Who else knew?"

"You were there the day I told Leo. An incognito unit was going to retrieve it from a place Emily and I use."

Daniel opened his computer to Leopold's classified files. "Leo said he'd post anything of significance here . . ." His face went ashen.

"What is it, Daniel?"

"They sent two agents to Montmartre two nights ago. I'm afraid that both agents were reported missing. A follow-up unit searched for the cylinder, but it was gone. This morning, they found one of the agents dead in the tunnels. He was tied to a chair with a taunting note."

"Is Leo calling us in?"

"No, we are to stay on stake-out as chatter indicates drone movement soon, and this is the only airfield in their training."

"Terrible about the poor agent. Is it someone you know, Daniel?" Joseph knew by Daniel's silence.

"Didier ordered the assassination," he replied.

"I need to call Emily, and I must talk to Leo," Joseph said.

"We can't. We can't give away this much work to let them mock us further."

Half an hour later, the men poured out of the conference onto the airfield. Eight insurgents ran straight to a large tarp at center field. Pulling it back, they unveiled at least eight bales of hay, each painted on top in red with a large alphabetic letter. They dragged each one to a symmetrical location that they paced out in two rows.

In the north sky, Joseph saw geese forming a dark V like he remembered back in America. His imagination took him to the banks of the Hudson River near Albany, where he'd watch the magnificent event. He was mesmerized as they approached.

Two of the lead geese dropped down and went to the back, and the next pair at the front took on the leadership. He remembered their instinct, with the strong ones falling back to wait for those behind.

He described their nature to Daniel. "If a weaker goose needs rest, a leader escorts it to a resting spot and waits until it regains strength. It is survival and respect, Daniel. Why can't humans be as supportive as birds?"

Daniel lifted his binoculars. "They're not geese at all. They're incoming drones. Cover yourself with shrubs."

The PA system boomed from the cement house. "Prepare for target demolition."

Didier was at the controls of a portable keyboard with the ability to take over remote landing. Wearing aviator ear muffs, he pushed a flash drive into the computer.

Seconds later, classical music boomed as drones swooped in under Didier's control. In sequence, they dropped grenades on Bale B, Bale B, Bale B, Bale B, Bale E, Bale F, Bale G, and lastly Bale B again.

That's a familiar tune!

The music subsided and the insurgents cheered their victorious rehearsal.

Didier raised his rifle. "Eight out of eight!"

At that moment, Leo's surveillance drone lifted from the ground for its preprogrammed timed flight.

"Really bad timing!" Daniel said, expecting Didier to notice an extra drone in the sky. Fortunately, the group was too busy celebrating and the surveillance mission returned undetected to the construction ditch.

Seventeen

Joseph returned to the safe house troubled by the airfield events, yet he couldn't get the tune out of his head. The surveillance van was parked down the street, and the main floor agent unlatched the front door as he approached.

"Agent Black, set up a meeting for me with Leopold," Joseph said. "I must speak to him privately."

The man nodded. "Certainly . . . I'm Agent Brown, by the way."

This is ridiculous.

At their apartment, Emily greeted him with a long overdue hug and a soft kiss. Pulling back, she knew the signs she'd seen before of worry on his face.

"Leo will be coming soon," he said.

She held tightly to his arm. "I insist on joining you. Joseph, I don't like how this mission has gotten out of control. Leo said the original blueprint is back in terrorist hands."

"It's haunting me too. My first conclusion is that we missed an embedded microchip. We know there are three layers: the first from 1855 with tunnels used in the French Revolution between 1789 and 1799; the second in the 19th century when the catacombs were packed with cemetery bones; and the third is more recent, about 2005."

Emily was still puzzled. "But if we don't have the original, it's impossible to peel back time."

"Not impossible, Em. As detectives, we never put our eggs all in one basket. This is no different."

"So what have you done?"

"Notice how the living room light flickers? I was sure you'd be safer if I didn't tell you, but I hid an encrypted flash drive in the base fixture. I took pictures that night before I called Daniel."

Emily hugged Joseph. "I feel safer when I'm with you. You're my David, slaying Goliath."

Leo arrived at the door, but not alone, as a wired man stood behind with an earphone.

"No, Leo, our meeting must be private. Ask your agent to go downstairs while we talk."

"There isn't anything left just between us, Joseph. You and Emily are on our team, and we have to back up one another."

Leo saw the defiance on Emily's face that he recognized from their first meeting in Montmartre. "Alright, we'll have it your way." He took a seat by the window and removed his earpiece. "I assume you have Daniel's report from Le Bourget?"

"Yes, it was unsettling."

"You know, when I was in high school back in the States, I wanted to play in the band. My parents bought me piano lessons for after school. I had an ear for music but I struggled reading notes."

"You never told me, Joseph," Emily said, surprised at the revelation.

"I hadn't thought about it. Not until I was on stake-out at the airfield."

"I'm lost, Joseph," Leo said.

"For the Djinns to go to such lengths to retrieve the original blueprint means something. Something critical that we've missed," Joseph said. I need a secure location, your best computer people, and code breakers, a concert pianist, and operatives outside of Paris. Set up a meeting and I'll give you what you want."

Leo's face reddened. "Joseph, you're not withholding data, are you?"

"Everything is alright," Emily said, putting her hand on Leo's arm. "We guarantee our loyalty."

"Of course, I know that."

"Let me know when you're ready," Joseph said. "Only those involved can be notified, and the purpose and whereabouts of the meeting must be top secret. There are too many leaks."

"Yes, I know. Two agents disappeared from Montmartre because of a leak. Be ready at six a.m. and the van will be outside. I'll charter a private plane."

He studied Emily longer. "You asked for a security clearance on Stephen Cahill at the lab. Your hunch was right, he has credentials, but his photo was altered. Fingerprints don't match. It's not him, but they match to a drug raid in Brussels before the Bataclan."

"Leave him in place for now. I'll go into the office on the pretense of having data on the terrorists, and we'll set a trap. Follow his movements, see who he calls and where he goes. We can feed him false data right away and use him as a pipeline to the insurgents."

"I'll drop you there now," Leo said, gratified with her constant diligence.

A private limo arrived for them in the morning. Emily stepped outside letting her thoughts escape to a different world, with songbirds, bright skies, and spring buds.

There's nothing like a choir of birds on a spring morning.

"Good morning, Emily and Joseph. I've booked flights from De Gaulle to Nice, then a one hour shuttle to the quaint town of Saint-Martin-Vesubie. Searching for a pianist to be of the highest standard, I contacted the Zodiac Music Academy in Valdeblore, a short drive from our lodge."

"Where will we stay?" Emily said.

"I can't name it yet. At De Gaulle, we'll be joined by two of Interpol's top code breakers, and at Nice, by an international operative, a man I've known for many years. As I don't know the details of our meeting, I was able to be absolutely discreet," he said in jest. The academy will give us consultative services of a master concert pianist this evening. It was the best I could arrange on short demand."

"Leo, it's amazing," Joseph said. "I never expected this to come together so quickly."

"As you didn't mention Daniel, I didn't include him here. Besides, with the tunnel activity, we need him in Paris."

In a window seat of the Mercedes, Emily pondered this change in direction.

Two officers from the French Aviation Authority met the limo and led the group through the back halls, downstairs, and to the tarmac. A pilot and attendant stood at the mobile ramp.

"No need to hurry, it can't leave without us," Leo joked.

"Well there are line-ups," Emily said. "Leo, many times we could have used your inside help through airports."

"Yes, security lines are indeed tedious. My wife rarely flew with me, although she liked to cruise the Mediterranean. You'll like the Côte d'Azur, Emily, the heart of the French Riviera."

Emily was warmed by Leo's personal tidbit. "I'm sure I'd like your wife. She must be a patient woman. My parents and sister are back in New York and I miss them greatly."

His warm smile faded and he recovered his stern demeanor. "I didn't mean to mention her. It's a number of years since I lost her."

"I'm so sorry, Leo," Emily whispered with genuine compassion.

The plane stopped briefly at Nice, picking up an Italian Interpol agent, Enio, a gregarious man of at least forty-five, short in stature, but with a booming voice.

Before taking off, Leo stood before them with an update. "This will be fast and efficient. We'll remain incognito and return to Paris tomorrow afternoon. By then, we should have a clearer picture of the terrorist scheme. We have a lodge close to Valdeblore."

Emily was glued to the scenery as they flew over the French coast, with the land rising abruptly from the sea into the hills. "We're going to the mountains, right?"

"Yes, and it's magnificent," Leo said. "Valdeblore is a historic mountain village high in the Alps. From the air, you'll see the snow-capped peaks, a stark white contrast to the brilliant blue of the sky."

In a case involving art, Emily had dealt with the works of Cézanne and Picasso. Looking out of the private jet, she understood how the artists would be inspired by the passion and scenery of France.

From the gracious lobby entrance, La Bonne Auberge lodge welcomed them with a roaring fire in its grand floor-to-ceiling hearth. Leo returned with keys and room assignments.

"I have booked a private area in the dining room where we'll convene in forty-five minutes, and the hosts will serve us a luncheon while we work."

Leo looked at the agents, Maurice, Alphonse, Georges, and Enio. "Rules . . . we'll have no outside communication, and do not notify anyone of your whereabouts. Transmitters, receivers, or any recording devices are strictly banned while we're here. Leave any electronics you have with me now."

As Joseph left for his room, Leo called him back. "If we may have a talk beforehand, I don't like being blindsided. My room has an adjoining conference area to talk."

"Of course, Leo."

At a light tap, Leo opened his door and led Joseph and Emily to a meeting table.

Barely in the room, Joseph started, "Nothing added up about this whole tunnel catacomb escapade until I was lying on the farmer's field, listening to a mad tyrant boasting of jihad to his insurgents. Did you review that transcript?"

"Yes, but as you say, it was revolutionary ranting."

"Well, it was more than that. He said too much."

"You're talking in riddles," Leo said.

"We've been looking at the blueprints as a map in three layers."

"Yes," Leo said, and Emily's curiosity peaked beside him.

"It's very much more in fact," Joseph said. "Didier boasted of the key to the scheme. He said the codes are encrypted in the scales at a high frequency that is 'unbreakable.' Just after that, a fleet of drones flew over the field dropping grenades onto targeted hay bales, each one dead on, in a specific order. Large red letters were painted on each bale, and the grenades were dropped in this order: Bale B B B B E F G, then a pause, and B again. It was exactly in this order. It came to me from my elementary piano lessons."

Emily gasped, "Joseph, I see what you're getting at. It's a musical scale, Leo!"

"I'm still not grasping this."

Joseph surprised him with a flash drive from a compartment in the sole of his shoe. "Here this is a backup of the blueprints. Your technicians can sort out the layers."

Leo hadn't yet reacted, still struggling with the concept.

"The codes in the map are musical notes of an Overture. Your piano master consultant will know it. We must find out where and when an orchestra will be playing it. That could be the trigger of the mass domino explosions in the network of the tunnels."

Leo paced to the window.

"Mon Dieu, incredible!"

Eighteen

Leo and Enio conferred to weigh up and determine the course of action. Two secured laptops were provided for the technicians' work, both property of Interpol and scrubbed of classified data.

"Maurice and Alphonse, we have a flash drive with a backup of a map of Paris," Leo said. "It has three generations of tunnels overlaid, from the French Revolution up to the last renovation of the catacombs in 2005. Peel the map into layers, and then consider the codes in the alphabetical range from A to G?

"Georges, you'll work with the technicians to isolate a code. We don't have a starting point. So be thorough."

The three worked until lunch at 12:30, when Joseph and Emily joined the group with the two Interpol agents for a progress update.

The chef, dressed in an impeccable white apron and crisp traditional puffed hat, was accompanied by a server in brilliant folk costume. An elegant lunch was delivered on platters, with trout meunière, duchess potatoes, and a salad of corn, tomato, pepper, and olives. Crème caramel came later with coffee and tea, but no alcohol.

After lunch, the code-breaking trio resumed, and Enio took the limo to the Valdeblore Music Academy to pick up Giovanni Picolini, a third-year masters student working on his operatic thesis.

Giovanni waited in the main foyer with a violin case, distinctive with shoulder-length curls under a red woolen ski hat. An uppity attitude subsided within seconds when Enio introduced himself.

"Thank you for assisting us, Giovanni. I hear you're from Milan working on an opera. You must love music. I'm from Florence myself. France is beautiful, but nothing like the hills of Tuscany and my mother's home cooking."

At Enio's genuine interest, Giovanni was at ease with his new friend, and a nervous tick in his left leg abated.

"The Maestro says you need me to identify a classical music piece from the 18th century?"

"Yes, yes, in due course. But please enjoy the scenery; we are not going far."

"Ah, La Bonne Auberge! I ski here in the winter with friends from campus."

"Yes, it is quite suitable. We have a room for you to work in, and we will be honored if you will dine with us this evening."

Leo and Joseph were in the lobby when Giovanni arrived. The new group adjourned to Leo's suite to work.

Joseph offered his hand. "Giovanni, I heard a few notes that I am certain are from an old Overture. Only eight notes, but a student of your experience with orchestras will determine the piece."

Settled to work, Giovanni brought out his violin and opened a case of reference books of symphony scores.

"I wasn't sure if a piano would be provided so I brought my own instrument."

Leo was impressed with the professionalism of the young musician. "Excellent," he proclaimed.

Joseph attempted to hum the sound he had heard and jotted down the sequence of letters from the hay bales: B B B B E F G B in quick succession.

Giovanni took a tuning pitch from his pocket. "I know what this is. With his tongue, he sang some notes. Da-da-dum-dum-dum. It is amusing."

Giovanni warmed up a few bow strokes on the violin, then dug into his case of symphony notes, to mull over a conductor's score. "It could either have 3 flats or 4 sharps. I'll go with the former, in the key of E flat."

The others all gave naïve approval and the room went silent as Giovanni closed his eyes and played the first section of the 'Finale of the'William Tell Overture'."

"Yes, that's it. Amazing!" Joseph left no doubt.

"You're right. It's from Rossini's opera Guillam Tell from the 19th century. You know it certainly, at least these eight notes. It's most magnificent when played by a full orchestra. I've played it many times."

"Great," Leo said, "but I'm afraid that was the easy part. Now we need to know if this can be programmed to coincide with remotely controlled cues from a device some distance away."

"It's in two-four time, likely fast at 150 beats a minute. Some maestros like different speeds and if we know what the orchestra uses, I can tell you how much time it takes."

Leo said, "Specifically, how long 'til we get to these notes?"

"I can calculate that exactly," Giovanni said.

Emily had heard the violin from outside and arrived to whisper in Joseph's ear. "It's the 'Lone Ranger' theme."

"Yes," he grinned." I didn't want to fizzle on this great classic."

"I remember something else," she said. "When you were at the airfield, I followed two insurgents into the tunnels through a buried basement access under the Petite Montparnasse Theater. But what's important was the billboard posted by the front entrance . . . a recruitment poster for musicians to perform in an orchestra in April at the Luxembourg Gardens."

Joseph waved for Leo to listen.

"When I came above ground, this is the same music I heard from an upper tenement," she said. "The name is something like Starry Night Sonata, a gala at the Luxembourg Gardens, with proceeds for survivors of the November attacks and the one at Nice. The admission was high, with a champagne reception and dignitaries from across Europe."

Leo made a note. "It's more than coincidental. I'll have the event investigated, about the organizer and when it came together. Perhaps Djinn plans to use it to meddle in our culture."

"Should we broach Giovanni to see if he knows who the maestro might be?" Emily asked.

"Before dinner, I'll ask him to make a casual inquiry. Giovanni is preparing the timing for the Overture at a slower tempo to study. Then we'll coordinate it with the code-breaking team."

Retreating to a corner by the window, Leo googled for ads for the Luxembourg Gala in both Paris and Brussels. With his jamming device, he blocked the frequency surrounding the lodge and placed a phone call to Interpol.

At six, the group rallied in the dining room. Three serving platters were delivered by the chef, with grilled lamb chops and mint sauce over a rice pilaf, braised vegetables with anchovies, and a homemade egg twist with locally churned butter. He waited to watch the first bites.

"Mmm. The aroma . . . I didn't know I was so hungry," Emily announced to the chef's pleasure.

There was no business conversation over dinner, other than random discussions of orchestra music that put everyone at ease. Joseph wiped the last of the balsamic and olive oil onto his focaccia and looked toward the kitchen entrance. "The food is exceptional. We'll give compliments to the chef and his staff."

Within minutes, a tray of chocolate profiteroles with whipped cream arrived, escorted by plump strawberries and a platter of cheese.

Giovanni raised his hand to speak. "Thank you for inviting me this afternoon. I hope it was helpful and I'd be delighted to offer my services again in the future. Monsieur Enio mentioned the Spring Gala in Paris and perhaps I could participate myself."

The code-breakers were puzzled and Leo awkwardly left the matter vague, as he hadn't yet broached the musical theory with the technicians.

Maurice nudged Leo to join him at the coffee station, about a concern with the map layers.

"We're slicing the map in graphics by sections. The fourth map should be considered. The 1789 Revolutionary map went no further north than Rue de Mont Blanc, then through the center of Paris on Rue Montmartre. The coordinates run in a network, south to Les Invalides in the west and across Luxembourg Gardens, the Panthéon to the Jardin des Plantes at Quai Bernard. That differs from more recent maps."

"Why is this older map of significance? Wouldn't it be incorporated in the later version, Maurice?"

"Yes and no. There are miniature alpha symbols and numbers on the Revolutionary map, that bleed through to the current version. But since the old map was created, landmarks and buildings burned down or were replaced. Recent locations are more accurate to physically access coded points."

As Leo joined them, Maurice continued. "At dinner, I followed your discussion with the violin student with interest. An orchestral adaptation lends a different view of the codes. Every code deciphered is on the musical octave, and each letter also has a numeric partner that is never duplicated."

"Let me see, Maurice. Is it like you'd see on a vending machine? You put in a coin and press an alphabet letter and a number, then voila . . . the treat drops to the basket and another takes its place."

Maurice laughed. "That is a concise example, Mr. Harkness. You're correct."

"So you're going in the right direction," Leo said. "Maurice, discuss this with the others and let me know how many codes are found in total. A list will be valuable."

In the tunnel below the Jardin des Tuileries and Pont Royale, Daniel and the bomb squad descended deeper, on the heels of a suspect. Agitated and suspected he was being hounded, the man continually looked back. The damp tunnels smelled of methane gas, and sweat poured from Daniel's brow.

They could be detonated prematurely if this man has explosives.

Daniel forged ahead as fast as he could trust his feet in the dim light, stopping when the rebel turned to listen. Paranoid, the insurgent slithered to hide in a heap of discarded refuse to set his lair.

Leading the trio, Daniel was first to reach the ambush point, when the rebel clocked him into unconsciousness. Seconds later he revived himself and struggled to find his footing, but his head was swooning and his vision distorted.

"I'll be alright, just keep on his tail," he mumbled, encouraging the team to stay in pursuit. But it was too late, the assailant was as lithe as a jackrabbit and vanished into a shadow.

However, Daniel's delay sent in a rescue crew to locate him.

"Gas," the senior bomb officer said. "Get out now! Methane . . . stay close to the ground and find the first tunnel out of this cesspool."

He slung Daniel's arm over his shoulder to drag him. Daniel's legs were rubber, but he knew time was scarce. "There, that's a ladder to a manhole. Hurry up!"

The officer released the lid and pulled Daniel to the surface just as a whoosh of heat and light pursued them at lightning speed. The third man was blown into the air and the manhole lid flew twenty feet.

The lead officer knew it was the combination of methane and an accidental match. "The fool lit a cigarette."

Sirens roared to take away the injured men, and a search party entered with oxygen masks to hunt down other culprits. Daniel examined the dead man's face. "It's the one that struck me. I've seen him before. I don't know his name, but his picture is in the Interpol files on the watch list. He is with an ISIS cell in Molenbeek."

"You need to go to the hospital now, Monsieur Boisvert, but be assured we will follow up on his connections."

Nineteen

The Security meeting with Interpol and the detectives was held in the protected zone of the Dingo. Daniel arrived with a bruised forehead and sported a few stitches.

Emily greeted him an engaging smile. "Daniel, we leave you alone for one night and look what happens. You must have a whopper of a headache."

"Someone needed to stay behind and do the legwork while my comrades gad about on the French Riviera."

"Oddly, Daniel's mission and ours have coincided," Leo said. "We found an underground insurgent in Paris from a Belgium cell, attempting to deposit a bomb that appears to be in the grand scheme."

"That's helpful," Joseph said. "And our workshop at Valdeblore was fruitful, I'd say."

Leo elaborated with personal pride. "Yes, the bombings are connected to the musical notes of an Overture in an orchestra program on April 12th."

"That's a long stretch, Leo," Daniel interjected.

Leo endured his best explanation of the blueprints and octave notes, coordinated with points in the tunnels.

"I'm not musically inclined, Leo, so it's over my head."

"A new pertinent factor is that we've identified the maestro hired for the Starry Night Sonata. He is Victor Strabinsky, an Austrian conductor. Daniel, your attacker in the tunnel was in the same group that locals refer to as Jihad Central."

"Which came first, the audition for Stabinsky or the planned orchestra score?" Daniel asked. "Is Strabinski a pawn or a conspirator?"

"Exactly my thought," Joseph added.

"We've started top-level meetings with the French Government," Leo said. "My higher-ups have garnered international interest, looking under every rock to stop this deplorable plan, as local and national government dignitaries have been invited to the main event."

"Certainly, France will be doing everything to protect this information without leaks. If Djinn were to succeed, the population would direct their anger at government ineptness," Daniel said grimly.

"Belgium has offered plenty of support too," Leo said. They've opened the files on watch lists of immigrants exposed to radicalism."

In the northern Brussels suburb known as a hotbed for Jihad terrorist cells, a handful of men gathered in the vacant office of an abandoned factory.

The dilapidated warehouse didn't stand out from others, with broken windows, bars across doors, and weeds growing through the asphalt cracks. At the nexus of canals and railways, the street hadn't been used for some time.

Molenbeek had become a safe haven for migrants, with three-quarters of its immigrant population arriving on boats from Morocco. Many considered it a training ground for

Islamist radicalism, and the frustrated government struggled to combat the linguistic apartheid.

Of the insurgents gathered at the warehouse, four were Moroccans and the fifth was an Austrian with a prematurely grey beard and a bohemian lock of long strands clasped in a leather tie at the back.

He caressed a violin case under his arm and carried a canvas sling. Accompanying him was a German-born young man, his eyes flashing with the prospect of impending danger.

As tires crunched over the gravel below, one man alerted the others of the arrival of their guest of honor. It was Bekir, the Turkish man, dispatched from Paris to evaluate the program. A restrained mongrel heard the car and barred his teeth in warning.

Aziz and Sayed, his accomplice, abruptly led the Austrian and German men by the arm and shoved them toward a side door to a wooden freight elevator.

"We wait for you upstairs," Sayed said in German.

Using the manual pulley, Aziz took them to the vacant third floor. A few tables and chairs lingered sporadically, but the wall was covered in maps, codes, and directives. Among the maps was the Revolutionary Map of 18th century Paris, marked with colored pins. The wall was adjusted to have the ability to rise like a garage door and flip itself so that an unsuspecting vagrant wouldn't know of its existence.

Along the wall, a bank of computers was being monitored with live footage of various sights and listening devices. One of the men on the monitor was Stephen Cahill.

Bekir extended his hand. "Maestro Strabinsky, greetings!"

Strabinsky was unsure of the protocol. "Merci, Monsieur Bekir."

"We all go by first names, so I'll call you Victor in future and your comrade will be Guenther. We don't know where you live, and you don't know where we live. Agreed?"

"Yes, yes. That will be good."

Bekir pointed to the violin case. "Ah, you brought the music to us. The acoustics here will be excellent."

Aziz pulled up a chair for Strabinsky to rest his case.

Strabinsky explained the canvas sling as he opened the sack. "I like to use my own music stand, if that is alright, Bekir?"

"Of course. I appreciate that you've thought of the little things. It will make our session easier."

With extensions being pulled and knobs tightened, Strabinsky adjusted the stand for his height.

"As I was instructed, I brought with me a flash drive recording of the symphony you asked about—the 'William Tell Overture'. It's the Finale you want."

"Excellent."

Sayed arrived at Bekir's side to take the disk to a façade disguised as a wall safe. Pressing a combination, the door slid sideways, exposing a fully engaged computer system. Sayed inserted the drive in a laptop and turned up the audio, enveloping the room with a beautiful violin orchestration.

"Magnificent, Victor."

Strabinsky's eyes closed naturally with an imaginary baton in his hand, drinking in the euphoria of Rossini. When it finished, Bekir moved closer.

"I understand that music is an international language, yet the notes are in Roman letters. The octave is A, B, C, D, E, F, G, is that correct?"

Bekir's words confused Strabinsky, and he gave a simple reply to explain the music.

"There are different keys, but this score is in the key of E flat, with three flats, B, E, and A."

"E flat, I don't understand."

"It lowers the sound down a halftone as with each flat."

"Whatever you say, Victor. We all join the cause of exalting Mohammed. You are commended for your contribution to the eradication of our enemies."

Emily longed for freedom from the safe house, tiring of the gloom of constant terrorist talk. At her dresser mirror, she saw a girl she'd forgotten about, with memories of simpler times.

She imagined arising and opening her balcony door to the sounds of Montmartre, with the clatter of Marie's flower buckets and Toby's morning yawn.

Brushing her long tresses, she twisted the auburn strands into a pearl clamp at the back. Turning sideways, she realized she'd lost weight, with her clothes hanging from now boney shoulders and hips.

"Joseph, I need to be Rachel for a day, to shop and walk the avenues. Can I do it today? We've been cooped up undercover here for too long. You've been sweet not to mention that any sparkle in my eye has faded, and my smile is rarely used."

As she leaned on his shoulder, the familiar scent of lavender in her hair was a reminder of how long it had been since they were alone in their loft. Neither pulled away, wanting a few more minutes of solitude and comfort.

Emily slid her hand into his open shirt and rested on his chest, and the intimate sensation melted Joseph into intense longing. Holding her closer he whispered words she didn't want at this moment and sagged her weight against his body.

"Of course, Honey, it's time. But I'll need to let Leo know you'll still need a tail. The coast won't be clear until the grand encore on April 12th."

"I don't want this to pass, but I know it has to be."

Neither pulled away for a long moment as they remained lost in the past and enthralled with the memories.

Alexandre dropped Emily at a trendy shopping area on the Champs-Élysées, with explicit instructions for a rendezvous. The boulevard bustled with shoppers, tourists, and business people strutting in self-importance. The boutiques and restaurants that had been part of everyday life for Joseph and Emily, brimmed with activity.

At a shoe store, she admired the elegant window display. The last time she bought shoes was the day of the Bataclan.

Definitely not Fendi today.

At the Banana Republic, she was greeted by a concierge who offered her a glass of champagne and summoned a private representative. Emily giggled inside at the attention.

The store was a parade of mini-boutiques and Neo Art Deco fashion, and Emily fell totally into the enticement. An hour later she walked out with a complete wardrobe and stepped to the Champs-Élysées with a broad smile.

The sun shone over the boulevard and the birds were singing, but it all crashed with her sudden ominous sensation of dread. Alexandre should be waiting on the corner with the van. He wasn't there.

"Turn on surveillance mode." The words screamed at her.

Turning toward the window display she intended to make a phone call. The reflection in the glass warned her she was being observed, and she fumbled to recover the earphone Alexandre had given her.

"Alexandre, you there?"

There was nothing, and Emily felt a surge of panic.

A few doors down was the Restaurant du Rond Pointe where she'd lunched when working at the detective agency.

I'll wait there for the security van.

Scanning the street, she recognized Fernando Valois in a heated argument at the curb. It was a full dispute with another man over the right to the next fare.

With a lowered head, she scurried past a section of planter boxes, glancing back from down the block.

Valois was still in a debate but did a double-take as she turned. Immediately, he was on his phone, speaking excitedly.

"Alexandre! Christophe! I need your help."

Emily spoke clearly knowing she was in danger. After an agonizing pause, she heard Alexandre, but not through her earpiece. He was right behind her.

"Emily, I'm here. Don't look at me, but keep walking. We picked up your call and you've been targeted. We need to get you out of here now."

In her haste to get away, she accidentally bumped into a woman watching her from a bus bench.

Isabella.

They were suddenly face-to-face, with no denying the moment of recognition between them. Isabella was about to scream and hold Emily for her accomplices, but Alexandre was quicker and carefully eased Isabella back to the bench with an instant tranquilizer dart in her neck.

Alexandre waved his hand, and within seconds a plain older Honda, that Emily had seen outside The Dingo, pulled up to the curb.

He looked back from the car and Isabella was gone.

Twenty

An Interpol search in Paris for an undercover musician was a priority, eventually discovering a man within their own ranks, a retired agent that had turned to orchestra conducting in his hobby years.

Blending into another life, he knew to watch his back and avoid contacts from his career, as he'd made many enemies while at Interpol.

Leo placed the call to his old friend, hibernating in a luxury 17th-century residence on Île St. Louis, a panoramic island surrounded by the Seine, with a 180-degree view of the Louvre, Pompidou Center, Notre-Dame, the Eiffel Tower and the Latin and Marais quarters.

Heavy ornate wrought-iron glass doors led to the prestigious address off the Quai Bourbon. The architecture was from the era of Le Grand Siècle and Louis XIV, and within the sanctuary of opulence, the apartments were protected like a prison, needing an appointment with a resident to pass the concierge and security desk.

Leo entered the grand foyer with furrowed wrinkles at the corner of each eye. Worry had lent itself pre-maturely to him as a dedicated agent. With long strides and an erect back, he approached the charge desk to make his own introduction.

"Gilbert Bernard, s'il vous plait."

The concierge reviewed the computer log and verified Leo's ID against the records, and after a series of obsolete queries, he signaled to a second man who had blended into a corner of the lobby.

"The valet will escort you to Monsieur Bernard's suite."

The elevator access was invisible to him, but at the press of a button, a portion of marble wall slid aside and Leo was ushered into the lift for a speedy journey to the penthouse. Walls were ensconced with 18th-century oriental paintings and Chinese artifacts, befitting a museum.

The gloved valet lowered a heavy brass door knocker and waited until Gilbert Bernard appeared.

"Leo, mon ami, it is good to see you after so many years." The two embraced in a gentleman's hug.

"You certainly had a good pension plan," Leo teased as his eyes scanned the elegant trappings.

"Non non, mon ami. It is the world of the wealthy and cultured that provides my living. I get to travel throughout Europe at the expense of international hosts. Sit and relax, Leo. Tea and crumpets will be along momentarily. I acquired the passion in London in the last few years."

"Then you are a traitor to the cafés of Paris and our exquisite patisseries," Leo laughed.

"We are Interpol. That means we are international."

A French maid delivered a silver tray with a chintz teapot and a plate of crumpets. On a vintage serving table, she set out small tureens of honey, jam, whipped butter and Devonshire cream, and a bowl of fresh, chilled strawberries.

Leo devoured several crumpets before he reminded himself of the purpose of his visit. Wiping his mouth with a linen napkin, he started with the last bite still in his mouth.

"Gilbert, we have a serious situation developing in Paris. It is incredulous what may happen if we don't take steps to intervene."

"I can be trusted with your confidence, Leo."

Leo eyed the ceiling and windows. "Have you had your apartment swept for bugs recently?"

Gilbert's face fell. "This place is a fortress. It's impossible."

"May I?" Leo removed a thin instrument from his pocket. "This will surely answer my question."

"Please, go ahead."

Leo strode the entire living room, dining room, and parlor, and nodded that the results were negative.

"I was not at liberty to explain it in detail on the phone."

Leo recounted the critical points of the terrorist scheme: the tunnels, the drones, the musical code and Victor Strabinsky.

"Paris would be facing a mammoth catastrophic event that could disintegrate our entire city."

"You have already identified the critical piece, I'm not sure how I can help."

"It is a complicated smokescreen perpetrated by evil men. Would you consult with us? We have no room for error when we come to April 12th!"

"Yes, of course. I would not be French if I did not do everything to defend my homeland."

"We've identified thirty coded locations, maybe more. From an old map, the square stretches from Montmartre to Montparnasse, affecting the most populated arrondissements and historic buildings of Paris. We believe that each site will have a bomb coded to a master computer, each triggered by musical notes at the very moment Strabinsky plays the Finale to the 'William Tell Overture'. Drones will be used in the climax, like a grand domino effect!"

Gilbert stood and walked over to the glass wall looking down at Notre Dame as he rubbed his chin.

"Yes, I can see that it will be critical to have exact timing."

He was an exact man, with a finely coiffed mustache and a striking bone structure that made people turn to look, easily assuming he could be from royalty.

"We have Strabinsky under surveillance, but he is working for Djinn. Last week he was in their pit in Molenbeek."

"When you first mentioned Strabinsky, I was certain I hadn't heard the name. It would be folly to mix Strabinsky with the great Stravinsky. But as I think about Belgium, I recall a second-rate conductor I encountered several years back."

"You won't need to worry about him, Gilbert. Our undercover people will keep tabs on him, but he is the one to set the program—the musical version that is."

"Do you know how the bombs will be triggered?"

"The terrorists are not highly skilled but they've imported technicians to control computerized telephone numbers aligned with each site and manipulated by a fleet of drones."

"Each note would correlate to a bomb site and its own phone number?"

"Yes, that is the premise."

"Leave it with me for a day or two, and I will do my best to provide specifics. I'll create an orchestra score for you to work with. I've worked with music computerized programming before and have a few ideas."

"Thank you, Gilbert. This began with a detective couple that intercepted a drone drop at the Basilica. The woman is intuitive and sees the valleys, while we focus on mountaintops.

"We planted her in the defense surveillance department to feed false data and reveal an insurgent mole. She intercepted him quickly. Now we are tracking him and sending erroneous statistics and fake classified documents. If you don't object, I will ask her to work with you."

Gilbert gave a gleeful wink.

"That sounds refreshing, Leo. Send her along on Wednesday for tea and crumpets."

That evening, Leo invited Daniel, Joseph, and Emily to dine at L'Auberge de Venise. Since the Harknesses had gone into the safe house, a public gathering of the foursome had become rare, with communication mainly by phone or text.

"It's good to see you, Leo," Emily said. She looked splendid in a soft ecru chiffon dress hanging in fashionable uneven layers.

"Looks as if you have recovered from the incident on the Champs-Élysées with Isabella."

"I've been in that position and worse, too frequently, so I've learned to protect myself and squirm out of a tight situation."

Her eyes teased. "But I confess, Alexandre and Christophe have been diligent in keeping me safe." Leo couldn't help but smile at her infectious manner and zest.

"Good job Em, I hear that Isabella has been significant in leading us to one of their terrorist's hideouts," Daniel confirmed.

"I have? How so?" She turned to Leo for an answer.

"I'll include that in our dinner conversation."

Changing the tone of the conversation, he turned to Joseph. "They recommend the Ossobuco if you have a hearty appetite tonight."

A waiter centered bottles of mineral water and lemon for them, and a bottle of Cristal for Leo.

"You mentioned that you had something to tell me, Leo?" Emily prodded.

"Wait a moment, please." In the middle of the table, he placed a tiny, cubed speaker box. "This will jam any listening device and muffles our conversation."

When the sommelier finished pouring the champagne, Leo made a toast to the success of the unit.

"Yes, I met with a retired Interpol agent who is now seasoned in classical music. I explained the premise of our situation, and he will assist us, providing details corresponding to the orchestration of the notes coinciding with tunnel targets. I recommended you assist him, Emily, for your instincts and acumen for details. If you would be so kind, he will expect you for tea tomorrow morning. Alexandre will have the address."

"Of course, whatever you need me to do."

Emily looked at Joseph but already had her mind made up. "What about my work in the Protection and Defense lab?"

"No worry. The data reports you organized are now downloading automatically to my office, and the drone is still active at Le Bourget. For now, your alias Barbara Church is on a short leave, and Cahill is being followed under a microscope."

Leo broke to sip the champagne. "Daniel, can you update us on the tunnel searches?"

"With all the manpower, we now have a handle on the code points in the blueprints; the study by the technicians at Côte d'Azur was particularly helpful. We know the insurgents haven't gone below the secondary level in the tunnels.

"The city's historic core is vulnerable, and these landmarks could all be in jeopardy."

"They'd destroy a lot of history," Joseph said.

"Not to mention people killed. But there's more. It's a circuit under the city. The route continues at the war museum at Les Invalides, then Luxembourg Gardens, Denfert-Rochereau and the Jardin des Plantes on Quai Bernard. The entire targeted square we've identified would eradicate the structural history of Paris and hundreds of thousands of its populace."

"Have our units accounted for the C-4 plastic explosives or arsenals in the tunnels?" Joseph asked.

"Yes . . . at every site. The C-4 explosives have attached boxes that would fit a cell phone. The bomb squad's regular rounds make sure the ignition sensors are disabled up to the minute."

"The timing within their plan is precise," Joseph said, "It coordinates thirty target points, each with its own phone numbers, and thirty notes played by the orchestra. Every phone will be programmed to a different location."

Leo continued the report. "Our progress is not only in the tunnels but in tracking terrorist cells. When our cleanup crew collected Isabella, she was interviewed but not charged. Like a jack in the box, she went directly back to Saint-Denis. We waited and watched, then she made the ultimate mistake and ordered a quantity of pizza to Didier's apartment.

"Our surveillance tracked down the pizza delivery and had a SWAT unit enact a raid on the apartment. Unfortunately, Didier and Bekir escaped in the chaos."

"Did you make arrests?" Joseph asked.

"At first they fired back, then we charged the door with a battering ram and tossed in smoke bombs. Isabella surrendered as a decoy, and Didier must have exited through a false door. At the same time, Belgium authorities in Molenbeek raided an abandoned factory, with a few arrests. But the coup of the day was a master plotting map on the factory wall."

"Do you think this was enough to splinter the group and deter their scheme?" Daniel asked.

"Not at all," Joseph added. "They are like a nest of ants that will rebound to become even more violent, splitting into groups and attacking where we least expect."

"International and Paris security will ramp up in the days before April 12th," Leo said. "Today we heard that a bus is chartered two days ahead leaving Molenbeek. We'll have roadblocks on the main routes and car inspections, and intelligence will track most movements. We need to prepare for anything, in the air, and on the ground."

"Photos of known radicals are on the Interpol site," Daniel said, "and we all need to review the updates by the hour. Also, tracking Cahill has produced new contacts."

Joseph was in thought. "Leo, if they are sending a busload of insurgents, there must be a secondary plan to use the tunnels' caches of weapons and ammunition."

"A smokescreen?" Leo said.

Twenty-one

Bekir's wife, Isabella, was raised in Morocco under rigid laws that demean the value of women in society, with strict subservience to her husband.

At barely twelve years of age, she was sold in Marrakech to Bekir for two cows, a paltry sum even in Morocco for a child bride. In subsequent years, she bore four daughters and was deemed a disgrace by her father for not providing a male heir.

One night when Bekir was asleep, she slipped from her home with the four girls and begged a nearby mission to take her daughters at the orphanage. She hoped for a better future for them, perhaps even education.

The next morning, Isabella told Bekir that bondage thieves took the girls in the night, threatening her at knifepoint not to follow or tell her husband. Bekir was skeptical but did not long for the return of his daughters, as he had greater things in mind.

The Islamic religion was ingrained in her, and she was taught to handle a Kalashnikov rifle while in a Syrian camp.

Moving about Europe as a poor emigrant, she arrived in Paris two years before the November 15th massacre. Since the Saint-Denis raid, she was under constant watch by Interpol, waiting for her to expose Didier.

It was a warm day in early April in northeastern Paris, as Isabella sat isolated and handcuffed in an interview room at an interrogation facility. A red welt was a reminder of the tranquilizer dart she'd received on the Champs-Élysees.

A stern, bloated officer entered the room huffing and grunting, with a cigarette dangling from his mouth. He took the seat opposite her and placed a lukewarm coffee on the table. On the wall was a two-way mirror, where Joseph, Emily, and an Interpol agent observed.

The investigator threw a fat file onto the table.

"Isabella, it will go much better for you if you choose to cooperate. You see, we've been watching you for some time. Youssif and Bekir made a fatal mistake, remaining in Saint-Denis in your fortified tenement for too long."

The officer removed a series of glossy black and white photographs and lined them up in front of Isabella. Her eyes glanced at each in succession.

"Here's one taken shortly after the Bataclan massacre. This man, Fernando Valois, is operating an eagle kite over a public area. It was lacking discretion and we were able to identify him as the operator of the remote-controlled drone tracking an unsuspecting woman - the same woman you bumped into yesterday."

"That wasn't me, and I don't know her. You've mistaken my identification."

"In this next one, you are talking to the woman you claim to have never met. It was immediately after the Saint-Denis raid, where Abaaoud was holed up."

Isabella was trembling, and her fingers tapping.

"We'll skip to another, Isabella. This is a photo of you on the surveillance video of a pizza shop, where you placed a large order to be delivered to the hideout of Youssif Didier."

"I want a lawyer."

"It will be better if you cooperate. We need information, so help us and we'll reduce your sentence substantially. By association, you are an accomplice in the Bataclan murders? Although you didn't directly act, you did nothing to impair the criminal activity of an impending event. Since you didn't contact authorities, you're as guilty as if you pulled the trigger yourself."

"I don't know anything."

"Let's give it a try and see what you know that you aren't aware of. Is that okay?"

The interviewer slid another black and white of four smiling girls but didn't say a word. Isabella gasped, and for a long time, she caressed the photo. Overpowering her intended stoic demeanor, a few tears ran down her cheeks.

"Are they safe? Yes, what is the question?"

"Do you know where Youssif and Bekir are hiding out now?"

"You are correct, they were in Saint-Denis. Bekir arranged for the apartment, but Youssif was always in charge. A man named Aziz told him that police were coming, but it was too late to escape. The apartment has a secret door at the back of the bedroom closet. It has stairs that go down many floors to the basement. They say the building has an old history of bootlegs."

"Bootlegging?"

"Yes."

"Where did he go?"

"I haven't been there, but I hear them talking about it."

"Take your time, Isabella."

"They go into those death tunnels and find their way to a theater in Montparnasse. That's how they got out."

The detective thumbed through the file and stopped at an aerial view of the Le Bourget airfield.

"Did you overhear them talk about a drone airfield northeast of Paris?"

"Yes, they talked about that a lot, and I listened to everything while I hid in the bedroom or the kitchen. They talked to a man in Molenbeek who was bringing underground soldiers to Paris next week. Jihadists—they are prepared to commit suicide for their cause. I know of one hideout where the radicals will stay, waiting for the day."

"Where is that?"

"May I have a piece of paper and a map?"

Isabella wrote four names, an apartment address, and the description of a vehicle she had helped to obtain.

"Here on the map—this is the house. It has a secret space down to the tunnels, just as Didier had. If anything goes bad, they are to remain in the cave. It's a tiny room with rations and a bed, sealed off by a broken monument. They could hide out there for up to a week."

"Very good, Isabella. This will be helpful." The interviewer softened, "Would you like something to drink?"

"Water, please."

Seconds later, a tap on the door brought a cup of water, and the investigator continued.

"Did you hear them talk about an orchestra?"

"Yes, they laughed at how easy it was going to be. I heard the music, it was beautiful. A man, Sayed, came from Belgium with a shipment of cell phones and what he called a modulator. Munitions have already been hidden but they wanted more. They stole a load of bullets left over from the Balkan Wars and even took a cache from a U.S. military base.

"With a ten-second delay, the modulator will connect a recording of the orchestra music being played at the Luxembourg Gardens into the computer, triggering a bank of phone numbers. They met with the conductor in Molenbeek last week at an abandoned building."

"Where will they meet on April 12th?"

"They won't actually gather together. Each man is assigned a location to install that phone, then he gives his code to the master computer operator. I believe that is Sayed. Five men will coordinate six numbers each, then feed them into another number to start a series of bombs."

The door tapped again, and an agent delivered a surprise sandwich and strong coffee. "Please be comfortable," the interrogator said in a more gentle voice.

"Yes, and thank you." Isabella gratefully took a bite of the sandwich and held the steaming coffee up to her lips.

"A helicopter will land on the 56th-floor observation terrace of the Tour Maine-Montparnasse, a skyscraper high above a Metro station. They'll control the roof access in advance. The coordinator will be waiting in the restaurant at the top of the Maine.

"He'll be evacuated when the chopper departs. And if everything goes as planned, the Maine itself will be collapsed within minutes of the drone launch. It too sits over a tunnel." She bit into her sandwich. "I listen well and I remember details. Bekir never thought to know that about me."

"Who is the coordinator?"

"Didier of course! He talks on his computer a lot to the jihadists in Syria. I don't know the man's name . . . maybe I heard of Salim."

The officer opened a book of photos of suspected Islamic terrorists.

"Who are these people?"

Isabella carefully thumbed through the pictures, providing names for almost two dozen men, mostly from Morocco, Syria, Turkey or Belgium.

"This one will be at the concert, the master computer man. He has arranged for a helicopter to pick him up before the last explosion at the Denfert-Rochereau. Immediately after that, a fleet of drones will sweep over the area and drop grenades and chlorine gas.

"They laughed when they talked of the maestro Strabinsky. They promised to send a chopper to lift him out of the carnage and whisk him to safety." She looked up feeling great shame. "They have no intention of rescuing him, just as they will not rescue me. They will either put a bomb in the orchestra pit or one of the musicians will have a suicide belt."

While the conversation was being recorded, the mention of the Maine-Montparnasse skyscraper sent one the detectives to dispatch a unit to the 15th arrondissement to check out Isabella's story.

"My worth is that of a cow. Although I am not educated, I pride myself on my memory. It is a relief to unburden my soul and tell you this today."

She sat back and finished the sandwich with renewed hope. "What will happen to my children? Once Bekir hears that I have spoken here, my life is over."

The interviewer did his best to offer hope. "We'll keep you in protective custody. A good situation would be to extradite you to a compassionate country where you could be reunited with your daughters."

"I will pray for that, thank you."

Emily looked on silently.

Poor Isabella, what will happen to you? I pray you will not be deported to Morocco. It will surely be your death.

Joseph put his arm around Emily's waist, as she was far away in thought.

A two-man surveillance crew had been holed up in the construction shack at Didier's airfield for many days, without as much as a bumble bee on their radar.

Stale perspiration and burnt coffee permeated the vinyl walls of the trailer. The construction crew had taken a hiatus, at the request of local government, placed on alert by national defense.

In spite of an overcast sky, the younger member reached for the ceiling crank to pop open an air ventilation fan. It was planting time, tractors would normally be furrowing in their fields, but silence had been purchased all around the Van Dame farm.

At 8 a.m., Alain Van Dame's pickup made its morning run around the circumference of the training field. He stopped at several poles to reset the security cameras, knowing Didier would double-check.

He's paranoid! I should never have sold out to such an evil man.

Van Dame removed a keychain from around his neck and unlocked the cement house. Bringing out several loads, he mounted controls on the row of podiums used to land and fire at the drones.

"There must be a training exercise soon," the lead agent said, as he directed the binoculars away from Van Dame to the southwest, the flight plan of the drones. "They're coming. Are you sure that the drone detection prototype is ready to record?"

"Yes, of course. It's camouflaged over there in the barbed wire. We'll download the flight plan at 400 feet. Last week we collected two dozen different eagle drones, and intercepted communication through the gamers back to a terrorist cell in Syria."

"What can these drones do?" the second agent asked.

"A report from Interpol says they're capable of dropping live grenades and chlorine gas over the entire city of Paris."

"Incredible. Where do they get the payload?"

"If the authorities had the answer, we wouldn't be here."

Didier's usual contingent insurgents arrived on cue, and the fleet of eight drones once again dropped markers on the field targets. The process didn't take more than ten minutes. A celebration followed, as the men, all in black camouflage, raised their arms in victory, then prepared to leave.

During the ten minute lapse and celebration, the younger agent crawled onto the field and placed trackers on three of the pickup trucks.

After the drone demonstration, Didier's men made close mechanical inspections of each unit, applying oil and tightening screws where necessary. Three of the drones had some level of malfunction.

"Munir, take these to Rafi at Drone Volt on Rue de la Perdrix in Roissy for diagnostics. Get the cameras stabilized in the undercarriage and adapted to a timed release. Perfection is imperative for the final launch. Take Sayed with you."

Each drone was fitted into its own snug compartment of shaped Styrofoam, then packed into a boxed frame in the back of one of the pickups and secured with a locked lid.

Their conversation was picked up by a transmitter that alerted crew in the center of Paris of the upcoming move. Leo and Daniel were notified by text.

"Daniel, check out the Moulineaux drone facility," Leo said. "If it's the one I remember, it has a number of helipads and landing strips for light aircraft and helicopters. Take a crew with you to make an on-site inspection."

Daniel rounded up Christophe at a row of monitors Alexandre had already left to transport Emily to her meeting with the retired orchestra conductor on Rue St. Louis Island.

"Christophe! Come and join me for a field inspection."

"One moment. A feed is coming through from the drone detection prototype at the construction site." Christophe swung his chair back to listen and a young woman leaned sideways to retrieve the report from a printer.

"Eureka!, she shouted. "The machine picked up all eight registration numbers and there's a graph of the flight routing for each drone—D'Issy les Moulineaux helipads."

"There's a secondary report from the prototype," Leo said to them. "The drones came from the Moulineaux helipad. The base is on the ring road and covers six hectares with four hangers. Daniel and Christopher, go quickly and be thorough. Possibly you'll locate the Attack Apache choppers too."

"We'll check in within the hour."

Twenty-two

Madge Bitteridge had just finished an interview with one of her clients and was returning phone calls when two dark-haired Turkish men entered the detective agency. The office on Rue Euler was a short walk from the Champs-Élysées and walk-in queries kept the office bustling.

The first man carried his shoulders high in a nervous stance, while the second stayed behind. In spite of the warm spring temperature, they wore woolen toques and black clothing.

"Can I help you, Gentlemen?"

"We've come to see Mr. Harkness."

The second man moved closer to the wall of the private offices to search for occupants.

"I'm afraid he's not in the office. Mr. Carter will be along shortly and I'm sure he'd be happy to assist you."

From their suspect behavior, Madge's instincts were on high alert, sensing an untoward intention by the two men.

"We'll wait," the first man stated and took a chair. "Go about your business. We'll be here when Mr. Carter arrives."

Madge texted Carter. "Suspicious men in the office, alert the police."

Carter's text came right back. "I understand. I'm parking now. Be up in about five minutes."

The men asked if they could have coffee, and Madge reluctantly went to the utility area to pour two mugs. The hairs on her neck stood up when she noticed a sound of movement. First, feet shuffling, then rapid feet and the door slammed, as the men were out the door with Madge's handbag and cell phone.

Madge dropped the first mug on the floor and took off after the last man.

"Come back, you thief! You won't get away with this." Madge was still yelling in the main floor lobby when she bumped into Carter arriving with a policeman.

"I knew something was wrong," she said shaking with disappointment that she had been taken. "They didn't come to see Mr. Harkness; they knew he wasn't here. They came for information and I fell into their trap!"

"Don't beat yourself up, Madge, I would have done the same thing."

"Well, I certainly hope not!"

Blocks away, Aziz and Sayed gloated to Didier of their success.

"The Harkness detective made a call to the agency two days ago. We're tracking the origin to a house on Boulevard Garibaldi in the 7th arrondissement. Aziz will go and stake out the site for the man."

Emily was charmed by Gilbert Bernard's old-fashioned social graces and his fastidiousness etiquette in ensuring she was comfortable.

Seated in an overstuffed, pale yellow patterned chintz armchair by the window, the pair prattled about delicacies. Before getting to matters of business, a maid brought trays of teas and crumpets on fine china.

"Oh, Monsieur Bernard, I haven't enjoyed such a treat since I was in London with my husband more than a year ago. I see you honor the true British tradition. Is that genuine Devonshire cream?"

"Of course, I never cheat," Gilbert chortled, delighted to see her pleasure.

When the tea-things were removed, Gilbert walked over to an instrument panel on the wall, and within seconds the room was enveloped with an astounding exhibit of classical music.

"It's Rossini, my dear. He was inspired by the great Emperor Napoleon Bonaparte, and wrote many Neapolitan operas during his time, inspired by victory and rebellion, and the scourge of the soul. Do you hear it, Emily?"

Gilbert looked sympathetically at Emily's wistful attempt to relate to her soul. "Don't worry, it takes time to open the windows and let your heart listen to the music."

"You certainly found a niche to nourish you in retirement."

"I did indeed. I travel throughout Europe and meet amazing people and hear the sounds of angels. It is truly living and enjoying people and life."

"Have you yet examined the William Tell . . . from the unpleasant perspective of this plot?" Emily asked.

"Leo was right to be concerned. It is a clever plan. The terrorists have schemed a cunning plot. And from what I know of Strabinsky he's not clever enough to deviate from instruction."

From an antique Victrola cabinet, Bernard took out a sheaf of music with notations and laid them on a coffee table with a copy of the map.

"The red X's mark points on the map where Interpol has detected a bomb placement or expect them. The green marks correspond to the music. The sequence B1, B2, B3, B4, E1, F1, G1, and B5 is the opening phrase for the explosions, starting at bar 14, and I've marked the first notes.

"Everything will be exact without any hesitation, however, it must be slowed slightly to permit the proper orchestration and conductor's movements."

Emily examined the notes, marks, and the bars that followed. "I see the pattern." She laughed. "It's the 'Lone Ranger' song too, you know, so I can hum the tune from Saturday morning TV."

Bernard smirked at her experience, a world apart from his.

"Tell me, will anyone on our side have control over the maestro?"

I don't really know, I'm sorry."

"I will propose that I go undercover as a member of the orchestra, perhaps with my violin, and I would get his music to compare. It's a possibility they could use an understudy."

"That puts you in grave danger if Interpol even agreed."

"Of course, it gets me back in the game. Danger can be exhilarating, Emily. I used to partner with Leo when we worked out of Lyon. There's an ultimate thrill of capturing a case at its climax, and I have yet to find a replacement for it."

Her brow wrinkled at the thought of placing this dear man in harm's way.

"Here is a flash drive, coded as I see it now, with the triggering of cell phones in sequence."

"Leo will be calling you soon, Monsieur Bernard."

"Emily, we have gone to the brink of death in our discussion. The least it has earned me is to call me by my first name."

"Merci, Gilbert. I wish you safety and success."

Emily offered him an affectionate hug after he escorted her to the main foyer on the secret elevator.

Alexandre was waiting outside the main gate.

"Was our entire conversation recorded, Alexandre?"

"Yes, Leo has already heard of Monsieur Bernard's offer to go undercover. You were quite persuasive, Emily."

She handed the flash drive to Alexandre and sat quietly on the way back to the safe house.

Funny how a sense of accomplishment is not always the result you hoped for. Do I really want an apple on my head and trust the arrow?

Outside the safe house, she looked up at the window hoping to see Joseph watching for her.

For the first time, she noticed a flower bed under the main floor living room window. Red and yellow tulips turned their faces toward the morning sun, and it reminded her of being at home in Montmartre, of their long walks through the winding streets and feeding the birds from a park bench.

The parlor window curtain on the first floor fluttered. It was the security agent checking on her safe arrival. She nodded in recognition but realized she didn't even know the agent's name.

As she turned her front door key, she heard a car engine pull up behind her. She'd been trained to immediately secure herself, and without looking back, she opened the door and latched the security bolt after her.

Joseph rapped at the door.

"Em, it's me."

"Thank goodness it's you." She wrapped her arms around his neck and clung in a long embrace.

"What's the matter, Honey?"

"Come upstairs. We need to talk. I'll make a pot of coffee and hot biscuits."

Joseph sat in the living room while Emily made a quick scone from the pantry's sparse ingredients and set the pot to brew. As it percolated, she returned to Joseph.

"We've been consumed for weeks and now months with this impending disaster, yet we have never talked of what will happen to us on April 12th. Where will we be? How will we escape? I'm not ready to die a heroine."

"I talked to Daniel and Leo about that yesterday. Right before the concert, Daniel and I will scour the tunnels with an elite team. Each cell phone will be blocked, and the C-4 line cut. All of that will be done well before the concert begins at 7 p.m. It is straightforward and we will not be in danger.

"You will accompany Leo to the restaurant at Maine-Montparnasse. A team of agents will overcome the insurgents on the roof, then guide the copter in as it lands. Watch for Didier or Bekir."

"So I'll be a lame duck?" Emily deduced with sarcasm. "Isn't there more?"

"Leo expects you to convince the chopper pilot to cooperate and abandon his mission. Our own pilot will be ready to take over, and he'll take you and Leo to the Luxembourg Gardens. Daniel and I will rendezvous there.

"Everything is accounted for with no injuries to authorities or civilians. Isabella described a busload coming from Molenbeek, and we'll follow the passengers. Each person will be watched . . . if one gets on a bus, an agent will be right behind him. We don't want to begin arrests too early and alert Didier of our interception."

"Will Monsieur Bernard be alright?"

"Yes, Em. The flash drive gives us what we need. Bernard will ensure that Strabinsky doesn't stray from our plan."

The oven timer beeped, and Joseph checked the oven. "Your famous scones, are they too hot to eat?"

"The things I can always count on," she laughed. "My man, café au lait, and French pastries. Together."

They had just buttered their scones when Joseph's cell rang.

"It's Daniel. I need backup right now at the D'Issy les Moulineaux helipad. A busload of Syrian emigrants is bustling around. Christophe and I have taken cover in Hanger No. 4."

"Okay, Daniel. Emily and I will be there straight away."

"And let Leo know. My battery is low."

On the way out, she grabbed two sets of earphones and hurried downstairs behind Joseph. The van with Alexandre was parked down the block, and they stepped out to be picked up. As Joseph whistled, a man got out of a navy BMW parked in the shade. He was vaguely familiar from surveillance at the Dingo, with blonde, curly hair and short in stature, a typical Frenchman that blends into a crowd.

Emily's eyes momentarily met his.

He has dark steely eyes.

"Monsieur Harkness, it's not necessary to summon your van." He tossed a ring of keys to Joseph. "Take the car and I'll ride back to headquarters with my friends."

Joseph watched him open the cube van's passenger door to join Alexandre, but never gave a second look back at the struggle in the driver's seat.

Emily set the GPS for D'Issy les Moulineaux port in Roissy, then googled for more about the heliport.

"Daniel said the Attack Apaches were under preparations for Friday's mission. I wonder who the front man is in Belgium."

The BMW veered onto a dusty lane, parallel to the main entrance of the airport. When Joseph put the brakes on, the glove compartment popped open and a folder fell to the floor.

"Joseph, this is a car rental from Molenbeek! We've been duped."

"We'll leave it here then and walk in by foot. Maybe they won't notice us from their control tower," Joseph said, as he pulled a revolver from his leg holster. "Is your pistol loaded, Em?"

"Don't even ask, Joseph." He accepted the admonishment and made a sweep of the tarmac with the binoculars.

"I see a refueling tanker parked over there. I'm going for it. When I'm there, I'll signal for you to follow."

"No need to signal, just turn on the earphone volume. I've got the jammer for the camera and our audio."

Hunched behind the tanker wheels, the pair had a clear view of activity in front of Hanger No. 4, watching two guards pacing nervously, with rifles. Seconds later, a third ran out from the hanger to a rusted brown cube van and sped across the pavement before coming to a sudden halt.

"They've taken Christophe hostage," Emily gasped. "I see a man shoving him with the butt of a rifle."

"What about Daniel?"

Emily closed her eyes. "There's no sign of him."

Joseph's binoculars focused on a military TJ jeep parked at a stack of loading crates. A body was tied and slumped in the boot. He watched a few seconds more before reporting it to Emily.

"It's okay—one of the guards was taken out by Daniel. He's changed into the insurgent's clothing . . . now walking boldly toward the others with a pilot's helmet under his arm and a parachute on his back."

When the sun momentarily hit the binocular lenses, Daniel stopped and made a hand signal back, that Joseph would easily interpret 'as cover me from this side, I'm going straight in'.

"He's brash and cocky walking into the middle of mayhem to rescue Christophe, yet expecting not to get himself killed," Emily moaned.

"Good news, at last," she said as she scanned the property. "Alexandre is here with the other agent from this morning. They're parking in the lane behind the BMW. More backup for Daniel."

"And for us," Joseph said. In his earpiece, he heard Daniel bark in Arabic at the man pointing the rifle at Christophe.

"He still surprises me, Emily. Did you know he spoke this language?"

Still holding binoculars, Daniel motioned with his other hand. Joseph said, "Stay low and we'll run closer, a few yards at a time, then down to the grass."

When they stopped to focus again, Emily discerned the outline of a lumbering man in the distance with an assault rifle.

"Look. The man walking from the hanger—that's Waldo."

"Pilot! Prepare the Apache," Waldo demanded.

Emily said, "He doesn't recognize Daniel from their encounter in the tunnels."

Inside the hanger, two combat helicopters waited under tarps, both four blade choppers with twin turbo, shaft tail wheels, and with missile carriers loaded in the undercarriage.

Daniel's black baseball cap had a micro cam in the visor and what he saw was being downloaded in real time at Interpol headquarters.

The outside guards were spaced apart, enabling Joseph and Emily to disable them without notice, then duct tape and lug them to a covered luggage cart.

As two mechanics attended to the repairs of the Apaches, Waldo focused on Christophe, lying on the floor of the hangar.

He looked up to the pilot. "Have you completed your checklist, Monsieur?"

"A few more minutes," Daniel replied in like dialect.

Christophe had given no trouble to the insurgents up to now, assured that the backup team could surprise them at any time. Recognizing Daniel, his confidence was bolstered. Digging in his feet, he resisted the next shove by the insurgent.

Inflamed, the guard yelled, "Move or I shoot!"

Christophe rolled back in a combat tumble against the guard's feet, leaving him off balance and vulnerable. Daniel didn't make a move, but the guard was shot from behind and felled to the floor. The two mechanics took shelter behind a metal cabinet, leaving Daniel standing behind Waldo.

"Fernando Valois, how did you get out of prison again?"

Waldo froze, feeling Daniel's gun in his rib. "And who is your contact on the inside that allows you to meddle in terrorism?"

Valois squirmed to get his revolver out, and now both men held guns at each other, within arm's length.

With Emily behind, Joseph advanced to the hangar door, and he lifted his revolver to fire if it came to it. He stepped closer. "Put your gun down, Valois!"

Waldo cursed. "So you think I am outnumbered, Monsieur Harkness?" An evil sneer took control of his lips.

Joseph called to Daniel, "Take care of this!"

He turned back expecting Emily, but there was no sign of her. "Em! Emily!"

Waldo laughed mockingly.

The tarmac was bare, and at the gravel lane where they had parked the BMW, both the car and the cable van were speeding away, with Emily's face pressed against the back passenger window of the car.

Twenty-three

Emily's senses were on alert, listening to road sounds, passing vehicles, the radio and anything to distract her, hoping to stumble on any tidbit to help in her escape.

When the BMW pulled into the alley in Montparnasse, she was blindfolded, and her mouth taped. Neither abductor spoke to her but boasted to each other in a foreign language. Nearby was another vehicle, and she recognized the feel of the door as they tossed her in.

I'm in the cable van.

Her fingers ran along the floor for her bearings and a chance of an escape tool. Instead, she felt the dead weight of someone beside her.

It has to be Alexandre. He still has some body heat—he must be unconscious. That's a good sign. They are not murderers.

Calculating that about twenty minutes had passed since she was taken, she visualized a layout of the city map and where she could be.

I hear a street sweeper but no vehicles; must be residential. From street cameras and sensors, there will be video footage when we pass major intersections. Surely Leo will search for the cable van.

After a bumpy ride, she was dragged down six concrete steps to a basement, into an odor of dampness and smoked meat. Still blindfolded, she was pulled to another room and shoved onto a cot.

A man tugged to remove her hood, and she turned her head to balk. Opening her eyes, she was face to face with Aziz.

This is not a good sign. They know I can recognize them. That makes me highly disposable.

"You make noise again and I tape you up. Nod if you agree." Aziz looked into her blue eyes and felt a pang of sympathy for this helpless young woman.

"Water," Aziz said, and gestured to a basin on the nightstand, then left her alone in the room. The futon bed had wooden slats, with a blanket at the end.

Not much here for comfort.

Next to the metal basin was a hand towel, but the room had nothing else, with no windows or way out other than the door.

The deadbolt latched, then the key rotated in the lock. Her memory took her to the black tower near Rouen, where she'd been held captive and in spite of the odds, had found a way out.

Her handbag and cell had been taken away, but she knew her phone signal could be active. In her pockets, she found two hairpins, a hair elastic, two euros, lipstick, a crumpled metro ticket, her house key, and earphone.

Earphone! I wonder if it works from here!

Leo texted Daniel that he'd followed the hangar events live. "Head back to the office. We recorded all of it—Waldo's takedown and Emily's disappearance.

He then called Joseph. "Don't go to the safe house. You and Emily have been compromised. The burner phones should have protected you from being traced, but Didier's men stole Mrs. Bitteridge's purse and cell phone at the detective agency."

In an instant of silence, Joseph remembered his call with Madge two days before to let her know they were safe.

"I wasn't thinking. I should have used the jammer," he said, his confession sorrowful and guilt-ridden.

"What's done is done. Come in with Daniel. Minutes ago, I received a call from the kidnappers. We need to talk urgently."

The Interpol office was a whirl of activity, pulling security footage from the helipad and at points on the Paris ring road.

"Hello, Joseph. We found the BMW at a back alley in Montparnasse, and a tow truck and forensic unit are on the way. Emily was not there. Wait, there's something else."

Leo read a trailer of progress notes running across the bottom of his monitor. "Traffic cameras sighted the cable van in the northeastern sector!"

"Whatever it takes, Leo. Get her back!"

"Joseph, you have every right to be angry. We are pulling all available units to find her." Joseph paced beside the desk, then sat to watch Leo's monitor with him.

"You know we'll find her," Daniel added.

"You two take a break," Leo said. "Be back at four, as the kidnappers will call then with a ransom demand."

"No," Joseph said. "I need to be here to see what's going on."

Daniel gestured, "Joseph, let's go downstairs for a coffee. Leo will call us back when he hears anything."

"You're right. She's resourceful, and we've always got her back safe."

The words sounded hollow but gave him hope.

At 3:30 p.m. Joseph and Daniel returned to Leo's office to await the kidnapper's call.

"Gentlemen, we've traced the BMW rental to a depot in Molenbeek. It left three days ago, and the video from the rental office shows two men. The signature is illegible, but we have confirmed that the driver is Aziz Ibrahim from the watch-list. He has connections to the terrorist cell operating in Paris and from Le Bourget. There's an all-points bulletin to find him.

"Daniel, go back to the retrieval site for the van and see if you find anything my men have missed."

Leo fumbled for words for Joseph. "I won't color coat anything. Online chatter says that Didier's group is responsible for taking Emily. They are aware of our investigations and noticed us following their footsteps."

A technician burst past and whispered to Leo, who looked up at Joseph. "Good news. We have a static signal that my security team believes to be from Emily's earphone."

"Where?"

"They're working on it."

Daniel checked his watch. "Half an hour before they call."

The minutes crept by with awkward interruptions, then a tap on the office window of an incoming call for Leo.

"Bonjour. This is Leo Desjardins, who am I speaking to?" He switched on the speaker button.

"It's not important who I am—we have Emily Harkness."

"Can I speak with her? Is she unharmed?"

"Don't play any stalling tactics. I'll ask the questions and you answer."

"We need confirmation that Ms. Harkness is alive and well. That's not negotiable."

"A photo will be delivered to you within the hour. I'll call back then to give you our demands."

"No. Tell us your demands so we can make preparations for an exchange."

"Is the husband there too?"

"Yes, he is listening."

"We uncovered a tantalizing detail about you and your wife, Monsieur Harkness. We did a little of our own detective work." Didier dallied the ambiguity of his words. "You don't want an international incident, do you?"

The suggestion floored Joseph.

Our aliases are secure, Leo assured us.

In the scheme of things, it seemed trivial without Emily. Glancing at Leo, it was agreed not to challenge this new threat.

"Please don't hurt her. Take me in trade," he begged.

"No. We toyed with the idea of taking you, but a woman gathers more concern and sympathy than a wayward detective. Americans are repulsed by the thought of a woman being tortured in a foreign country."

"Please, I beg you not to hurt her."

"Enough, Mr. Harkness. Now, Monsieur Desjardins, we have five demands. I will provide each to you in sequence and we'll see how you cooperate. The first is that you order all your men and local authorities out of the tunnels. We will watch and have ways to detect your presence, ways that you have not discovered. You are foolish to assume we don't have contacts within your system."

Leo was biting his tongue, not to say. "Like Stephen Cahill in our Defense department!" Instead, he said. "There are many people involved. I need half an hour to make some phone calls. What's next?"

"You do that first then I'll tell you more." The receiver was disconnected, and Leo summoned his assistant.

"Were you able to trace that?"

"They used a jammer. Looks like the one you gave to Ms. Harkness."

"Keep working on it then." He motioned to come closer, and whispered, "Get me a report on the movements of Cahill."

At the kitchen table of a farmhouse near Goussainville, west of Charles de Gaulle airport, Yousiff Didier sipped on his sweet Moroccan tea and devoured a goat tagine with vegetables and couscous. With a piece of flatbread, he wiped the plate clean and pulled toward him a bowl of stuffed dates and sweet purple grapes.

"We have reason to celebrate! We have taken a hostage— an American no less." Didier waited for the women to leave the room, then addressed the five other radicals.

"Bekir, go to Aziz and get a photograph of the woman holding today's issue of Le Monde. I need proof of life."

Aziz and another man were playing cards upstairs when Bekir knocked at the door of the basement hideout. He was carrying a newspaper, take-out green tea and a bag of food from a burger joint.

Aziz peered through a peephole. "Welcome, comrade. You bring news and food."

"Didier needs proof of her life for Interpol, and I must deliver a photograph within the hour."

"She is of no value, Bekir. Women are but chattels to their husbands in Syria and Morocco. If you choose to keep her, send her to Morocco and you'll get livestock in trade."

"Yes, Isabella cost me two cows," Bekir sneered, leaking his hatred toward women.

"And now you have no wife and no cows," Aziz joked.

"This Harkness woman deserves whatever she gets for being an accomplice to her husband when they interfered with the transfer of our blueprint."

"Yes, Bekir. If they had minded their business, we would not be under the thumb of the authorities. Our leaders will seek tribulation from the French and all Christians when the ultimate bombing takes places under the very feet of France."

"Have you talked to the hostage since this morning?"

"No. She has water but I have nothing to feed her."

"Unlock the door."

Emily overheard parts of the conversation, but her spirit was unwavering, with hope there might also be progress.

"What is it that you want? You are interfering with my privacy."

Bekir scoffed, "You're nothing to us. The Interpol boss wants a photograph of you with today's newspaper to prove you are still alive." She paced her breathing slowly to present a calm superior attitude to Bekir.

Angered at her demeanor, he yanked her to the middle of the room to hold the paper. She held her elbows high, hoping Joseph would know it meant planes from Charles de Gaulle. In the background was the metro ticket, pinned to the wall, with words in faint lipstick: old commune, church bells. She tilted her head as Bekir snapped the photo on his cell.

As he left, she observed shelving and waxed wooden crates in the outer room. She listened for the deadbolt to fall into place, but this time there wasn't a key lock after it.

Footsteps of two men ascended the stairs, then she heard Bekir leave for his rendezvous with Didier.

The smoked meat smell—it's a butcher shop or grocery store. When Joseph and I went to the Le Bourget airfield, we passed a commune called Goussainville, near the Station of Louvres, a transit hub to the airport. The town had old deserted buildings and castle remnants, with crumbling chimneys and broken stone fences.

She made another attempt with the earphone.

"Calling Leo! Emily here at Goussainville. Old butcher or grocery basement. Send help!"

She repeated it clearly and slowly but heard only static gaps in return. She put her ear to the door, but there was no sound of movement above.

Twenty-four

Emily did her best to stay prepared and maintain strength, with squats, sit-ups and knee presses. Scratching lines at the door frame, she accounted for the hours of the first three days she was held in the basement.

The image of Emily with the newspaper was sent by an untraceable email account to the Interpol offices precisely at five o'clock and was immediately dissected for clues.

Her lipstick note created a slight cheer of optimism for Joseph, and he interpreted it for Leo. "Old commune with church bells. Her hands are up like she means to flap her arms. Got it—airport."

Leo shook his head. *Two peas in a pod.*

Minutes later, Leo's phone rang, with a scrambled call using a voice modifier.

"Monsieur Desjardins, we completed our part of the bargain, now how do I have the assurance that you kept yours? We have eyes on the tunnel access points. Motion sensors are set and we will detect anything than moves larger than a rat."

He must be using Cahill as the monitor. Time to cut the ties.

Leo replied, "I've instructed government security, police and Interpol in Paris to cease and desist activity in the tunnels from Montmartre to Denfert-Rochereau for the next twenty-four hours."

"Twenty-four hours? You are reckless to determine that."

"It's a step only. I trust we can complete our terms as soon as possible to effect the release of Emily Harkness. But there's another issue now—we have disturbing news regarding the missing agent we refer to as Alexandre."

Didier sounded confused. "Explain!"

"He was found a short distance from the cable van, face down in a ditch filled with water. What do you think I'm saying?"

Didier's voice trembled. "That's his own fault. He made a run for it. If he can't stay on his own feet, that's not on us. He was alive when we last saw him."

"Circumstances tell us a different story," Leo replied. "You said you have five demands. What is the second?"

"We require the release of five insurgents from Syria and Morocco that you have held since the massacre in November. We will send photos and names by email. At twelve midnight, the five men will walk into the arrival level of Gare du Nord, unaccompanied."

"I can't answer that as I don't know who they are or where they are held. It will be impossible to commute murder charges. I would, however, agree to release five insurgents held in Molenbeek assuming I get agreement from Brussels. They can be flown here under guard for your midnight deadline."

The line went dead.

Leo looked up at Joseph and Daniel. "He's playing the game, he'll call back in a few minutes."

Right on cue, it rang.

"Five insurgents—we've sent you the list. At the same time, you will deliver ten million euros in both cash and gold."

"You ask the impossible. Interpol isn't a bank, and we don't have access to any funding like you suggest."

"Perhaps you should call the Prime Minister . . . surely he would find the funds if it were his daughter. I believe she attends Neuchatel."

Leo sighed in frustration. "I'll make some calls. Call in two hours and I'll let you know if I've have made progress."

"Five o'clock."

Alexandre was shielded under a trench coat and helped into a briefing room on the fourth floor. A nurse was applying dressings to his wounds when Leo walked in with Joseph.

"Alexandre, it's good to see you looking so well. We've insinuated to Emily's hostage takers that you perished at their hands. It gives us a wild card."

"Is she alright? What can you tell me?" Joseph asked.

"The rogue jumped into the van outside the safe house and clocked me good. I woke up parked by the heliport and they stuck me with a needle to put me out again. I remember Emily telling me to hang in, then she was gone. I struggled out of the van and tried to make a run. One fellow chased me, but I tripped over a large tree root and knocked myself out."

He was sipping on a glass of water when Daniel burst in.

"Leo! Joseph! We have bits of a message from Emily's earphone. I'm certain she's in Goussainville. It's close enough to Charles de Gaulle that she would hear aircraft overhead and the Church of Saint-Pierre Saint-Paul still has its bells. It only tolls on Sunday morning though."

"Daniel, get a chopper for us for an aerial of the commune."

"If I can't get one from Interpol, I can get an Apache."

Leo wasn't humored. "Regular resources please, so we don't alert the thugs."

"There's also a company with Paris helicopter tours. It's close and might be faster to commandeer a flight."

"Whatever you do is fine if it's quick. We'll wait on the roof in half an hour, Daniel."

Emily decided an offensive position could give her an upper hand, and leaned against the door to draw attention.

"Hello, I need to talk to you," she shouted.

She counted the steps as Aziz came down from upstairs.

He's turned at the landing which must be the front door, then six more stairs, and another five steps in the basement to my door.

"What's the trouble?" Emily listened for the deadbolt to release.

"First, I'm hungry. It's cruel to let your hostage starve. Something please, even a bowl of soup and some crackers."

Aziz hadn't thought of feeding her and reacted as she hoped.

"Of course, Madame. I'll find something to bring you."

When he left, she scratched the number of on the top of the door frame, then eyed the hinges on the back of the door.

I hope he brings utensils too. I'm going to start a collection of escape tools. Resourceful ones.

She laughed at the memory of her words on the evening of Leo's introduction.

Leo, I'm trusting you!

Ten minutes later, Aziz set the tray on the floor outside the door. He unlocked it and placed the soup and saltines on the nightstand. The door was wide open and Emily studied the outer room and the lower hand railing for the stairs.

She inched forward, but Aziz was alert and stepped in front of her, preparing to pull his revolver from his belt.

"Don't think of escaping, Madame. Move to the corner."

She toyed with a surprise karate chop, but relented, seeing the revolver. When she relaxed her body, Aziz backed down.

"What should I call you?" Emily asked.

"No need to know my name, but you can call me Bob for the time being."

They both had a chuckle over the sound of his new name.

"Alright, Bob, thanks for the soup."

Emily drank the bland soup from the cup and devoured the stale crackers.

It's important to keep up my energy.

Joseph had a flashback to Emily's escape from the Black Tower in Rouen. He briefly recapped the scenario to Leo, of her return to Paris to get Toby, the bloodhound, who then tracked him down by his scent.

"Excellent idea, Joseph . . . a canine unit. They use them at the airports," Leo replied. "Do you have one of Emily's scarves or something with her scent?"

Joseph turned to Alexandre. "Was anything left in the van?"

Alexandre thought carefully. "Nothing today, but when I took her to St. Louis island, she left a sweater behind."

Leo accessed the intercom. "There's a woman's sweater in the cable van. I need it pronto."

"Yes, Sir. Everything from the van has been bagged and sent as evidence to the basement. I'll have it delivered to your office right away."

Belgium was reluctant, but Leo's superiors were persuasive about the collection of the five named prisoners, to be transferred to Gare du Nord that night.

But the arrangement of the ten million euro ransom from the Government of France was not so easy, despite high levels of Interpol requests that bared the potential risk to the country.

"Sorry, Director, but since the kidnappings in Afghanistan, France's position in paying ransom has been opposed by parliament, like the policies in Britain and the USA. The fact that Ms. Harkness is both a French and American citizen makes no difference. If we did it once, they would continue to kidnap more often. Where would the world be in ten years?"

"I'm not interested in ten years. We have a young woman tonight that has given much to save the people of Paris. Have you been briefed on the sensitivity of this situation?"

The bureaucrat was cautious with his words, "I'm unable to confirm what I know."

"Of course," the Director replied. "I hear in your voice that you don't know, and that bodes well for the level of security in our intelligence units."

The Interpol commander ended the call quickly.

Leo was in his office, about to leave to meet the chopper on the roof when a call flashed on his display—Gilbert Bernard.

I'm too busy for Bernard right now!

Almost out the door, he had a change of heart.

"What is it Gilbert? We are in a crisis."

"That's what I'm calling about. I heard through secure channels that the kidnappers asked for a large ransom. I know you'll have a hard time coming up with that."

Leo was becoming overly anxious and a bit short-tempered. "I'm trying to outrun the clock, Gilbert!"

"I have access to six million euros. I'll put it up for Emily."

"Gilbert! How and where would you get that kind of money?"

"I invested well and performed for a significant fee. Don't ask more, just take the money. I can have it to you in an hour."

Leo was stunned and perplexed.

"God bless you, Gilbert! I didn't know what to say to her husband. It's not looking good right now. You have no idea the relief this will be."

"Did they specify denominations?"

"Not exactly, they said a combination of cash and gold, if that makes any difference to you."

"I'll see you at your office. Send a car to meet me outside the Assurance Lloyds de Londres on Rue Lamennais."

An armored car waited for him curbside at the bank. Emanating confidence, Bernard strode inside, with a wooden violin case under his arm. At the foyer, he was greeted by a distinguished man in a bespoke black suit, drawing attention both for his fine attire and receding long white hair that was tied at the back of his neck.

"We can settle the transaction in the Manager's office."

Gilbert gestured to a reception officer, who led them to a private office with a security guard on both sides of the door."

The bidder in the black suit was accompanied by a Lloyd's appraiser who would seal the offer between Bernard and the buyer, transferring the 1697 Molitar Stradivarius, once owned by Napoleon Bonaparte, to the Italian.

"Your Stradivarius, Monsieur VanHolt. This is of supreme craftsmanship and rarest quality. Just two years ago a violin by the master Antonio Stradivari sold at Sotheby's for $16 million. We will register this with the Stradivarius organization as they keep track of the location of the last 600 violins in existence."

"Thank you, I will treasure this in my personal collection. I have longed for this day. Six million euros are easier for me to part with, than for you to give up an incredible instrument."

The banker placed a briefcase full of currency on the desk and the documents were again signed before Bernard departed.

Gilbert was content with the conclusion of the transaction and brushed off a moment of separation from his beloved violin.

Money has no real value, but the life of a friend is immeasurable.

Twenty-five

Daniel returned to Leo's office in the copter, ready to pilot Joseph and Leo to Goussainville Vieux Pays. "I'm sorry boys, you'll need to go ahead without me. I have too much to do before the five o'clock deadline."

"You can watch. I've secured a high-resolution camera to the undercarriage, and thermal detection that can isolate buildings that are occupied. Monitor what we see as we go, Leo."

"The thermal imaging cameras are better than the naked eye. A recent archaeology expedition even deciphered activity and layers below ground level."

As they left, he phoned the Department of Defense.

"Blake, are you certain the data Cahill receives is only what we discussed?"

"Absolutely. His monitor access tells him there's no current Interpol activity in the tunnels and that our tracking was halted."

"Perfect way to send fake updates to the insurgents," Leo said. "He's a useful espionage deviant without his knowledge."

"From the data your Ms. Church provided, we can intercept their codes to take control of the master drone, once it enters airspace over Paris. They will be disabled like a lame duck on our cue."

"And they won't detect anything?"

"There's no way they would know."

On the roof, Daniel took the pilot's seat, and the helicopter lifted up over the city, heading north to Goussainville Vieux Pays.

Soon they were lofting over heavily treed farms and decrepit vineyards that were abandoned when Charles de Gaulle airport was built forty years before, forcing residents out of the quaint village.

From the air, the Main Street looked eerily abandoned, almost ghostly. They swooped low over the village to get their bearings, passing over the rooftop of the Au Paradis Café, once the cornerstone of a vibrant town.

Many houses were decayed, overgrown with weeds, and boarded up or secured with metal grates from curious looters. At the cathedral of Saint Pierre and Saint Paul, fields of wildflowers had created a picturesque natural tranquility.

"Some cottages are obviously occupied, by clothes flapping on the backyard line. If you wanted to escape the pace of the city, this would be paradise," Joseph said.

Lowering over a small commercial building, Daniel pointed out a parked vehicle.

"That shop is occupied as the thermal detection shows definite shapes. Considering how isolated the town is, my bet is that it is Emily, and this is the butcher shop."

"Land in the Church courtyard, Daniel. We can approach it on foot from there."

"I understand your urgency about Emily, but the insurgents don't value lives. The house could be booby-trapped or under remote surveillance. We can't risk danger to Emily."

Leo was listening from his office.

"Daniel is right. Come back in, and lead a ground crew to enter the building, with a pair of scent hounds and a backup force. You've done the task you were sent to do. Our highest priority is Emily's safety."

Daniel's eyes widened as he looked at a barn on the ground. "Leo, do you see this? 'C1' is painted on the roof and number 17."

"I see, Daniel. We'll dispatch a ground crew with caution. That could be the deadly chlorine gas intended for Paris the night of the concert. '17' is the atomic value. Glad you sighted that; it narrows our search considerably."

Joseph didn't respond but was in thought as the Apache rose to turn back to central Paris. Daniel's vision was abruptly struck by a laser beam, and he shielded his eyes from the red stream.

"What's that, Joseph?"

"It's from a pickup truck near the church. It's black like the ones at the airfield. The man's arm is pointing a remote control toward us. Watch out!"

"An eagle drone is hurtling toward us," Daniel shouted and lifted the copter straight up. "It's about two hundred feet away and coming fast."

"It's armed. Can we shoot it down?"

"This chopper isn't loaded with firepower."

Daniel jerked it in and out of its flight path to avoid the line of fire. "There's a rifle behind the seat. Take a shot out your side window."

Joseph had a visual on the ground location, where two men stood watching the sky.

"You devil!"

Joseph aimed and fired, not at the drone but at the man with the remote. "It's easier to shoot a stationary target than the drone."

Leveling six rounds into the courtyard, he forced the men to take cover in the truck.

Didier was livid at the news of the helicopter over the kidnapper's roost and that one of his men was struck by a bullet in the arm and taken to the hospital.

"Bekir! Has the motorcoach left Brussels yet?"

"Sayed and Munir went there this morning. We hired a Setra 511 coach from Mowbray to bring the Molenbeek group. The contract says the passengers are scholars and university students on a study trip. Each was vetted for many months, and all are Islamic radicals between sixteen and forty years, recruited in Syria, Turkey, and North Africa."

"When do they travel?"

"The bus will leave the Marché du Midi at the South Railway depot at noon and arrive at Paris Gare du Nord this evening."

"That works well with our rendezvous plan for the ransom at midnight."

Leo watched the phone on his desk as he waited for the five o'clock call from the kidnappers. Gilbert Bernard had joined him in the office and was sipping a tea when it rang.

"Hello, Leo Desjardins here."

"Monsieur Desjardins, I trust you have been successful in obtaining our ransom."

"Sir, we have done our best and can only offer you six million euros in unmarked cash, received from Lloyd's Bank."

"Six million? But we asked for ten."

"I understood your request, but you must be aware that government resources do not participate in ransom for a hostage—it's not acceptable internationally. Six million is still a large sum. Certainly, you can still do whatever it is that the money is for. You take the six million, or we begin retaliatory measures to retrieve Ms. Harkness."

"Don't threaten me, Monsieur Desjardins. That's unwise."

"The ball is in your court," Leo challenged.

"What assurances do you offer for the safety of my men at Gare du Nord, if we decide to go ahead with the meeting?"

"We live in a world with eyes and ears everywhere. How can I control that? I have no influence over the internet or your own leaks."

"For insurance, we will bring Ms. Harkness at midnight. She will be placed in a neutral location, strapped to a bomb. If she's approached, it will go off."

The kidnapper waited for Leo's reaction but hearing none he continued. "Twelve hours after midnight, I will give you the code to disable the bomb—only if you have complied by evacuating the tunnels, releasing my prisoners, and paying with untainted money."

"No. At midnight tonight, we get Ms. Harkness without a bomb. That is my final deal."

"Non, non. We have your precious cargo and it will be on our terms."

The kidnapper abruptly ended the call and Gilbert Bernard was speechless observing it.

As soon as the Apache touched down, Leo summoned Daniel and Joseph to his office.

"You are certain it is the kidnappers' hideout?"

"Ninety-nine percent," Joseph replied.

"It's after five now, and you have to retrieve her before ten. Once she's moved, our chances diminish for a safe recovery. Not only is Emily's life at stake, but the entire scheme to collapse Paris hangs on your success."

"We'll get her out," Daniel said. "Give us eight men, vehicles and security equipment." He scratched a list for Leo.

Joseph's fists were clenched. "No matter what it takes, we will get her out, Leo."

Thirty minutes later, the entourage headed north: two SWAT vans armed with state of the art espionage devices and equipment, a canine unit SUV, plus a nondescript black sedan lead vehicle.

Aziz was caught up with a TV show on the upper level when Joseph and Daniel approached the butcher shop.

Checking the perimeter, they found the back door barricaded with boards and leaving the front door as the only access. The two windows facing Main Street were covered with metal grates over plywood.

Joseph tugged at a window grate causing the rusted bolts to yield. Reacting quickly, the detectives caught the falling scraps to avoid a clatter to the sidewalk. The plywood sheeting felt weak to the hand from years of exposure to the elements without glass windows for protection. Joseph silently bore a small hole with a manual pin punch to see inside.

Lounging on a lazy boy in the living room was a young Middle Eastern man, holding a can of beer. Shelving, debris, and boxes littered the floor.

"The man is alone," Joseph said.

Left of the door was a staircase into the basement, but Joseph focused directly ahead on a door with a deadbolt.

The cement and stone building was wedged between others of the same vintage, with no side alley access. He signaled for a team to cover the backyard, and motioned for two others to back them up from Main Street.

Daniel whispered. "Two choices. We could use a blow horn and demand that he surrender. In that scenario, his only chance of escape would be to use Emily as a human shield. These insurgents would rather die for their cause than be arrested."

"And what's the second method? I hope it's better," Joseph quipped.

"With a battering ram, we'll plow down the front door, and I'll take the upstairs man by surprise. Then you get Emily from the basement."

Consulting with the SWAT commander, they prepared a heavy beam for a raid through the front. Four men swung the heavy lumber, splintering the door on the second swing.

Aziz was stunned and on his feet, yelling in Arabic. Before he could get to reach his revolver on the television, he was rushed by black uniforms. Ranting and yelling, he was subdued by Daniel, who yanked his arms behind him and clamped on handcuffs.

Joseph bounded down to the hostage room coming to an abrupt halt in disbelief. The door was slightly ajar, with no sign of Emily.

We're too late, she's been moved. They must have gotten skittish when we fired from the chopper.

Twenty-six

Police and Interpol personnel converged in the 10th arrondissement to circle the Gare du Nord Metro. All buildings within visual range had rooftop gunmen watching through telescopic lenses for anything that moved. In the parking lot, the bomb squad technicians walked vehicle to vehicle, sweeping for incendiary devices.

Over the public address, passengers were asked to exit the terminal, announcing that trains were temporarily suspended due to an impending security threat. At the exits, plainclothes police and tactical snipers were in a position to monitor anyone hesitating.

Daniel and Joseph arrived back at Leo's office disheartened that Emily had been moved. Leo and Gilbert listened to the raid. "Don't worry, Joseph, we'll have her back tonight."

Daniel, Joseph, and Gilbert rode with Leo from the downtown Interpol office to the train depot an hour before the scheduled ransom drop.

A seasoned kidnapping negotiator suggested that Leo should pad the briefcase cash with counterfeit or newspaper bundles instead of the full €6 million that Bernard provided. Leo vetoed it, with support from his friend Gilbert Bernard.

"We must build the trust of the kidnappers. These are smart people if they're clever enough to plot a takedown of our great city with a few musical notes."

Gilbert was firm on it. "I put up the ransom, fully expecting I may never see any of it again. Leo has my confidence."

"Alright, the cash goes as it is. Let's proceed. Are you tuned in to my instructions, Monsieur Desjardins?" the negotiator asked.

"I'll be able to hear you, but you mustn't interfere with my command of my agents."

Two combat vehicles followed Leo, carrying the five criminals to be released. Guards wore body armor and carried assault weapons as they marched the five men into the terminal.

"Lie on the floor, everyone. Hands behind your head," the SWAT commander shouted at the confused men. Disheveled and tired, the sneering convicts muttered in Arabic of their looming victory.

"You're being treated better than how your leader handled my agents," Leo mocked.

Just like Alexandre's mouth had been taped, he ordered the offenders' mouths sealed and lined them on their bellies on the cold cement floor of the platform.

By 11:45 p.m., the train terminal was ghostly quiet.

"It doesn't mean there's no one here," Leo said. In every alcove and under the ticket booths, tactical agents were posted to react to any sound or if anything moved.

Leo and Joseph took up a vantage point on the mezzanine level, and Daniel remained outside with police to survey the streets and walkways.

Didier's men will surely be arriving by car or truck.

By the stroke of midnight, nothing had changed. Ten seconds later, the roar of a lone train engine emerged on the track reserved for the Lyon train of the French National Railroad.

The engine ground forward into the terminal.

Joseph had a clear view of the engineer that was manually operating the cab. Behind him, Emily came into sight, with her mouth taped and hands at her back.

Bekir stood in the middle, staunch and ready for battle. Two men in dark clothing and balaclavas were further back with rifles pointed out the windows. Showing they would relish a battle, their cheeks were streaked with black war paint, and they wore bullet-proof vests.

On earphones, Leo cautioned his men, "Hold positions until we see what they're going to do."

Emily's eyes exposed her fear as she searched for Joseph.

The brakes seized and a sliding door opened, followed by a sigh of pressure from the hydraulics.

Bekir called out, "Monsieur Desjardins, step forward."

Leo acknowledged his position from an upper level of the terminal. "I am coming."

He raised the briefcase over his head in a gesture of compliance.

"Alone. No one else with you."

"My men understand."

In a foreign language, Bekir ordered the five prisoners to stand and board the waiting carriage, one at a time.

He called each one by name and checked with his accomplice for a visual match of the names and faces to their records, then removed the tapes from their mouths.

Leo continued to the platform, then stopped. Joseph was positioned out of sight, with his rifle targeted at Bekir's head.

"No money until you give us Ms. Harkness."

"That was not the term of my leader," Bekir challenged.

Another man stepped forward using Emily as a shield and took her to the nearest bench.

"Sit," he commanded and laughed. "Like a dog."

A suicide bomb had been attached to her chest, and she was bound to the bench rails. They watched as an accomplice installed a series of wires and laser dimensions to isolate her.

Bekir pointed to an invisible location on the floor fifteen feet in front of him. "Bring the suitcase here."

Leo objected, "Take one of my men in place of Ms. Harkness."

Gilbert Bernard moved to center stage. "I volunteer to become a hostage."

Leo was surprised by Gilbert's impromptu move but waited for the response.

"No exchange! Your woman will not be harmed if you continue to follow instructions. My leader will contact you with the code to abort the bomb when he is satisfied the money is genuine and you meet his final instructions. She will remain here on this bench until noon tomorrow. When I leave, I will set the timer. Either you receive the code, or if we are not satisfied, your hostage will die by your own hand."

Joseph was outraged but knew it was imperative to remain calm.

"Furthermore, if anyone comes within twenty feet, they will activate a motion sensor to trigger it."

An accomplice collected the case, and Bekir checked to see that the prisoners were onboard, then backed into the waiting train car. For effect, he held his watch high and set the timer.

The train roared as it backed out from the platform, leaving a stunned audience of policemen.

The weight of the world hung over Leo Desjardins as he looked over at Emily. He placed his hand over his heart and mouthed the words, "I'm sorry."

Gilbert Bernard crouched over his knees with his hands covering his face, feeling a failure after his efforts of many years for the cause of justice and peace.

Joseph went immediately to the rim of the motion sensor boundary. "Em, are you alright?"

Aware of the motion sensor, she was afraid to move, and with her mouth taped, she could only blink her eyes in acknowledgment.

"Honey, don't worry. We'll get you out of this. This morning we were so close. We found the house in Goussainville and organized a raid, but were too late, as they had moved you." Joseph's voice cracked with emotion. "Love you, Babe."

Leo's negotiator came close and asked to speak with Emily.

"Yes, but you see she can't talk."

Ignoring Leo's sarcasm, he proceeded. "Although your hands are tied, we can see your fingers. I have some questions. Please answer by pointing your index finger if the reply is positive, and your first two digits if it's negative."

Emily pointed her index finger.

"Did you watch them prepare the suicide vest?"

A series of mundane questions followed, allowing the negotiator to deduce the bomb was made by amateurs.

"Daniel, we have two big problems," Leo said, "a noon deadline tomorrow for Emily, and also tomorrow is April 12th, the day of reckoning for Paris.

"You agreed to hold back officers from the tunnels."

"Yes, but I agreed to twenty-four hours, and by my clock that has expired. I don't expect another phone call from the kidnappers. This is simply a ruse to keep us from the main event at the Luxembourg Gardens. Our tunnel activity won't be visible to the insurgents—we're supplying false images."

"What if there's a slip-up? A miscalculation."

"Joseph, we have an open door to the tunnels but we won't take foolish risks."

"We can't take that chance, Leo."

"Here's the bomb demolition crew . . . perhaps we won't need to."

Leo explained the kidnappers' instructions, and yellow tape was placed to mark the twenty-foot perimeter for motion detection.

Calls flooded his phone from the Ministry of Foreign Affairs, the Department of Defense, the CIA's team in Paris, and the chief of Interpol in Lyon. Each wanted instant updates and coordinates of the kidnappers.

"Gilbert, this is getting out of hand. I'd like you to field these security calls so I can concentrate on Emily and the impending catastrophe."

"Absolutely, Leo. I'm honored to serve you again."

Daniel stood fifty feet back, making mental notes and measurements. Years before, in training to evacuate Iranian hostages, he was up against impossible odds and found a way through it. The complete scenario was replaying in his mind.

The atrium ceilings and the cooing of doves and pigeons from the rafters brought the idea, and he looked back up. The train station was protected by a glass ceiling and surrounding windows to bring in natural light during daylight hours.

"Glass reflects infrared beams," he muttered, imagining aerobatics swinging from the highest beams with bungee cords without ever touching the ground.

Emily's bench was centered on a peninsula island, and he noted a light standard with large glass globes on both sides of her, with parallel train platforms.

"I've got it, Leo!"

Leo rushed back. "What do you have, Daniel?"

"Replay the hostage-takers words if you like. The motion sensor's range was within twenty feet of Emily, correct?"

"Yes, he said that."

"Once, in the field, I was in a unit to evacuate an American diplomat in the Middle East that was facing certain death by a firing squad. We completed the operation successfully, and we can do it here too.

"The thought occurred to me when you and I were watching from the Mezzanine, as the train came in. I respect that the bomb is an authentic suicide vest. But today I watched them set the motion detector. It's a twenty feet perimeter . . . at ground level.

"So we'll come down from the ceiling like my unit did. I'll need scaffolding and tension wires secured from each side of the Mezzanine. Look up at those hooks and grappling lines like window cleaners use. We can anchor there."

Joseph had moved in to hear the aerial plan. "I'm good with it, Leo. I understand how this would work and it gives us a fighting chance."

Emily watched the discussion and gave a light groan for attention, curious about their next step. It had been many hours since she'd had a drink of water or even a shift of her body weight.

Joseph reassured her.

"We'll rescue you from above. I know we can do this. Do you trust me, Em?"

Her index finger gave her agreement.

Twenty-seven

Didier and his Syrian counterpart were jubilant about the outcome of the mission at Gare du Nord. At a safe house, the funds were recounted to ensure the six million euros were real, and the five prisoners were debriefed and grilled about their confinement and contacts in prison.

Unbeknown to his aides, Didier booked himself on a flight out of Paris for late Friday evening.

His grandiose plan of Paris lighting up with bombs and grenades would be spectacular from the air, and he reveled in a narcissistic vision of death spewing across the city while he languished in the sky with a glass of champagne.

"We'll use the Belgium prisoners in the tunnels tomorrow night," Didier told Bekir.

"What about the girl in the meantime?"

"It will occupy them long enough for us to reset the bombs in the tunnels and get ready for the concert. The distraction is part of the bigger plan to keep authorities spread thin and out of our way. Bring Strabinsky for a final review. It's critical that he focused as the plan hangs in his musical acumen."

"Yes, Sir. I'll send Munir for him. I 'll go to Moulineaux for a final check on the drones and to load the grenades," Bekir replied.

"Take Aziz with you, and tell Sayed to come here with the blueprints."

Munir and Aziz jumped into a rusted Honda in the alley and drove to a cheap hotel in the west end of Paris where Strabinsky had an upper floor room. He'd been warned to stay out of sight and rarely left the hotel, except for take-out food.

"The success of the mission depends on the Maestro," Munir said. "He won't be expecting us."

"Then we will take him by surprise. When least expecting, the truth is told on a man's face. We'll stop on the way. Didier ordered a tuxedo for the conductor to wear. It shouldn't take too long."

In the early morning, the lives of Parisian commuters were disrupted, finding Gare du Nord still paralyzed, and trains diverted with a contingent of buses. By afternoon, a photo of an unidentified woman spread online—tied to a bench in the train station, thought to be a terrorist with a suicide belt.

A TV man read a simple script, "Parisians are resilient and denounce the principles of radical terrorism. We will not let fear change us or alter our lives." It did little to satisfy the public, clamoring for facts.

At the main entrance, guards cleared each arriving delivery truck, bringing pole beams and planks to build a structure in the frame of a massive hovercraft over Emily's bench.

Tension lines were anchored from the Mezzanine's sides, with ratchets and pulley weights. With deep breaths, both Joseph and Daniel repelled down, suspending themselves close enough over Emily to study it first.

"I can do this, Joseph. Your eyes on the situation are critical, but I'm lighter and used to tenuous situations."

"She's my wife."

"And you are a very lucky man. Let me help return her to you, Joseph."

"If you balance the weights, we'll go together. That way, I'll focus on the mechanical to remove the bomb. A camera is rolling attached to my armored vest, and I'm connected to the bomb specialist for instructions."

Leo nodded his consent.

"Suit these men up with blast protection vests."

"Leo, only the minimum. The weight could interfere."

By zip line, Joseph traveled from the east side and Daniel from the west, until they were suspended ten feet from the other over the bench.

Emily was fraught with pain and unable to flex her muscles or turn her head. Gilbert sat cross-legged on the floor outside the safe boundary and talked to her softly and hummed some classical tunes to ease her anxiety.

"Concentrate on me, Emily," Bernard said. "Joseph and Daniel are highly skilled. I wished the men had taken me instead of you, but they don't compromise. When this is over, I owe you another round of crumpets and tea."

Emily blinked her eyes for him.

"I once had a daughter. If she were still alive she'd be about your age. Unfortunately, my career put my family in jeopardy and I regretfully gave her the keys to my car, not knowing some sinister people had placed a bomb there for me."

Emily's eyes watered, and she blinked it away.

"No Emily. I'm sorry. I was trying to console you."

Gilbert's words were cut short by Leo. "Bernard, we're ready for a final sweep of the tunnels and need your help."

Bernard rose carefully to avoid any sudden motion affecting the sensors. "Whatever is needed, of course."

"We're confident that we've pinpointed every location, using data from the factory in Brussels and our constant investigations. But I need you to work with our coordinators today. Their complex plan has multiple steps to be checked and rechecked."

"I've studied the network route in the map intimately from Rue de Mont Blanc to Invalides and Luxembourg Gardens. I'll meet with your staffers right away."

"Good man. There are thirty bombs in all. See that the C-4 explosive's wires are disconnected and the cell phones are removed at the last minute, so the insurgents won't have the time or opportunity to replace or reset them."

Leo called back to Bernard as he was leaving. "One more thing. Send a unit to bring in their conductor, Strabinsky. I have questions for him."

On headphones, Victor Strabinsky listened critically over and over to the opening notes for his conductor's wand. His dirty hair was askew and his clothes hadn't been washed or changed for several days.

There was no door knock or sound to alert him. With one swift kick, a squad of policemen broke down the door with guns aimed his way.

"What the heck? You've got the wrong place, I've done nothing wrong," he protested, raising his hands high.

Gilbert confirmed to the officers that this was indeed the man Leo wanted, and they cuffed him and led him downstairs to a waiting black sedan. He went willingly, almost relieved to be freed from his prison.

As they led Victor out, an old Honda pulled up across the street, with Munir and Aziz, to bring Strabinsky to Didier. They were alarmed and watched as the conductor was deposited in the back of a police van. When Gilbert looked across, he made a fateful mistake of eye contact with Munir.

I've blown it. Will Munir remember my face? How can I now be a substitute for the Sonata? Surely if Strabinsky doesn't turn up soon, they will call the understudy.

Seething hatred burned inside Munir as he sped away.

En route to Interpol's detention center, Bernard fired a series of questions at Victor. "So you are a Maestro. Have you ever played that great Rossini score, the 'William Tell Overture'?"

Strabinsky raised his eyebrows. "No, I'm not familiar with that."

"Every maestro knows it," Bernard shouted. "Even the youngest student musician. You're lying poorly."

Gilbert watched Victor squirm with the guilt of his fib.

"Do I need to ask for a lawyer?"

"I don't know, do you? I recognize you from a concert I saw years ago. As I remember, you are from Austria, the great nation of musicians."

As Victor chewed on his lip, Bernard sensed he was on the verge of co-operation.

"Come on, Victor. May I call you by your first name? I hear there's a musical gala at the Luxembourg Gardens tonight. Were you planning to attend?"

"Perhaps I did hear about that."

"If I didn't properly introduce myself, my name is Gilbert Bernard, and I am quite proficient at the violin, as well as conducting."

"My main instrument is also violin."

"So you are a musician after all." Victor was falling into Gilbert's trap.

"I am a retired Interpol agent and I have been recalled, due to rumors of a massive terrorist plot in Paris. It may even happen this very evening. The potential loss of life and devastation to Paris is unfathomable. I'm sure if the police received a credible tip from a bystander, they would view charges in a more lenient light."

Victor continued to stare outside as in a trance.

"We are near the detention center, Victor. Would you like to go to the cells in the basement, or would you prefer to join us in our interview room as our guest?"

"Perhaps I'll listen to your offer of an interview and let you know my decision."

Gilbert's soft nature turned to a stern glare as adrenaline pulsed through his veins.

"Non, Victor. What happens to you from this point forward is most definitely not your decision."

I've missed using my negotiating skills.

Twenty-eight

Suspended high at the Gare du Nord terminal, Joseph and Daniel moved gingerly to avoid triggering the motion detector. Even a sound or temperature change could be critical factors.

With a canister, Daniel sprayed a light mist over the area until the infrared beams glowed in pinkish spokes that emanated from the vest. Timing the pulses of the beams, they calculated the seconds available in each lapse.

A zip line delivered a mechanical arm to Joseph's reach, and he cinched the D-ring to his equipment belt. A few feet away, Daniel prepared a series of weights to balance Joseph as he would be lowered to remove the explosive vest.

A railway management operator manned the overhead digital message board used for arrivals, departures and gate changes. Instead, it began messages to Emily.

"Emily, if the motion sensor is operated by a battery pack, signal yes. Or if wired to the actual bomb, signal no."

She raised her index finger in reply.

"Good," the bomb expert radioed to Joseph. "Dismantling it is a possibility."

An inch at a time, Joseph dropped the mini-cam, stopping directly in front of Emily. Across the stadium, the mobile bomb crew watched. Next, he maneuvered the mechanical hand, easing it down like a spider in search of a web. With great attention by the robot operator, it extracted a slicer that cut the taped bonds from her wrists, then meticulously peeled tape from her mouth.

Although circulation could, at last, creep back into her fingers, she refused the temptation to clench her fist while the robot hand and camera remained to examine the vest.

"X-rays show the belt is packed with ball bearings, nails, screws, and bolts, enough to create deadly shrapnel," the robot operator observed.

The bomb squad studied the x-ray of wires connected to the C-4 explosive, as Joseph and Daniel remained suspended.

"We can see the outline of the battery pack with nodules at the top," the operator said. "We can manipulate copper wire to drain the charge, then we'll dismantle the sensor detection circuit."

Emily looked into Joseph's eyes, sending the message, "I'm ready."

"We're sending up a contraption now to drain the battery, Joseph. Lower yourself and hold the mechanical hand a few inches from the electrodes. Do you see them?"

"Yes, I see them." He glanced at Daniel for moral support.

"Take it slow and easy, pal."

"Alright, here we go."

Sweat began to trickle from Joseph's temples, blurring his vision. He took long, deep breaths to slow his heart rate and perspiration.

"Keep going, you're in the correct zone," the instructor said. "Don't speak, we don't want any vibration right now."

Joseph nodded.

"Put the copper wire on the clamp and go closer. More . . . down a speck. You've got it. Hold the wire there for a count of thirty. Steady does it."

The beeping green light on the battery pack started to fade, then slowly pulsed until there was nothing.

The remote operator gave a thumbs up. "Fantastic, fellows. Now we can attend to removing the bomb."

Emily whispered, "Can I speak now?"

"We're not finished yet, Madame."

"Sorry," she mouthed.

Joseph moved closer to locate the detonator to determine how it could be safely extracted.

The bomb commander spoke slowly. "Shunt the bare wires with another piece of wire? Keep it on the detonator wires."

"Done."

"Okay. Keep it there, and sever the wires on the bomb side. Slowly though, as a sudden movement or initiation with radio waves could trigger the blasting cap."

Joseph's hand was steady but his voice was feeble.

"Alright, done."

"Good. Let me know if the clock starts to count down."

"It just started and says thirty minutes."

Daniel eased himself closer, clenching the cable of weights.

Joseph sped up, deciphering the wire combinations and following delicate procedures.

"Cut the red and yellow wires at the same time!"

Joseph looked at Emily and shared her panic. The world then came to a silent full stop, and he unhooked himself from the zip line and dropped to the ground.

He knew Emily would be unable to move and picked her up and carried her as far away as he thought would be safe. Daniel was with him, prepared to throw himself on his friends if they'd miscalculated.

The bomb squad swooped in for the remnants of the vest and contained it in a resistant mobile unit for removal and fingerprints at the forensic lab.

A pair of medics rushed to Emily, but she delayed their assistance as she clung to Joseph.

Leo issued an immediate order for re-entry into the tunnels, to search for any new activity or arsenals, and detonate any new explosives.

"The order to stay at arm's length is rescinded."

Leo's phone flashed with a call from Bernard Gilbert.

"Strabinsky has been captured by us and has agreed to cooperate during a pressing interview. It's likely that the Djinn will call me as Strabinsky's understudy for the concert. But I may have been recognized."

"We could cancel the entire event at the Luxembourg Gardens," Leo said. "But it's an opportunity to round up mass proportions of insurgents in one evening. Otherwise, they'll go back to their lairs to plan another one. Besides, they surely would intend to set off bombs in spite of the concert."

"They've come to Paris like bees to honey," Gilbert said. "The Belgians, the Moroccans, and the Syrians. We are so close."

"I'll won't ask you to risk your life, Gilbert."

"Are you forgetting I'm an Interpol agent? It's my commitment to defend the people of Paris."

"I know you've perfected the right appearance as a conductor, but I must convince you at this moment to get your hair cut and colored to change your appearance."

"Oh Leo, you are hitting where it hurts. But, yes, it will be the best façade under the circumstances. I looked one of Didier's close insurgents directly in the eye today, and he peered back with a hatred I haven't seen before. Perhaps you could send Emily to my loft at St. Louis to help me if she's up to it. Few people know where I live."

Gilbert looked at an incoming text. "Aha, there's a note that I am to contact Youssif Didier urgently. It's addressed to my musician alias, Montague Dunsmuir."

"He's the kingpin, Gil. And as soon as Emily is ready, I'll see that she gets to your apartment discreetly. No one will be looking for her. They'll be expecting the bomb to go off."

"The six million euros was well worth it."

"We'll do our best to recover the ransom, but I must say you are a real stand up guy."

Twenty-nine

Didier was smug with his briefcase full of cash on his return to his west end hideout but became outraged by Munir's failure to get Strabinsky from his seedy loft across town.

"What good is a tuxedo without a Maestro?"

In a rage, he threw the suit for Strabinsky on the floor.

"We can use the understudy. It may even be better since he's not been privy to the plot. Set up the meet and I assure you, Boss, there will be no mistakes this time."

Didier stood at the window to calm himself and organize his thoughts. Across town, the Eiffel Tower stood tall, taunting onlookers with its heritage and durability.

"Paris will pay tonight," he muttered and put out a text to the understudy, Montague Dunsmuir, who had auditioned at the Petit Montparnasse Theater. He picked up the resume.

"The man has no political leanings, but is against excessive government and restrictions on immigrants to France."

Gilbert replied right away. "I'll be delighted to conduct the orchestra this evening. I am well-rehearsed and can rendezvous at the Denfert-Rochereau at 2 p.m.

"The cats in the bag!" Youssif boasted.

"I'll go at 1:30 p.m. to check him out," Munir volunteered. "Where's Bekir?"

"Arranging for cars for the men tonight."

"Does he have all the cells? Help him with that before you go to the catacomb museum. We need to have six zones . . . never mind, Munir. I prefer to talk with him directly."

There was no answer at Bekir's phone, and Didier put it in a long text to him.

"The tunnel areas must be broken into six zones controlling five points each, using four quadrants and a central point for the core. Send me all cell numbers now for the programmer. Double-check everything. Send Aziz to be sure the drone fleet is ready at Moulineaux with its cargo. Confirm Apache pilots for the timing of their movements at Maine-Montparnasse."

Bekir was sipping sweet tea with his terrorist colleagues in a café in Montparnasse when the text came in.

"He wants a hundred things done at the same time. Didier sometimes forgets he's not Allah." The men all broke into laughter.

He stood to leave, but first addressed Sayed. "You must be at the roof restaurant at 6:45 p.m. exactly. Remove the roof security guard and barricade the access door. Take the landing flags with you, to bring the chopper onto the helipad."

An agent in the Interpol building printed a transcript of Bekir's conversation, with his voice detected from the nearby Dingo café. Interpol had already been forewarned of the helicopter plan, and a mini-cam and sound transmitter were planted in a ventilation shaft on the Maine-Montparnasse roof.

At the St. Louis luxury residence of the retired Interpol agent, Emily was transforming Gilbert Bernard into Montague Dunsmuir, who looked considerably younger with a tint of dark hair, and the removal of his mustaches and the beloved ponytail he had kept for years. Rossini's classical music played in the background. Gilbert's eyes were closed.

"Now it's my turn to rescue you," she teased. "At the right moment, Leo and I will come for you with a chopper."

She clasped her hand over her mouth to admire her finished transformation of the Maestro.

"If I didn't know the truth, I absolutely would not recognize you."

Gilbert was tall and lean and strikingly handsome, yet the character lines and wisdom showed his age.

"So I look like a stranger to you—well for me it is worse. Who is that man in the mirror?" he joked.

The new Montague Dunsmuir arrived early at Luxembourg Gardens, ahead of his appointment with the Djinn boss.

He surveyed the orchestra pit and the seating bleachers and envisioned the musical euphoria under a starry night sky. The concert would begin with a pop symphony preceding classical renditions of the 17th and 18th century.

In several hours, dignitaries and guests of the wealthy and elite would arrive in limousines for the black tie affair, with patrons met in champagne tents by tuxedoed waiters. Floral boughs and telescopes were placed strategically to encourage views of the star formations. The sky was clear and predicted to be star-studded with a gentle breeze over the lush landscape.

Many contributors volunteered to be part of the musical showcase that would raise funds to repair the terror of November, and orchestra members auditioned locally for the privileged opportunity.

Gilbert stepped back outside the Denfert-Rochereau museum, recognizable only by the violin case and a folding conductor's music stand. He hoped he would not look into the eyes of Munir.

A rusted Honda stopped at the curb and two men crossed the open lawn to Gilbert's bench. He put on his usual sunglasses hoping they'd protect him from more than the sun.

The shorter of the two men approached him in an Emperor's fashion.

"Monsieur Dunsmuir?"

"Oui, I am the understudy for Monsieur Strabinsky. Will he be coming?"

Munir was abrupt. "Non. Monsieur Strabinsky has taken ill. You will be going on tonight in his place. Did my Boss not explain that to you?"

"Yes, something like that. I was so excited to have the opportunity that I don't recall the precise words leading up to this moment."

"Come with us. We'll walk to the orchestra pit to give you a better understanding of your role."

"Yes, I would like that."

Across the field, Bernard saw a glint of glass or mirror and hoped that it was Interpol backup and no one else.

"This is your music stand. See the X on the floor. That is for you," Munir said.

"I always bring my own director stand." Gilbert lowered its tripod and widened the bookplate surface on both sides. "It was measured exactly for me, and is wide enough to lay out a full orchestral score."

Munir shrugged with indifference.

"When you get to the last piece, the 'William Tell Overture', you must count precisely according to the beat. As the grand finale, this will be the pièce de la résistance, the most substantial dish in the meal. The ending will be extraordinary, but you are the key to the success. Here's the music with the phrasing marked. Each time you raise your conductor's wand, a man is cued to ignite fireworks to your music."

"Fireworks! Yes, that will be a suitable finale. I can perform the piece with perfection; I have studied every note and practiced diligently. Would you like me to play some bars with my violin?"

"Go ahead."

Munir and Aziz listened only for a moment before Munir raised his hand.

"Study William Tell to perfection, Monsieur Dunsmuir. Be back here in the orchestra pit no later than 6 p.m. Understood?"

Daniel and Joseph teamed up at the Avenue de Breteuil entrance of the Esplanade des Invalides, the access point to the labyrinth. The morning air was still, but through the trees, they heard a surveillance drone.

"Must be a dry run from Moulineaux," Daniel grumbled. He pointed a jamming signal into the west and watched as the eagle kit plummeted to the ground.

"The operator is running for the Metro," Joseph said.

"Let him go, we have bigger fish."

Like ants, the search crews had descended into the tunnels to cut wires and remove SIM cards from phone detonators. Despite no sleep for twenty-four hours, Daniel and Joseph were tirelessly on point.

"Leo's team has turned over every rock, and there is now zero chance the Djinn can succeed. I'd like to see Didier's face at his moment of realization," Joseph said.

Crouching at a monument, they waited for an approaching commotion of men. Two Moroccan men talked in gibberish, one holding a case of cell phones, and the other a map.

Daniel whispered, "We'll follow them closely and undo their work." An hour later, with the Moroccans' new devices dismantled, Daniel stepped out of the darkness with his gun.

"Hands over your head! You're under arrest! Don't think of touching your phones."

With a supply of C-4 still in the pack, they didn't try to make a break and were quickly taken over by two policemen at the ladder.

"We've arrested more than a dozen this morning," an officer said. "Perhaps these will like to talk."

"There's always one in the bunch willing to guarantee the safety of a wife or parents," Joseph said.

"Yes, and it's time for Fernando Valois to tell us a story."

The Prefect Commissioner of the Paris police leaned over Leo's desk, for the twice-daily update, which today had evolved to hourly.

Together, they scrolled online photos of suspicious new immigrants, snapped at airports, train stations, bus terminals, and car entry points.

"It's more than the thirty Didier indicated were necessary to complete the scheme," Leo said.

The two then examined the wall map, now fully filled with red pins that identified dismantled bombs and phones retrieved.

"We're satisfied the misleading data fed to Cahill impacted the Djinn's manoeuvers," Leo said. On his computer, he ran the footage captured by surveillance drones of the department of defense. "You can run, but you can't hide!"

Leo pressed his back into the armchair with contentment.

"We raided a property on Boulevard Carnot and arrested a man and a woman, then surrounded a flat with suspects on Rue de Corbillion near February's Saint-Denis raid and found others outside a pizzeria. Two other restaurants on Rue Bichat are being evacuated, as the owner reported suspicious men carrying a weapons satchel."

The commissioner stood back to proclaim some credit for his people. "The suspects will for now be held together in a downtown cell with their conversations recorded as we might pick up some private chatter."

"We'll send in a mole to learn more about the zone locations," Leo said. "They are likely at cafés or Metro platforms. Meanwhile, we have eyes at the helipad and our undercover man in the orchestra."

Thirty

Dressed in full pilot's uniform, Daniel steered across the tarmac at D'Issy les Moulineaux and parked beside two Apaches, waiting in the hanger. A mechanic was making one last check, with the wheels secured by locks.

"Bonjour!" Daniel greeted the man. "Is she ready for me?" He continued his confident stride, with his pilot's helmet dangling from the strap.

"My manifest doesn't show a flight plan until seven tonight. You're a bit early, Mister."

"Oui, oui, good man. I'm just doing a trial run; two others will be coming for the choppers later. Which one is the master of the fleet?"

Hearing the far-off sound of a vehicle, Daniel made a nonchalant exit, without waiting for a reply. Through binoculars, he watched two black pickups from the Van Dame Farm.

They parked in the overgrown farm lane at the hangar, and several men unloaded the truck's cargo of wooden crates inside. He zoomed in on the open doorway at the racks of drones hoisted and ready for grenade installation. Five men in overalls delicately carried the grenades to the first row.

Daniel focused on them and whispered to Leo on his audio, "Look at the second bank . . . zoom on my footage and send it to a dismantling bomb expert. These are second World War RDG-5 fragmentation grenades and a box of Thermite grenades. Russian-made."

"I'm watching," Leo said. "The Thermite ones were stolen from a US military base last August. A team is on the way, Daniel. Stay there—these can't be moved live. Plant a mini-cam on the site and do a count."

"Twenty-eight, twenty-nine . . . thirty, definitely."

"We coerced enough from detainees that it appears Didier is on the run. He's booked on a flight after the concert. Interesting, however—yesterday Didier entered the tunnels alone in the Montmartre zone and went directly to a spot on the blueprint."

"What's he up to, Leo?"

"I've been suspicious for some time about what was on the treasure map. He appeared to come out empty handed but we studied it more. The older map had a marking, N.B., that could be interpreted for years as the Latin 'nota bene' for 'note well', meaning important to pay attention. But it was actually Napoleon Bonaparte's escape cache. I'm sure Didier knew it."

"A cache of coins?"

"Yes, coins. If he found a few for himself, it was only a distraction to the domino plan and pales to the scheme of collapsing the Paris underground. When your backup arrives, I need you to join Joseph in tracking Didier. Our final trap will be when Emily and I go to the Maine-Montparnasse restaurant."

Emily waited at the St. Louis residence for Gilbert to return from his understudy meeting.

"How was it, Maestro? You look twenty years younger and very handsome," she teased.

"It was a pleasant piece of cake," Bernard replied, "and you briefly restored some youth. I brought back the musical score if you can lift the prints for Leo."

"Certainly. If you have an agent's kit, I'll need the black powder, lifting tape, and a glossy card."

"You do know your stuff, little lady."

Emily flipped her head and from the look she gave him, Bernard knew he would never address her in that way again. He passed her the kit from an inlay Marie Antoinette desk.

Laying the materials on a glass table, she picked a fiberglass brush with tiny filaments and a canister of brushing powder.

"Every one of us leaves DNA behind on a coffee mug, a spoon or a hand on a subway grip. We give away much of ourselves in a single day."

Slowly, Emily poured a tad of powder onto a paper towel and swept the brush over it lightly until she was satisfied she had the correct amount. Spinning the brush she dabbed pressure to the corners of the music sheet where it was likely multiple users had handled it.

Satisfied with her work, she photographed and emailed the prints to the forensic lab. Applying the lifting tape, she smoothed it with a credit card to release the air bubbles. Pressing the tape to the glossy card, she marked the data line with the date and time.

"Done. I'll get this to Interpol on my way to meet Joseph."

With her hands on her face, she looked at Gilbert painfully.

"It's okay, kiddo," he said. "Leo has the best men on this and it's about to end. Nothing will happen to the good people."

Emily gave him a long hug. "I believe in you, Gilbert."

At a café patio on Rue Bichat, Didier and Bekir reviewed their final day checklist. Didier was edgy and fiddled with a cartomizer of Turkish tobacco juice to refill the vapor chamber of his e-cigarette, then sucked in a long draw. White circles of mist formed over their heads.

A crowd of five boisterous young girls squeezed past on the sidewalk, and one of the girls accidentally bumped the back of Didier's chair. He turned with a horrified look, astonished that she would dare to inconvenience him in this manner.

"Mademoiselle, you intrude on my space," he shrieked, expecting an apology, but she laughed in his face and quickened her pace to catch her friends.

In his fury, he felt for his switchblade in his rear pocket, but Bekir placed his hand on his arm. "Youssif, she is not worth it, compared to the unwanted attention this will bring. Besides, she will suffer in another way tonight."

His face was still puffed with rage and arrogance, but he listened to the wise advice of his friend.

"Oui, she is not worth it! Bekir, get us some sweet tea. I need to relax."

A burgundy Passat stopped across the street, seeing Didier alone. Sayad got out and walked to the patio table, and two other Middle Eastern men stayed to smoke cigarettes against the car's hood.

"Didier, I was on the lookout in the tunnel exit after your crew finished up. A team of local police went in through a manhole and brought out several men in handcuffs."

"Have they been charged? Where are they?"

"I don't know anything else, but the police can hold anyone for twenty-four hours without charges. We need all the men we have for the mission tonight."

"We have plenty of men to take care of the job. Are all the men in custody guaranteed not to talk?"

"There's one I'm unsure about—an emigrant recruited when he crossed over on a boat from North Africa. He made his way into Germany where he became sympathetic to Djinn. Says he doesn't know his birth name but refers to himself as Thoren. He does stay in contact with his mother."

"What do you suggest, Sayed?"

"Send in a lawyer of sorts to question him—I could do it myself. We still have some of those suicide pins if needed. One little scratch and the life quickly fades away."

"Then you should take care of that, Sayed."

Didier threw some euros on the table and followed Bekir to their car in the alley. "It should be done within the hour."

Sayed, dressed in a borrowed business suit, presented himself as a visitor for Thoren at the detaining center.

The senior officer at central booking was cued about the arrival of a decoy asking to see one particular prisoner who was arrested that afternoon. They decided to let the visit play out, hoping to glean further information.

Sayed presented his business card in an alias, identifying himself as a criminal lawyer representing Thoren Sharif.

As time passed, sitting on a wooden bench in the outer area, his anxiety grew and his eyes shifted constantly to the door, waiting for the man to be brought to a visitors' booth.

Finally, Thoren shuffled in, looking haggard and fearful. He instantly recognized the lawyer as one of the jihadists' insurgents.

"Speak softly. This area is supposed to be privileged but I don't trust those protestant proletariats. What have you said?" Sayed asked.

Thoren looked over his shoulder then leaned forward. I said only that I was innocent, that they had the wrong man. We ditched the trap bag in the tunnel at the last minute, so I had nothing on me."

"Did you say you were an immigrant from Morocco, and that you came from Africa by boat and landed in Greece?"

"No, I said nothing," Thoren pleaded, but his eyes betrayed him. The police had extracted enough from him to contact his mother in Germany. She confessed that her son had been in Syria for training, and feared he was brain-washed as a potential suicide bomber.

After a painful pause, Sayed leaned forward. "You did well, my friend."

Sayed patted Thoren on the face as a friendly gesture as he stood up. The prisoner barely felt the scratch as he struggled to his feet.

The world spun for a moment, then nothing. A guard rushed to help Thoren and sent an emergency medical alarm.

By the time they figured that something was sinister at hand, Sayed had left the building.

Thirty-one

Emily changed to an elegant, black dinner dress, with a diamond pendant and earrings that Joseph had given her on their last anniversary. The rendezvous with Leo would be a short walk from the Eiffel Tower, and she settled on simple black patent pumps instead of the stilettos that tempted from her closet.

At the mirror, she straightened a sheer silver shawl and went to the lobby. A taxi driver waited inside, not your everyday driver, but an undercover Interpol agent.

At Tour Maine-Montparnasse, she was escorted to a secure area for the elevator ride to the Ceil de Paris restaurant, the pride of Chef Christophe Karachais.

When the doors opened, Leo was waiting, with a different look than she'd seen, in his finest black silk suit and dress tie.

"You look lovely, Emily, but I shouldn't be surprised."

The evening's events were about to become serious, but his smile still exuded a charm he had kept back until now.

The luxurious venue had a muted, spherical architecture, with the restaurant revolving past the Eiffel Tower, Arc de Triomphe, and the tiled rooftops of cathedrals, monuments, and regal edifices. From her window seat, Emily kept track of the time of a full rotation.

By heart, the waiter recited the specialties of the four-course menu, recommending the chef's creation of foie gras, with spice crostini, melon chutney, and brioche.

Leo tasted the Chardonnay, then the pair sipped slowly with eyes focused on the exit doors and roof elevator.

"What time is it, Leo? I'm so nervous, not knowing what's going on with Joseph and Daniel."

"Relax, Emily. The final tunnel sweep will be well underway and the concert has begun. It's seven-thirty."

The bow tie waiter brought the first of several covered silver tureens to the table, presenting roasted sea bass with polenta, baby pickled tomato, stewed fennel with saffron and Noilly Prat sauce for Emily. For Leo, there was roasted breast of duck with baby parsnips, roasted sucrine lettuce, purple baby potatoes with tonka beans and honey in lime sauce.

"It's all magnificent!" Emily beamed. "But Leo, I'm afraid I don't have much of an appetite. Playing with her fork, she sampled the exquisite tastes.

"It takes Parisians months to even get a reservation here, but working for a reputable firm, it is one of the perks. You understand, for business reasons," he teased.

Emily whispered, "Two men in white jackets and pants are loitering at the roof exit. They have black hair that's unkempt and unshaven beards, a caliber of hygiene this restaurant would not tolerate. And across the room, someone else is watching us; a lone occupant near the hostess station."

"That's our imposter, Stephen Cahill," Leo said.

"He has a small laptop with him." Emily gritted her teeth. "The dastardly snitch is intercepting tracking sensors."

Leo grinned. "No, he isn't. But he thinks he is. I disabled the active line, so what he is seeing is old tape. Blake Uberon at the analysis unit is an old friend, and I do owe him."

"I'm still watching the two men near the exit. There they go."

The first man pressed the release bar on the No Exit door and ran out onto the roof. Through the window, they were exposed to a full room of diners, and Emily's eyes followed every movement.

Inside, two undercover officers, dressed as waiters, yanked Cahill's arms behind his back. In an instant, he glared at Emily, realizing he'd been as a patsy. His first reaction was to bolt, but he was overcome by the strength of the officers in the melee of scattered and broken dishes.

Staying low, Leo and Emily squeezed through the roof access door, to watch from behind a ventilation shaft.

One of the men jammed a metal rod into the door handle to barricade restaurant access, then on claiming a strong wind warning, the insurgents shooed all the patrons from the viewing telescopes to the elevators, sending them to the main floor with the control boxes locked.

Emily poised herself behind the shaft, as Leo attacked the first man. Before the second could turn, Emily surprised him with a small stun gun. Two of Leo's agents arrived to take away the white jacket insurgents.

Minutes later, the police team donned white overalls to assume the roles of flight navigators.

"I hear the distant chopper. Do you see it yet?" Leo asked.

Emily tilted her head and searched the sky. "It's dusky, but yes, I see red blinking lights at two o'clock. A few miles out, I'd say."

The blast from the rotator blades became fierce as it lowered to the roof, and the navigation crew braced themselves to wave the Apache to the helipad.

An Interpol agent rushed to the pilot's door and yanked him from the cockpit. Protesting and confused by the aggression, he claimed to be a local pilot from Moulineaux.

"Who do you work for?" the agent demanded.

The pilot refused eye contact. "I don't know the customer. The boss gave us this manifest and warned us to be exactly on time or there'd be consequences."

Resisting, he shuffled his feet and turned his head to the restaurant.

He's looking for someone else," Leo whispered in Emily's ear, "Perhaps a person in the dining room. Check it out."

Emily and the agents took a count of inside occupants. Many had left, except a few curious stragglers and employees.

In spite of the man's denials, Leo knew a guilty look and narrowed his questioning.

"Show me the manifest."

The man produced a simple, incomplete form issued by D'Issy les Moulineaux with only the time and date, and a notation, 'verbal instructions'.

"This doesn't show a destination. Where to next?"

"My cargo was to be two passengers for a city tour, from the roof of Maine-Montparnasse. I've done this several times before. It's not irregular." The pilot's demeanor suddenly was conciliatory, hoping his cooperation might spare him.

"Over the city of Paris, you must register a flight plan. Where is it?" Leo fumbled quickly through the attached papers.

"I must have forgotten it. Call my boss if you like."

"Yes, I would like."

The pilot scratched a phone number at the top, and Leo looked at it with suspicion.

"Who shall I ask for?"

"I never talked to him. The name was Bashir or sounded like that. He'll be angry that I failed, and I fear for my life."

Leo signaled for a policeman to make the call.

"See who answers, and trace it."

He turned back to the pilot. "It so happens that we do need your services tonight. You will fly the lady and me to the Luxembourg Gardens."

The pilot raised his eyebrows in recognition of the destination and took a sigh of relief.

"Yes, I see you know where that will be," Leo said.

"Everyone knows. I heard there was to be a concert there tonight. When the fireworks begin, it will be dangerous to fly."

Fireworks! How ironic.

The policeman returned quickly. "Sir, the voice was deliberately muffled and refused to speak, but we've traced it to the Charles de Gaulle airport."

Leo opened digital photos of Didier and Bekir for the investigator. "Alert the airport authorities to find and hold these men."

The policeman whispered to Leo, "This second one, Sir, the one you say is Bekir—he's watching from inside, at a window table."

"Lock down the restaurant so no one can leave, and sweep it for explosives. These men are not afraid to use suicide belts."

Bekir was clean-shaven, dressed in a tailored business suit and gentlemen's dress hat, but it was clearly the same man. His voice was rapid and staccato on his phone to warn Didier. He assumed he was unnoticed, and Leo kept it that way, avoiding eye contact.

Leaving Bekir's apprehension with the police, Emily and Leo boarded the chopper and demanded the direct route to Luxembourg Gardens. The lift over the city was exhilarating, rising above the magnificent steel structure of the Eiffel Tower.

"We need to be overhead at the concert at precisely twenty hours, eight o'clock—not a minute earlier or later. Do you understand?"

Leo pressed a revolver into his ribs for an answer.

"Yes, Sir, no problem."

"After you pick-up at the concert, where would you take your passengers?"

"It was a need to know basis, with instructions on arrival. After completing my task, I was to meet at a café in Montparnasse for payment."

"Are you carrying any weapons cargo?"

The pilot shook his head. "No, Sir. None."

"You realize the chances of your surviving this mission are slim, don't you? My sources indicate you are carrying grenades and possibly some chlorine gas canisters. After eight o'clock, you would fly over a pre-planned route and drop your cargo onto coordinates. Correct?"

"Yes, Sir."

"How did you get yourself into this mess? Are you Islamic, and are you sympathetic to jihadists?"

"No, absolutely not. They promised to pay me one million American dollars to do as I was told. That's enough for me to leave the country and retire."

"Did you really think you would live to collect it?"

The dawning of reality struck the pilot, and his face reddened in a rage with his temple throbbing.

"I can identify these men in a line-up if you guarantee my safety."

Leo laughed. "*If?* No, no, no, you've got this all wrong."

The Paris lights were breathtaking, and as the helicopter neared the gala, Emily scoured the scene with binoculars—her heart accelerating as they got close enough to see the lights in the garden.

"Leo, we've passed the time for the tunnel explosions and all looks calm."

"Don't be too sure. They are a colony of ants! Those stars on the horizon are military drones giving us a private escort."

The incoming lines at Interpol were flooding with data, as Uberon's team directed the airborne drone fleet over the abandoned airfield near Orly.

Across town, a minor eruption raised a false alarm in the 18th arrondissement, as an old quarry mine shuddered, leaving fault lines on the road.

Emergency crews routed traffic away, fearing a roadway collapse. The activity in the tunnel during the evacuation had weakened major support beams, causing a gas line to explode and sporadic fires. The only victims were two unoccupied vehicles that became submerged.

At Goussainville, fleets of military vehicles were carting away the storage containers of chlorine for destruction at a certified location.

Leo bellyached to himself. "It's like playing ten-pin bowling but we've covered half the field already."

Thirty-two

Joseph, in combat gear, was attached to a SWAT unit. The raiding team was going door to door on foot to known insurgent locations. Reports of sporadic gunfire led the team to the Paris Gare Lyon, then to the Pont de la Concorde.

Joseph's unit searched the perimeter of every building around the Assemblée Nationale on Bercy Street. Pedestrians had taken cover in restaurants, transit stations, and alleys looking for safety.

A frightened, young girl cowered under a newsstand by the bridge.

"Three men with weapons are firing continuously, yelling slogans in Islamic, things like 'Allah Akbar'. They have heavy coats and threatened to blow us all up."

Hearing gunshots inside a grocery store, the lead Commando, Jean-Baptiste, entered with Joseph and signaled to customers to exit at the front. One of the insurgents realized they were trapped, and fled to a rear refrigeration room, yelling in defiance, "You cannot kill us. Our souls belong to a higher authority in the name of Allah." The freezer door slammed shut, holding them inside.

The store manager had ducked behind his counter, refusing to leave, but Jean-Baptiste would not have it.

"Joseph, get him out of here."

"No, don't let them blow up my store," he pleaded, resisting and dragging his feet. "There's no exit from the cooler room."

With all his might, Joseph grabbed the manager and forced him out the front. "Go directly to that SWAT truck. You will be safe there."

A team of agents huddled with Jean-Baptiste. "Remember procedures men. We have civilians to protect."

Joseph remembered his own undercover military training when it was ingrained in him to improve his dexterity and tactical responses.

"If we force open the freezer door, three of them will come out blazing," Joseph said. "These bullet-proof vests won't protect us one hundred percent. I saw their weapons, the same as the assault rifles from the tunnel cache."

"We'll wait it out then. A thermometer is on the wall outside the door. Turn up the temperature. My men will hold cover here. Harkness, you're to call the boss at headquarters."

Outside, Joseph called Leo. "What's happening at Charles de Gaulle? Do they need tactical operations? Yes, I'll go."

"I'll fill you in as you drive, and Daniel will join you there. He's working with Uberon and the Department of Defense to gain control of the terrorists' drone fleet, inputting suggested deactivation codes. The analyses lab team is trying to reprogram the master drone to a new frequency."

With the police siren blaring, Joseph sped north to the airport. On speaker, Leo filled him in on the reported sighting of Youssif Didier, at a gate to an Istanbul flight.

"The airport is surrounded, with passengers evacuated from a cordoned area. Unfortunately, SWAT units are largely occupied in the downtown core. Emily is with me and everything is going according to plan. There's intermittent gunfire in some subways, but no lives lost," Leo said.

"And the concert?"

"It will come to its grand finale momentarily."

"Text me on the airport progress. I'm getting close." Joseph said.

"You'll get instant news. Snipers are in position, and a unit is ready with smoke grenades. He's a dangerous man and capable of planning this type of catastrophe all over again, so do whatever is necessary to immobilize Didier."

Daniel Boisvert sped across the Moulineaux tarmac and parked behind the control tower. He listened at the door, then burst inside, raising the revolver to the operator's head. The man hastily raised his hands, with tears of fear, then relief, on handing over the reins of the fleet of destruction.

"Stop it all!" Daniel yelled as the man cowered on his knees.

"It's impossible. All the grenades are ready to go. Once the programmer sets his code, each drone will find its target . . . then oblivion on the ground. You'd need the abort code to intercept, and I don't know it. Bekir said he'd tell me only if I need to know."

"You're lying. You know how to stop it," Daniel said.

He flung the inner office doors open to ensure they were alone. The man was sweating, knowing his future was in jeopardy in either case.

"He tapped in the access requests as sweat dripped from his brow. Yes, I'm past the firewall . . . we're in."

Two officers arrived and cuffed the operator. Daniel assumed the computer's controls and called Blake Uberon.

Slowly, he entered the first code possibility that Uberon produced, then waited.

"Nothing, Blake. Give me the next."

As he entered the second series, the pressure was building. Again it did not deactivate, and he tried a third.

"We have more," Blake said. "They're computer-generated and one will work. Stay at it."

Uberon was sweating as he continued frantically. At his side, his best programmer suggested, "I call the Commander of the gendarme to see if they have expertise. They have their own drones and may be able to override the program."

"I'm still trying to deactivate the master drone," Daniel said on the line to Leo. "The codes haven't worked and I'm entering them as fast as Blake tells me. Also, the gendarme is providing support. Has Bekir talked?"

"Bekir's in custody in Montparnasse. He's refusing to say a word and we haven't found the incentive yet to push him our way," Leo said.

"Incentive . . . or threat. What can destroy a man dedicated to terrorism?" Daniel mused. "There isn't time to grill Isabella for something to use, but we could say she volunteered every dirty secret about him that a wife could know. Tell him she has a remarkable memory for conversations and details, heard behind the curtain."

"In Islamic society, that does not bear the weight you might assume," Leo said. "The right bait could get Bekir to talk."

"All men want others to believe in them, so they reveal themselves to close friends and family. I was about to say that Bekir doesn't have materialistic values, but that's not true. Isabella saw one of the Napoleon coins from the cache in his possession. It's likely he stole it from his boss—I doubt Didier would forgive that."

"To be sold out by a friend for money is the ultimate insult!" Leo said.

"That tidbit should cause Bekir to shake in his boots," Daniel said. "And as the pickup man for the six million, he no doubt expects to share in some portion of the ransom."

"Since Bekir was arrested, he's had no contact with Didier. He won't know that Didier fled to the airport, or whether he made a safe escape. If the kingpin gets away, he takes all the glory and praise from fellow jihadists, allowing Bekir to fade into obscurity in jail, without a penny."

Daniel said, "We can tell Bekir that Didier sold him out and his morsel of vindication could be to have Didier's grand plan fail, and be disgraced among his people."

"It's worth a shot, Daniel. We'll give Bekir a life or death ultimatum."

Bekir was belligerent and shook with anger at the insult of being placed in handcuffs. Leo knew he could capitalize on his humiliation. "Bekir, I'm afraid it's all over."

"Our cause will never be over, and I will soon be freed."

"You don't understand," Leo said. "Didier was arrested leaving town. He said you have the grenade codes and he will turn evidence to send you to prison for the rest of your life if we provide him safe exit by air with his €6 million. He says you were the kingpin all along, and you used him."

Bekir's eyes shifted back and forth.

"I don't believe you."

Leo watched the minutes on the clock, but remained calm, refusing to let Bekir detect any anxiety.

"Suit yourself. You'll be transferred to a hard labor prison in a few hours. The prison population is sympathetic to the French victims and will seek revenge on any perpetrator in their realm.

"This is your chance to clear your name if you decide to refute Didier's claim. Do you choose to live out your days there, no matter how short that may be?

"By the way, your wife remembers seeing a stolen Napoleon coin in your possession. I doubt that Didier will take kindly to that when we tell him. Perhaps you should reassess the wrath of your boss, versus the police."

Leo shrugged and prepared to leave, with every second now an eternity. At the last glance, he saw the brink of collapse.

"Perhaps, we could talk longer," Bekir said softly.

Blake Uberon's call interrupted Leo at the right moment. "The Defense Department has successfully overridden Bekir's codes. We don't need him anymore."

Leo turned back to Bekir. "I'm glad you might be reconsidering your cooperation, but for now I'll send in one of my detectives to interview you. There's someplace else I need to be."

Daniel texted Leo. "Let the sot rot—we've broken the codes. Grenades are being deactivated now, and the Department of Defense has an interceptor drone in the air to down anything in Paris airspace without a clearance."

"Fantastic. The chlorine has all been accounted for and the army can pack up the helipad and dismantle the drones' cargo. Can you go to the airport to back up Joseph?"

"Going now. Is Didier in custody?"

"He's surrounded but not captured."

Outside Luxembourg Gardens, sirens resounded with the swarming of combat vehicles and ambulances as a portion of the historic Passage d'Enfer fell into its own subterranean landscape, spewing dust into the air within sight of the concert.

As the maestro conducted the second last symphony, Gilbert Bernard closed his eyes to soak in the emotion and swell of the strings. Then, looking up past the orchestra, he saw a line of policemen moving across the back of the audience.

Overhead, the helicopter's lights flashed as it came into range. It was a magnificent, starry night under the moonlight, with the light breeze a welcome relief to the audience of dignitaries. In their finery, many groaned and complained at the distraction of the police chopper.

Gilbert hushed the crowd to announce his finale and say a few words to relax his appreciative patrons.

"Ladies and Gentlemen, tonight will be an evening in Parisian history, in defiance of jihadist terrorism efforts to quash the liberty of our people.

"It is appropriate that my finale is Rossini's 'William Tell Overture'. He composed this at only 37 years as his musical farewell and as the introduction to the Guillaume Tell opera, a passionate story of a Swiss hero seeking liberation for the cruelties of Austrian occupation.

"Governor Tesler sadistically forces Tell to shoot an apple off the head of his son, for rebelliously refusing to bow sans chapeau to the Governor. Imagine the choice he endured? He was ordered to succeed with his first arrow, or they would both be put to death. He fired only one arrow, and Tesler asked why he had another inside his jacket. He replied that if perchance he struck his son, the second arrow would be for Tesler. We are heartened to know that the son survived. Tell's subsequent arrest rallies his fellow revolutionaries to gather and fight for Swiss liberty. Tell lives on to lead a victorious uprising."

The audience was spell-bound by the legend.

"Tonight, you all have survived an uprising of hatred against France's freedom, equality, and fraternity, the same cry from the revolutionists—liberté, égalité et fraternité. France's President has said, 'No barbarians will prevent us from living or how we have decided to live. To live fully. Terrorism will never destroy the Republic because the Republic will destroy terrorism. We are no different than we were two hundred years ago, seeking life and liberty'.

"Tomorrow you will read in the newspapers of heroic stories of the events of tonight, while you sat here under the heavens, with the music of the masters. Our police and security forces intercepted a scheme that would have devoured the underground tunnels of Paris."

As murmurs spread, some patrons fretted and stood.

"There's no cause to panic or leave. Please stay and listen to the tale of a great patriot in this orchestral rendition of the 'William Tell Overture'. Give gratitude to the men in uniform and to those not seen, who are dedicated to your freedom.

"Over to the right watch that string of seven or eight lights in the distance, coming nearer and nearer. That's the French military doing a victorious flyover and each is ready for combat by any militant in our great city."

Gilbert never felt so patriotic. A stand-up applause radiated through the patrons, some spell-bound and tearful, and others chanting Vive la France, as a fleet of military planes swept over the gardens in a salute formation.

Gilbert raised his baton to the violins, and the opening notes of the *Finale* filled the park. Due to the success of the defensive operation, the timing was irrelevant.

Leo's chopper pilot landed on a grassy knoll near the stage. Emily jumped out and they ran together to flag a security vehicle to the airport to unite with her husband.

The press flocked to Bernard, hungry for more about his fantastic claim of salvation to France. He deferred on details, knowing that news departments would get overnight releases.

But he privately basked in the unexpected respect and notoriety now as an orchestra conductor, realizing he could, at last, widen his career in the passion he had chosen.

In the days that followed, news of the Stradivarius leaked out, raising Gilbert to hero status. At the Versailles Festival, organizers adapted their operatic program to guest host Bernard, with international demand for his name.

Thirty-three

Didier had last been spotted in Terminal 2 at Charles de Gaulle in the Air France building. As Daniel neared the northeastern sector of Paris, the imposing seven floors of the airport's massive circular building of avant-garde architecture rose in his sight, with seven tram spokes connected to its surrounding buildings.

A police barricade restricted traffic, with most disgruntled drivers turning around, and others waiting out the closure on the boulevard. Surrounding the terminal, traffic was congested with police cars, riot vehicles, ambulances, news teams and a convoy of National Guard army trucks.

Inside, Joseph easily passed the checkpoints with his Interpol credentials, and looking at his watch, he wondered if Daniel would be near yet. One of Leo's men stopped him.

"Come this way. Didier evaded the security line in the transit hall." The two of them ran past the luggage conveyor belts as Didier disappeared over it and through security doors.

As a baggage investigator tried to hold him, he tossed a live grenade to the ground, escaping in the distraction and clouds of smoke.

Injuries were limited from the explosion that rocked the outer area, hurdling debris across the passenger area. A rash of emergency staff was there in seconds, then a bomb squad.

Security monitors showed movement behind the luggage wagons, with the outline of a person moving alongside a cart toward a private plane on the runway.

When Didier saw the combat commandoes, he took over a mobile cart, knocking the occupants to the ground. Changing his mind, he took two of them as a human shield.

"Do we have a positive identification on the suspect?" the onsite commander barked.

In a flash, he turned his head back to Joseph. "Who are you?"

"Joseph Harkness. I'm assisting in this case with Major Leo Desjardins of Interpol. The terrorist is Youssif Didier, responsible for a failed bomb plot in Paris tonight. Check my credentials with the head of national defense but you'll just be wasting valuable time."

"Does the assailant know who you are?"

"Yes. I foiled his drone scheme and I'm on his hit list. It's important that he not escape. He is the mastermind of the Paris murders. If we take him alive, there's hope of rounding up others."

"Mr. Harkness, if you look around, you'll see the firepower here. This fellow's chances of escape aren't too good."

The commander pressed on his earphones for an incoming call. "Yes, Mr. Harkness, it seems that you are in charge for the time being.

"I'd like to talk to him? He's escaped with a six million dollar kidnapping ransom. Desjardins has been monitoring their activities—I assure you that I have enough in common with him to initiate a conversation."

"A negotiator is on the way, but I'll listen to your plan if you have something specific."

"He has two hostages, let me offer myself in trade. I'll take the earphone, as he won't be fooled by a body wire. You have sharpshooters on the roof as a backup that can equalize the conditions at your call."

The commander weighed Joseph's request while he listened to static instructions from the terminal.

"It's certain suicide if you volunteer, Harkness."

"I am trained in strategic and tactical procedures. If I can get closer, I'll find his weak spot. I have his phone number from my wife's kidnapping. May I call him?"

The commander signaled for an isolated frequency channel to relay it. "It's your show, but as soon as the assailant fires a single bullet, we will retaliate."

Daniel ditched the car in an emergency zone and dashed through security.

He sent a text and scanned the area. "I'm here, Joseph." Daniel saw him through the glass on the far side, but with the intensity of negotiation, Joseph hadn't looked at texts.

"Let me through. That's my partner."

Daniel was too late. Joseph was already on his way, with his hands in the air, walking toward Didier on the tarmac.

An unmanned mobile staircase was on the edge of the tarmac, in the triangulation between Didier and Joseph, with his hands raised in surrender.

Skulking through the maintenance loading bays, Daniel crouched out of the line of vision and crawled up the stairs. He was close to the terrorist and examined the manual controls to consider options, then looked at the faces of the innocent hostages. Joseph was barely within reach, with his hands still in surrender.

The eyes of the male hostage, a baggage handler, were becoming wilder with fear, and he looked up pleadingly at Daniel. His arm was wrenched behind his back, and a gun was to his temple. The second, a female baggage tracker, was younger but clearly on the brink of collapse. Joseph attempted to silently whisper words of encouragement to her.

Youssif's pearly whites hid the face of a devil. "I didn't expect to see you again, Monsieur Harkness. Have you come to say goodbye?"

"Wouldn't you rather take me as your hostage, and let the girl go? She's no good to you in her condition. She's paralyzed with fear, and that makes her a loose cannon."

Joseph gestured to the snipers poised to shoot on the sound of the first shot. "Look up. It will give the commandoes on the roof assurance that you are willing to negotiate peacefully."

"Peacefully?" Didier laughed with rancor. "Nothing the Djinn does is peaceful. However, I'll play along with your little game. Take the woman, women are useless . . . not even worthy of the price of a cow."

Didier struggled with the offer, then shoved the woman to the ground. With a whimper, she gathered newfound strength and scampered toward the terminal, expecting a bullet in the back. An awaiting soldier picked her up, and she was quickly whisked out of sight.

"That was a good decision, Youssif?"

"Don't placate me. I'm in charge here, not you."

"I agree, you are the one with the gun to the hostage's temple. To the snipers on the roof, he's merely a man in the wrong place. Me, well I'm more valuable alive to Interpol."

Didier's eyes flashed back and forth, taking in the truth of Joseph's words. His eyes moved across the roof line and he was shaken by the sight of five snipers at different vantages.

"I'll make the trade if your people call off the snipers," Didier replied, "but it must be now with no tricks!" He looked at his watch again. It was synchronized to the master drone, and, unaware of Beker's failure, he was counting down to the spectacular moment the tunnels would collapse Paris.

"May I use my cell to make the request?" Joseph said, hiding the fact that the command center was hearing every word. His fingers touched a fuse and a small amount of C-4 explosive that he had secured in his phone, a strategy he'd used in Afghanistan.

"The command leaders are debating, but I'll try again," Joseph said, but instead sent a text to Daniel and Leo.

The text read, 'Don't use this cell number. Activating it with C-4. Remove visible snipers to show goodwill. Communicate by megaphone. Absolutely no phone calls on this line!'

The commander in the terminal blared over a bullhorn, "As requested, we have removed two snipers but it would not be a good chess game to remove all."

"Okay, Youssif. They'll withdraw two snipers. What's your plan?"

Didier laughed sardonically. "I said all the snipers, then I want a Cessna here. Twenty minutes, no later. Chess game, you have a sense of humor, I can appreciate."

"That shouldn't be a problem, Youssif, but you need to show good faith. Slowly release the baggage handler. I won't move and you can keep your gun on me. Deal?"

Didier glared at Joseph. "Alright, I'll agree to that."

The man stood up in fear.

"No sudden movement, Sir," Joseph said. "Walk slowly to the terminal, as your co-worker did." Joseph watched each step and relaxed as the hostage was sheltered out of sight.

Leo and Emily were now inside with the commander.

"I heard they want a Cessna. Several are sitting at Moulineaux. Send word and get one here."

Leo called back to Didier, "We'll provide the plane, but you have to find your own pilot."

"Bring Aziz from your dirty prison. He can fly a plane."

Leo nodded to one of the men. "He's detained at the headquarters downtown. Bring him in an armored vehicle."

"Monsieur Didier, arrangements are underway. The plane and your accomplice will join you in twenty minutes."

While Youssif was distracted with Leo, Joseph opened the briefcase at Didier's feet. "Six million euros as agreed," he confirmed and closed the case."

Joseph knew that once the plane left the runway, his value to Didier would be expendable and he couldn't take that chance. Out of the corner of his eye, he spied Daniel, poised in wait like a stalking lion.

Emily paced behind Leo but was tuned to every word, in her uncanny ability to step back and see the whole picture.

She looked at Daniel in the wings ready to rescue his friend, and Joseph, selfless and heroic to do the right thing and outwit the terrorist.

Intuitively, she knew his thoughts. Although she admired his bravery, she wished to be in his strong arms. The two of them against the world.

"Emily, what is he thinking?" Leo whispered.

"You do whatever your instinct tells you," she said. "If I gave away Joseph's plan, you might change how you react. That would upset the whole scheme of what he expects.Don't worry, he'll be in control of the situation. Didier is outwitted and distracted by the timing on his watch. The master of destruction always waits for his moment of glory. Joseph is waiting for the right instant to win. You'll see, all in good time."

Leo was puzzled but reassured.

"Joseph will come back to me; I'm sure of it," she said out loud to Leo but mostly to herself.

Thirty-four

Waiting for the Cessna, Leo made the gesture of offering food and water to Didier and Joseph. It was adamantly declined.

As the plane approached, its lights became visible, then its markings as it circled. I know that aircraft model, a Citation CJ 2, with the Matterhorn stripes," Emily said under her breath.

Leo was amused. "How do you know this? Do you google everything?"

She laughed. "Of course. But I was in one in California. I am curious, but not a nerd," she declared. "It's American made, with turbofan propulsion, twin-engine and reaches 760 km/hour. Fueled up, it can take Didier anywhere he wants."

"Fueled up?" Leo stopped. "We could short the fuel load."

"Don't even think it, Leo. If Aziz is really a pilot, it's the first thing he'll check when he sits in the pilot's chair."

Leo phoned the tower, for the Cessna to taxi close, and the command station set up for the two-man crew to disembark.

Aziz, haggard with tattered hair and a scraggly beard, watched the landing from the terminal. Stiffly hand-cuffed, he was led down the ramp and out onto the tarmac into Didier's view.

"He asked for me to be his pilot? Why me? He knows I've only flown a few times," Aziz argued. "What's a Cessna?"

"He's not interested in your credentials. You just have to get it off the ground, then land wherever he decides without a flight plan," the commando leader replied. "You've been approved as the pilot!"

"That can't be too hard," Aziz grunted, noticeably shaking, either from distress or nicotine withdrawal.

Leo begged one of the officers for a cigarette and handed it to Aziz, releasing him from the cuffs. "This will calm your nerves."

"Merci, Monsieur." Aziz was both fearful and grateful.

"We have your pilot, Didier," Leo called on the bullhorn.

Two commandoes walked Aziz part way to Didier. At the side, in the darkness, the mobile staircase was easing closer to Joseph with Daniel on board.

Joseph made eye contact with him, and in sync, each understood their anticipated moves.

Didier snapped at Aziz, "Get in and start the engine!"

Snuffing the cigarette with his shoe, Aziz scurried up the ladder and disappeared into the plane.

Didier backed toward the steps, with the barrel of his gun against Joseph's temple, and his other hand holding the ransom briefcase. His glances at his watch were now more frequent.

"You're coming with us as added security, Monsieur Harkness. Don't try to be smart, this gun has a full round."

The last sniper on the roof had his telescopic lens directly on Didier's forehead. "Permission to take the shot, Sir?"

Leo shook his head. "Denied! Hold your position. The negotiator has full control."

Didier held Joseph close to him as his shield as the two inched up the stairs. At the midpoint, a loud bang startled Didier. It was Daniel racing the ramp, close to the aircraft.

"Jump aboard, Joseph, and secure the door crank."

As Didier turned, Joseph elbowed him off his feet. Stumbling, his footing gave way and he fired wildly in the air.

Suddenly a S.W.A.T. helicopter neared the Cessna with gendarme snipers hanging out the side. They had been a holding pattern waiting for the sound of the first bullet. The stand down command was relayed from the terminal upon Leo's call.

Joseph dove for the release lever to stop the staircase as it rose quickly, but Didier scrambled past and climbed into the Cessna on his knees.

Through the crack in the closing door, he raised his gun. In the blink of an eye, Joseph leaped from the staircase, rolling onto the ground at the foot of Daniel's ramp.

Didier got two shots away before the door reached the top and sealed. Through the window, Joseph watched his emerging fury as he stamped about. Then he turned smug and raised the briefcase to taunt Joseph of his success.

Aziz eased the plane jerkily down the runway under the pressure of Didier's rants.

Emily ran across the tarmac into Joseph's arms and huddled in his embrace as they watched the Cessna lift off into the morning sun. Moments later, Leo joined the trio, admiring the clever escape.

Joseph shoved his hand into his pocket and brought out a wad of American one hundred dollar bills.

"Give that back to Gilbert. I needed to make room in the briefcase for my phone," Joseph gloated looking very satisfied with the outcome. "The flight is set to be over the ocean. When you track it over open water, Leo, you might want to dial my cell. I had leftover plastic and wire in my pocket from the tunnels that I put to good use."

"Soon, he'll be learning online that his catacombs scheme and drone plan were foiled, with many terrorists captured. I'd like to see his face when he presses his final code to ignite the tunnel bombs and nothing . . . not the slightest click," Leo said. "But he may never know the ultimate con if his plane goes down at sea."

"It's one of those expressions—what goes around comes around. Very apropos," Daniel added.

Far away, past the northern coast of France, the light aircraft was heading out over the vast North Sea. The day was forecast for clear skies, a perfect day for flying. Didier sneered with both hatred and self-congratulations on his financial coup.

Still unaware of his failure, he opened the case to touch the cash. He held a handful of bills and removed the phone on top.

"Just you wait, Aziz," he laughed. "This is just the beginning."

Back in Paris, Leo Desjardins walked to a north facing office window and made a long distance call to Joseph's cell.

On the horizon, whether he imagined it or the blast was that magnificent, the sky lit up like a field of flaming stars.

American currency with the face of Benjamin Franklin and the words 'In God We Trust' wafted down to the sea.

Never before, had Leo had such satisfaction closing a case.

Thirty-five

Blake Uberon stood at the head of the Treasury boardroom table with all eyes on him for a pronouncement.

"Ladies and Gentlemen, what I am about to show you is an ancient treasure map belonging to the great emperor Napoleon Bonaparte."

The executives and senior administrators remained silent in confusion and anticipation at the announcement.

"It is fitting that this piece of France's history is returned here to the Élysée Presidential Palace to be preserved for Parisians. Preserve and handle it with the greatest security and respect as it has a curse and has claimed the lives of several Interpol agents in attempts to save its integrity.

"Your department is aware of a sensitive security breach several months ago, and your vetting processes were corrected."

The Director stood beside him to reply.

"Monsieur Uberon, we are grateful to receive this valuable part of history back to our archives. Is there any way we can repay you for your patriotic efforts?"

"This is an honor to serve our President and our country. The Treasury Department and the government will want the map's existence and the security breach to be strictly classified.

"With a moratorium on this sensitive information, you may wish a private recognition in honor of our fallen men in protecting this artifact. I will forward the names of two foundations. A simple ceremony to honor these men will be held in the next few days."

As the sun rose with a glow over the city, the team members that had shared the common purpose of defeating the Paris network plot gathered at the fountains at Place de la Concorde. In the peace of the morning, they paid silent tribute.

An onlooker stood nearby and photographed the audience in attendance.

Joseph and Emily were free to be Thomas and Rachel once again and took the Metro home to their loft on Rue des Saules in Montmartre.

Months had passed since they lived a normal life of detectives in Paris, banished from their home by terrorists.

Toby, the bloodhound, bounded down the hill as they approached Marie's flower shop. Rachel bent and rubbed her face against Toby's soft, silky ears. Marie was not far behind.

"Joseph et Emily, I have been worried." She hugged them like long lost children.

"It's a long story, Marie. For now, we just want to be at home," Emily said.

"Here, take a lovely bouquet," Marie gushed, pushing a posy of gerberas and daisies at her favorite tenant.

The loft's stairs gave her a tingling sensation. "I didn't know how homesick I've been." He put his arms under her knees and carried her over the threshold.

On Montmartre's cobblestone streets, they loitered under the stars, stopping at the sounds of street entertainers at Place du Tertre.

At a patisserie, the aroma of croissants drifted to the walkway. They stopped to savor the posted menus of the restaurants that were taken from their lives in recent months.

Outside Le Basilic restaurant on Rue Lepic, Rachel's fingers touched the leaves of the climbing ivy that surrounded the doors. She looked through the open portal at the table candles, flickering as if to invite them inside.

"It's perfect for tonight," she said. "Can we eat here?"

With a chilled white wine, they gave in to the veal chops with blue cheese sauce and tagliatelle, and stuffed chicken with foie gras. Their conversation was subdued, satisfied to gaze into each other's eyes, both wanting the tension of Djinn to fade from their memories.

Rachel raised her hand. "Thomas, stop!"

Her nose was in the air, and her posture became rigid.

"Stand here. What do you smell?"

"It can't be," he laughed.

Next to them on a side table was a single, empty wine glass and an ashtray with cherry pipe tobacco. A crisp white card was tucked under a domino tile beside an ashtray.

It was a formal, embossed invitation for two to the Palace of Versailles, to a masquerade ball in the Hall of Mirrors.

"The tickets are for June 25th, Thomas!"

Look for the Count of Monte Cristo, he will be waiting for you. —D.B.

THE END

*Thanks for following my books. You might also like the many short chronicles
in my 620 page historical fiction.*

HOMAGE: CHRONICLES OF A HABITANT
A ten generation historical fiction, in a series of short chronological
stories, beginning in France in the 1500s. A 500 year journey based
on a family's lives, tragedies and immigration to North America.
Experience typical life as the early migrants travel from France to
settle in Quebec, with generational conflicts and cultural clashes in
the founding of the new land.

Shirley Burton

shirleyburtonbooks.com